GAYLORD DOLD

BAY OF SORROWS

ST. MARTIN'S PRESS

NEW  YORK

GAYLORD DOLD

BAY OF SORROWS

ST. MARTIN'S PRESS
NEW  YORK

Design by Judith A. Stagnitto

ISBN 0-312-11751-5

First edition: February 1995

10 9 8 7 6 5 4 3 2 1

Hide in cesspools, sleep well
on broken glass, and eat
shit. Kiss the whips,
hold the wife for rape,
and have good luck:
stumble behind a lamb
before the bomb bursts
and crawl out of the wreck
to be the epitaph:
"The good ones die first,
but I am not so bad:
Americans are worse."

Alan Dugan
"Qualifications of Survivors"

1

Tom Poole was tired of corpses. In those days death had become a way of life.

He had been driving north along the Port Arthur highway with the bay behind him, a long, shiny seam of water, heading home after a hard Saturday, when the call came over his radio. Dispatch said there was a dead guy in a fishing shack just down the beach from the old marina. Poole knew where that was, and something—he didn't know what—made him turn east, back toward the ocean. It took some driving around the barren dunes, sumps and oil pits, and tule groves, but he finally found the shack, and the corpse, and now he was waiting on the veranda for the sheriff.

Maybe he was heat-wilted, maybe just tired, but something made him focus on a bright orange gas flare coming from the stack of Port Arthur Oil and Pipe, a lick of flame just across the water. It was being rippled by a breeze whisking in from the bay, and when Poole closed his eyes, concentrating on the smell of the acrid gas, he lost his focus and sensed not the gas but only a dull ache in his head, a stab of pain between his shoulders, as if a knife had been plunged deliberately between the shoulder blade and his arm socket. You can't start thinking this way, he said to himself. *You have to float and relax and allow your feelings to coalesce around an object, make the pain come together on the head of something. Otherwise, it will eat you alive, like what happens to guys on the Jefferson County detective staff, pinheads who walk around with a hard-on for the world. It's only a job. You answer calls down on the Port Arthur highway; you see dead guys in fishing shacks—that's what you do for a living.* Poole knew, deep inside, that it was silly to complain about the things you choose to do, like making a living, but he was wishing just then that he had gone on home and left someone else the job of sitting up with a corpse.

He leaned on a rickety balustrade overlooking a brackish tide pool which led away to reeds and the sump that Port Arthur made of its waste. The palms along the beach were singing in the wind, a silky sound buried under the steady *clump-bump* of the oil tankers, pump engines running as they unloaded into pipelines, engines grinding away in the near background. Standing there, his mind's eye turning through the past like a bore, Poole was returning thirty-five years to a Gulf Coast that didn't exist anymore, except on fancy travel posters, on TV in modern momentary figments like sale items of the imagination that Poole knew happened only in the medium of advertising. Snap your fingers and the past is right there, then fleeing; you never get it.

Poole wanted a cigarette, but he had quit, one of many times. He turned his gaze down the beach toward the highway to Galveston where it ran past Sea Rim State Park, all the worn-out road shacks, fast-food joints now, shit that littered the seafront, with the palms dropping their fronds and the surf turning poisonous. The light, in times past that Poole remembered, would pour in over the bay and the ocean toward the offshore islands in a solid magenta wash, like varnish, and the sea looked emerald green, except when the wind was up or when hurricanes threatened in summer. Then the sea turned oxblood in color, like a pair of shoes that had been shined and then had gotten a layer of dust. When he was a kid, Poole had fished off the jetties down there, piles of rock, taking off his shoes and socks and shirt, leaving them on one of the dunes to get later, taking his casting rod and a box of tackle and a sack lunch to the end of the jetty to fish.

Poole could remember casting his jig and lead weights into the deep pull of the Gulf, letting the whole rig drop to the bottom with the bait, a chunk of mackerel, waiting on the rocks as the spray climbed around him. More than anything, he could remember the pull of a redfish as it hit the rig, down deep, the fish lying on the sand bottom, using the undertow while Poole backed away, setting his drag. Poole thought he could feel the past; his jaws were clenched. Back then . . . the Gulf didn't have a solid string of platforms pumping oil and gas, tankers flowing down to Galveston, up to New Orleans, wind that smelled of gas. Poole caught a lot of fish back then, and sometimes his father would grill the fish in the side yard of their house. Sometimes after his family had eaten, his father would take him to the movies in Beaumont, but that was a long time ago. Now, Poole was all grown up, sitting on a crime scene, baby-sitting an old man who was dead in a fishing shack—gunshot, from what Poole could see.

Suddenly, Poole felt amused by what he was doing, what he had tried to teach himself not to do anymore, which was not to romanticize the past but to keep clear the focus of each emotion so that he could avoid confusing himself with false feeling. More than anything, his past was shrouded with falsehood. It was simple. He had answered a call down on the highway and now he was doing his job. A daughter had found her father dead. She became hysterical, running down the beach, probably screaming bloody hell, and now Poole was waiting for the sheriff, looking around just to make sure the place was secure. He couldn't help it if the old man was stone dead, and Poole couldn't help the fact that his own wife had run away, and he couldn't help it if there weren't as many redfish in the surf as there used to be. Now, Poole was trying to live his life by a few simple rules, feeling that the simpler he made things for his internal life, his psyche, the better off he would be. He was afraid of becoming bitter if he didn't, and maybe even cynical, which Poole had discovered was an occupational hazard.

"Eat shit and die!" his wife had said once when he came home after three days away on police business. She had been drinking Tokay wine and crying, and there had been such a look of lost resentment on her face that Poole felt he couldn't ever change it no matter how hard he tried, nor did he quite know what he would do to change it if he had the chance, or the power, either one. "Eat shit and die!" she screamed, overwhelmed with tears, and Poole had tried to comfort her simply, putting his arms around her, but he had felt like a complete fool because the gesture had seemed false the instant he made it, and he knew he would have been better off not having tried to express an emotion he didn't feel, because people, his wife, Lisa Marie, included, eventually saw through false emotion, thinking you were a liar instead of being, as Poole was, confused and flattened by his life.

The word *corruption* crossed Poole's mind. He began to walk back and forth across the veranda like a caged panther, peering around the sun-shaded corner of the fishing shack,

4

studying the clean line of sand where it curved uphill to the dunes, broken sea grass, and tule. There was a ring of dark brown lumber piled against the side of the shack, and two oil drums were buried in the dune, sides tinged by charcoal fire where fishermen had burned some trash and garbage. The land on the other side of the dunes was gray and beige where oil roads ran through collections of shacks and storage sheds and abandoned oil equipment. It was ramshackle country, and Poole wondered if there was anyone out there, if anyone had seen anything or heard anything. It was so quiet, you'd think a gunshot would have carried a long way.

Some pelicans were flying over San Juan Island and Poole could faintly hear their wings beating against the wind. He could hear the clop of the oil derricks, too, but then the birds folded their wings and plunged down to the surface of the bay, smacking the water with an instantaneous whack, ripping back skyward where others were already disappearing into a ragged mangrove beyond the jetties.

The mangrove was a smudge of green just like the hump of a turtle shell. God, Poole was still remembering. . . . He had once seen a sea turtle that had been hooked by a fisherman on the Port Arthur pier. He could remember the flash of its shell as it rose through the water, foam rolling off its back, its flipper hooked next to the white underbelly, the flipper mottled gray and dangling helplessly out of the water as the turtle struggled against the weight of the line. Poole had watched for a long time while some young boys gathered around the fisherman, urging him to land the turtle, some of them throwing pop cans and cigarette butts at the helpless animal. Poole had pulled his knife and had walked over to the guy with the rod, a kid no more than fifteen years old. There was a rip of silence as Poole handed the knife to the kid, who just stood there silently for a time, until he had finally cut the turtle free as Poole stared right at him. There had been a surge of something electric, and then the turtle was gone to sea.

All the while, Poole knew what the crowd on the pier had been thinking, ruffians in cutoffs and tank tops, hard guys smoking cigarettes, throwing the butts off the pier, watching the butts wash in to the beach. Eat shit and die! Yeah, motherfucker, eat shit and die! The vector of their existence was like the point of many knives, a shiny explosion of intention. And how could Poole's actions have made any difference? And now Poole was looking around a crime scene distractedly, the pelicans re-forming over the mangrove, settling on pilings, all over the rock jetty near the marina store. Poole felt okay about the turtle. He just didn't want good things to have such a high price.

After fifteen years at the sheriff's office, maybe there weren't any good things left, anyway. He felt like he were a bundle of statistics, divorced, overeducated, stabbing pain behind the shoulder blade, not getting enough sleep, eating microwaved food. If given half a chance, Poole thought he might go back to those kids on the Port Arthur pier and ask forgiveness. He might try to explain himself from the perspective of time, kid them a little, have a smoke and toss the butt down to the surf.

Just then, right in the middle of the thought, Poole noticed an orange dinghy bumping over the waves toward the marina store, its outboard putting dully under the water. Pelicans rose as the small craft bounded into the wharf against a load of wave. The sky was turning gold and it was very hot.

Back in the dunes, a car lumbered over the oil roads. Poole stood up straight and tucked in his shirt, which was wet with sweat. He could feel the heat prickle on his skin, near the back where his pants were belted. The wind had picked up and the palms had begun to clack lounder along the edge of the surf. The water had turned dark purple in the low sun and slowly, along the circle of shore, lights began to flicker. Poole pushed his gun around to his back, above his suit trousers, and tucked down the holster flap so that he could sit down without pinching himself. His hands came away oily and he wiped them on his coat. The car stopped in some dune above the shack. Poole could hear its engine ticking and the door slam.

To Poole, the motion of Daddy John Lister climbing down the sand was disgusting. He looked like a balloon full of shit sliding down the incline, ice plants slick under his boots, the sheriff wearing a brown suit and a Stetson. Poole felt himself going stiff all over, and he realized that he had tucked in his shirt and had wiped off some sweat because Daddy John might make some snotty remark about the way he looked and Poole would have to back off his real feelings as always. He hated that kind of Tinkertoy game, and he knew he would resent it the rest of the Saturday night, which was supposed to be his. Poole felt small, having to tuck in his shirt that way, but it was nothing to the way he would feel if Daddy John said something about it. Whatever was screwing up his head at the present moment, Poole didn't want it to be resentment. Daddy John scuffled across the deep sand, smiling fatly like a tick full of blood.

"You been inside, Tom boy?" Lister asked, pausing to kick sand from his cuffs while he talked.

Poole flicked away a grin. Looking at Daddy John in his expensive brown cowboy suit with a big silver belt buckle, all Poole could think about was the face of the lank, ugly kid on the pier, the one Poole had handed the knife. Poole made a mental point that he was going to clean out his head tonight. Jesus! Here he was focusing on gas flames, thinking about the Gulf the way it was thirty-five years ago, remembering his own daddy, when what he needed to be thinking about was the old guy dead inside the shack. Poole realized there was no freedom inside your head. Freedom was being sheriff, wearing four-hundred-dollar cowboy suits, and whoever believed differently hadn't been around much.

Poole stood above the sheriff, looking down at the fat man, who was sweating. He told Daddy John that he had been inside the shack, that he'd had a look around. Poole stood there while Daddy John got his breath and wiped his face with a white handkerchief. Daddy John was wearing a fine cowboy suit all right, summer worsted blend, brown, with light red piping and black arrows on the pockets.

Poole told Daddy John the fisherman's daughter had found the old man and had made a call. The sheriff went around the veranda and walked up to the screen door, Poole standing back against the balustrade. Daddy John opened the screen door and stood there in a haze of sunlight.

"Smells like fucking fish," Daddy John said, his back to Poole.

2

It was a slow-motion pastiche, an imitation of something real, that had Daddy John leaning back against the screen door, his left hand inside his suit coat, reaching with the other hand for a white handkerchief, taking off his glasses, commencing to wipe them down, there in the half-light, which fell on the dead Vietnamese with the verisimilitude of pure drama. To Poole, the scene was like a filmstrip unwinding backward, so that for a while he was preserved from his own feelings by the perversity of what he was seeing, as though everything had screwed down to its essential negativity. It occurred to Poole then that it wasn't the smell of fish Daddy John had noticed, but fish sauce, and chili, and the deep aroma of citronella, and then the word *hooch* crossed his mind, in the same phenomenal crease in which the word *corruption* had reached him. Suddenly, things speeded up, until Daddy John was sitting in a wicker chair directly over the dead man, looking down at the corpse, still wiping his glasses, but distractedly, the room quiet and hot and close as the sun slanted down in diagonals from two jalousie windows.

There were clouds of gnats everywhere, and Poole thought he could actually hear them moving in the draftless hovel, along with the buzz of mosquitoes.

Poole felt himself fall backward in time toward the village of Duc Tho, where he used to go on Sundays, a solitary walk in the long, lonely afternoon, just to get away from the war. He could smell Asia, vaporous burning oil as helicopters hovered and then moved off, firing. There had been an old woman in a hooch, her plywood hovel at the end of a shady lane. She used to sit inside, surrounded by jerry-built shelving, on which she had managed to collect some black-market cassettes, cigarettes, a few tins of potted meat, chocolate, and even condoms. When Poole came through the door, she would smile hauntingly, revealing her ragged brown teeth, an ageless face that seemed both young and old, and entirely empty of expression as she rose and bowed while Poole glanced around nervously and without purpose. He would stand in the doorway of the hooch like a dust-ridden ape, trying to think of something useful to say, some greeting to make her understand even for a moment that he was lost, too, that he was estranged, not an enemy.

Then Poole twitched back to the present and came through the screen door and stood with his back against the jamb, staring at the old man lying dead in the sun, his body in a fetal pose, with a halo of dried blood around his head. The old man seemed to Poole as though he had gone to sleep and might wake at any moment. Poole felt in looking at him as if he was intruding on something terribly private, as if he had dropped suddenly through a trapdoor into a more personal space, where he was experiencing a feeling of shame. He could explain his feeling only in reference to the hooch, because it was compounded of both shame and embarrassment. He used to think about it at night, on his pallet below ground, hearing the incoming, the all-night rock and roll, dreary, spaced-out, and lost. Much later, on his way home over the Pacific in a C-135, Poole couldn't get the hooch out of his mind, even though he knew he should have been thinking about his wife, Lisa Marie, or about his mother. And even now the hooch kept coming back to him in waves of remembrance. Poole would think about the times he had purchased some cigarettes, cassettes, or potted meat. He would contemplate one Sunday when he had noticed the mysterious appearance on the shelves of a dozen bottles of airline scotch, some Gilbey's gin, each wrapped with a sprig of red ribbon. It was odd. It sent chills up his spine. And then another Sunday, the old woman had sold Poole a hand-stitched wallet, and another time a penknife, some flashlight batteries, baseball cards wrapped with a rubber band. Afterward, sitting down on Firebase Duc Tho one night, during a not-so-bad shelling, Poole realized that the items had been scavenged from dead GIs.

Near the end of his tour, Poole had been transferred to Saigon, and he had gone to the hooch on a Tuesday before he left, just to see the old woman. He wanted to say goodbye, but she wasn't there, and another old woman was there instead. Poole had been stunned, stumbling back to the base through the rising hot dust. It must have been just then, at the precise moment that Poole had gone through the doorway of the hooch, in the incredible scorching heat and din, that he had given up all hope of achieving an understanding of any of the subtle shades of things in Vietnam. He had stood still in the doorway of the hooch and had looked back at the old woman in disbelief while the woman considered him with absolute unknowing. Poole remembered thinking, Grandmother, sister, mother-in-law—what? For Poole, the infinite replaceability of human life had the regressive monotony of pi, but without the sense of rectitude. The old woman had opened her mouth and Poole saw that she had no teeth. All the way back to the firebase, he kept thinking, praying, Oh God, if you're there, if you exist, cast me away from this awful violence and anonymity. And then halfway back, in the middle of a brown field of grass, he realized that he hadn't bought anything from the old woman.

Daddy John was saying, "Well?" as Poole came back to himself, the screen door whisking shut. "Well, Tom boy, why don't you give me what you've got?" Daddy John had put on his glasses, and Poole could see dust forming on the lenses already, the sheriff's eyes bugging through the glass. Little pig eyes in reams of fat. "I would appreciate your attention to the matters at hand," Daddy John said, turning slightly. "If that wouldn't be too much trouble."

The Stetson was pushed back on Daddy John's head. The floor and walls were cypress planks, and in the sunshine the old Vietnamese seemed terribly small in death, still wearing worn black pajamas and a gray sweater with the sleeves cut off. Poole couldn't help looking around the room with a dull fascination, especially at the Vietnamese calendar on one wall.

"The daughter found him this way," Poole said. "Dispatch told me she's up at the family house. Down the beach somewhere. I don't quite know the location, but you take the oil road all the way to the swamp estuary." Poole felt as if he was reciting his lessons for a teacher. Poole had never liked Daddy John and whenever he was around the sheriff, Poole had a feeling of being under observation, that at any moment a wrong answer might bring down a ruler on his hand. Poole knew that Daddy John understood everything from a political slant, that Poole's veteran preference in getting the job had meant permanent probation somehow. "The dead guy's name is Nguyen Bao Do," Poole said, trying to lend the name some significance, trying to avert the essential namelessness of the old man, because down deep Poole knew that to Daddy John this old Vietnamese fisherman was utterly unimportant. Nothing was important to Daddy John except keeping his job, the joys of ass-kicking politics, and his only son, Darnell, who was already cashing in on Daddy John's place in Jefferson County, that pig-eyed son sitting drunk on the board of commissioners, feeding himself on the droppings from taxpayers' pockets. "Nguyen Bao Do," Poole said again, louder, when Daddy John asked him to speak up. Poole told Daddy John that the lab boys were on their way, that the county coroner was in Houston, gone up to catch the Astros playing the Mets, and wouldn't be back until tomorrow. Daddy John was in midsentence: ". . . one of these goddamn fishhead shrimpers." He was smiling up at Poole, sharing a confidence. Daddy John had a way of thinking: If a man had been in Vietnam, he had an automatic attitude. Poole didn't allow him to doubt it about himself, though he knew it was more complicated than that. Poole knew that he didn't have an attitude, at least not one that Daddy John would trust, so he hid his real feelings from the sheriff. Poole let Daddy John believe he might be a Rice Owl fan, a lover of good bourbon. "And how many of these fishheads do you reckon live in the home place? Quite a mess, I'd reckon."

Poole knew Daddy John was asking him something about the old man's family. A mess, Poole mused to himself, like fish. And Daddy John had been talking about children, humans, not abstractions like numbers. Human beings like the old woman in the hooch. But there was some common ground, an irony about death itself that Poole could share with Daddy John. The thing that sets me apart from you, you fat bastard, Poole was thinking, is that I can't abstract from this shit, this corpse, no matter how tired I am of all of it. Just after that, Poole recalled that the freedom in your head wasn't worth spit.

Poole made his first inventory while Daddy John sat in

the wicker chair and watched. Poole wrote everything down in a spiral notebook, one eye on Daddy John, who was wiping his face with a handkerchief. He noted all the fishing gear, tackle, seines, rods and reels, cooking utensils, cans of motor oil, one old kerosene lamp, some outboard motor parts, a broken-down inboard in one corner, Vietnamese tapes and magazines. The .22 Colt target pistol he found beside the body surprised Poole because it was so new. There was no rust on it, which you'd expect on the Gulf, and it was an expensive gun, not a Saturday-night special.

Poole made a diagram, putting chalk marks around the old man, X's at his shoulders, at the tips of his toes, the old man's feet bare, thongs lying on the floor as if he had just stepped out of them. Poole put the pistol in a freezer bag and left the bag on the floor for the lab boys. He was trying to focus on being a cop again despite the fact that Daddy John was watching him the way a cattleman might judge livestock. Poole studied the entry wound in the old man's skull, a dark blue hole in the temple just ahead of the vein, but he didn't touch the body. He examined the wound, the ears, the fingernails, which he found unusually long for a working man. The way the body was positioned meant the exit wound would be behind the right ear, a part of the head Poole couldn't see. If Daddy John wanted to move the body and see the exit wound, he wouldn't hesitate to lift the body and look, fucking up the crime scene. Poole had seen Daddy John screw up a lot worse, shit so flagrant it was almost beautiful. Right now, though, Daddy John seemed content to sit and allow Poole to work without interference, the mosquitoes getting worse and worse as evening came on. Daddy John asked Poole if he had seen anyone around the shack and Poole answered that he hadn't, explaining that he'd checked for footprints, or broken glass, but there was nothing. And besides, the wind had kicked up and was tossing sand everywhere, covering over whatever might have been.

Poole put on some rubber gloves, which he always carried in the car. You never knew when you might need them, what with the AIDS thing, prisoners getting drunk, biting your hand, spitting in your face. He touched the Vietnamese at last, the man's skin soft and cool. Poole touched just under the jaw, lifting the old man's head, patting down the pajamas, but there weren't any pockets. Daddy John got out of his chair and stood above Poole while Poole patted down the old man. Poole cleared his throat, trying to jack up something to talk about with the sheriff, but it was tricky, like talking to your high school basketball coach, a stupid prick who gave out swats.

"I was on the Port Arthur highway," Poole said finally. He glanced up at Daddy. "I heard the call and came over. Do you want me to take the job?"

"May as well be you," the sheriff replied.

"May as well," Poole was saying, but just then Daddy John finished up, smiling: ". . . seeing as how you've had experience with dead gooks."

Now Poole knew Daddy John believed that they were sharing a private joke, not a confidence, but something much more terrible, a whole goddamn national experience, which was where Poole's secret attitude came in. There was a lot Poole wanted to say, like, How about this new gun, this expensive Colt target pistol that looks as if it just came out of the box, like a Christmas present? But Poole let it go.

"Get back with me in the morning. Maybe Monday," Daddy John said.

Poole followed Daddy John to a door in the back of the shack. The sheriff shoved it all the way open while Poole stood in the entry, Daddy John climbing down a staircase that was nothing more than an old gangway leaning against the back of the shack, nailed to the plank walls. Poole concluded that the gangway was salvage, propped against the back of the shack when erosion had slurried the beach away, raising the house three or four feet from ground level.

Poole walked around front, out on the veranda, and found the light failing fast. He heard Daddy John start his car and the car crunching over the oyster-shell sand, then later he heard more cars bouncing down the oil roads, maybe Mirabelli and Hernandez. Poole hoped it wasn't Hernandez, because one of the guy's kids had just died and it was hard to know what to say to him. Poole decided that he would go up the hill and talk to the daughter who had made the call, hoping that she had stopped crying by now if it came to that, because if there was one thing Poole hated, it was trying to deal with personal shit. But he decided he'd rather do that than stay in the fishing shack, which reminded him of the Duc Tho hooch. Poole pulled his holster around to his left side again. Yes, he thought, that was how he got rid of his personal shit, by not dealing with it, like he got rid of his wife.

The men coming down the dunes were laughing. Probably Mirabelli, maybe Hernandez. Then Poole froze, realizing that the old Vietnamese didn't have any teeth. The thought put him right back in the hooch with the old woman sitting behind her plywood counter in grainy heat. It occurred to Poole that he could not imagine the old woman a suicide, not even close, no matter how bad it got, and he couldn't imagine an old Vietnamese fisherman a suicide, either. That was one of the qualifications of the survivor: You survive.

It was Hernandez coming around the shack. From where he was standing on the veranda, Poole could see the gas flame of Port Arthur Oil and Pipe, dark red now. He tried to think what he was going to say to Hernandez, who was walking up the stairs.

3

Poole couldn't believe how sharp Mirabelli looked with his blazer and a red power tie, a pair of gray flannel slacks. Even in the heat, he looked as if he had just stepped out of *GQ*. Mirabelli flicked a fingernail at his suit pocket as if some sand had offended him. "The fuck," he yelled down to Poole, "my kids are playing Hansel and Gretel at Children's Theater in Beaumont." He smiled at Poole. "Here the fuck I am on Saturday night."

Poole was on the veranda. He could hear Hernandez moving around in the shack: a sneeze, the click of a shutter as he took some quick photos, then the sharp crackle of the car radio coming in over the wind, which had become steady. Poole walked up the dune path to where Mirabelli had parked his car next to Poole's on the top of the dunes, and he and Mirabelli relaxed against the hood. In the wind, some of the sweat finally cooled away from Poole's body.

"Who offed the old fart?" Mirabelli asked.

Poole had been telling him about the Vietnamese. Poole thought about the question, and when he didn't respond, both men leaned back in the sunshine, listening to Hernandez humming a weird tune down in the shack.

"Maybe the old fart offed himself," Mirabelli said.

The palms were working now, *clickety-click-click* in the wind, like billiard balls on a smooth felt table, and out on the ocean in the blue evening, the oil rigs made a chain up and down the Gulf, so many lights that Poole found himself astonished that there was any open water left between Port Arthur and Galveston. Poole was not surprised to see refuse out on the water, since he was used to seeing the sprawl of plastic suburbs between Spindletop and Beaumont, what had once been scrub creosote and black cotton land. It was phenomenal. Americans killed history as soon as it threatened to exist. Poole wondered if Mirabelli shared his perception in any way, but he doubted it, knowing that Mirabelli lived in Boomtown with his wife and kids, in a brick house that really didn't belong on the Gulf Coast, or anywhere in south Texas, a single-story ranch, some slotted windows at roof level, low ceilings, big heat pumps on concrete in the backyard.

When Poole had married, he and Lisa Marie rented a big house on Laurel Street in Beaumont, in an older neighborhood. The house was run-down in a nice way, with its peeling paint and genteel sagging porch, a breezeway with a good run of wind north to south, and, between the kitchen and the garage, a covered walk with trellis roses and honeysuckle, where Poole used to sit in the evenings and drink ale and listen to ball games on the radio. There were some old oaks that shaded the house in summer, and Poole thought the ten years he had lived there were his happiest times, though later when he thought about it, he realized that his happiness was either relative or utterly imagined—romanticized, at any rate.

Early on in their life together, Poole and Lisa Marie had taken to going to flea markets and antique shops, trying to find old things that fit their idea of what they would share as they got old, shopping for their future by rummaging in the past. They came back with some furniture—overstuffed chairs—and an old-fashioned Zenith tube radio that Poole had insisted on buying even though they couldn't afford it. Their forced effort to create a shared future, instead of sharing one, hadn't worked.

Poole had been to Mirabelli's house in Boomtown once for dinner and he'd never been invited back, probably because he had alienated Mirabelli's wife by going into a premature shell. That had happened, he thought, because of the family feel to the place: the flat beige paint on the walls, the kid noise, the smell of broccoli, and the TV that was playing while they ate. Even now, after all this time and distance, Poole would sometimes buy a twelve-pack and drive over to the house on Laurel Street and sit out in front in his Caprice, drinking the warm beer and smoking cigarettes one after another until his mind shut down, discovering later in the dawn that he had burned his suit coat, dropped some ash on his pants, wondering if he wasn't shutting down too much—turning off entirely was more like it.

"On the way," Mirabelli was saying over the car hood.

"What?" said Poole, startled.

"The ambulance," Mirabelli said, louder, looking at Poole as if he was deaf.

"Sorry," Poole muttered.

Mirabelli had one hand on the hood of his car, his shoe on the fender. Then Mirabelli put his hands on his knees and did a bongo beat, *tap-tap*, unconcerned and relaxed, as though the old Vietnamese down in the shack didn't exist.

"So," Mirabelli said in jazz tone. "The old fart offed himself?"

Poole was not Mirabelli's boss, but he had been in the department longer, and Mirabelli would more than likely

19

do what Poole told him to do, and besides, the implication from Daddy John was that Poole would lead any investigation. While Poole was pondering this fact, he looked up the beach at the marina, where some sailboats were bobbing up and down around a wharf. Dim lights shone inside the bait store and beside the jetty the rocks were black as obsidian. The jetty stuck out fifty yards into the surf. Below him, the fishing shack stood on a spit of land by an estuary that worked its way south to where it became a tidal basin of the Sabine River. Beyond that was some brackish land and a system of swamps and lakes that had been protected from drainage and development by the state parks along the beach. Back to the north, toward Louisiana, the oil roads cut a crazy quilt pattern around the bay. The land was high-water table, brush, and salt-encrusted with mounds of tule, saw grass, then the suburbs with houses like the one Mirabelli lived in.

Poole was trying to think what to say. "I don't know," he managed. "Maybe the old fart did off himself."

Mirabelli was still using his knees as bongos. Poole knew Mirabelli wanted to go home and see his kids in the play, and this knee tapping was a way of diverting his impatience. Poole was sympathetic.

"Work your way back to town on the back roads, would you? Make me a map of the shacks along the way. Maybe I'll knock on some doors in the morning." Poole smiled, splitting the difference with Mirabelli. He didn't want to be anybody's boss around here, but he didn't feel like letting the old Vietnamese go that easily, either. It was funny, Poole thought, talking to Mirabelli, how worked up people get over abstracts like flags, medals, battleships, even ideas, communism, freedom, but how real things never take a strong hold. Some guy sees a dog hit by a car in the street and he turns the other way, heading down to McDonald's for a burger and fries, not wanting to be delayed five minutes. There had been body counts and rocket fire on Walter

Cronkite for years, and then some chicken colonel blows a VC away for live TV and everybody goes apeshit. And now the old Vietnamese was turning into an abstraction, this dog in the street.

Mirabelli grinned at Poole. He nodded and hurried around his car, leaving Poole to take Hernandez back to Beaumont when they were through in the shack, unless Hernandez wanted to ride back in the ambulance. Poole hoped Hernandez *would* ride back in the ambulance, not only because he didn't feel like talking right now but because he wanted to be alone on the beach, knowing he was going to have to talk to the old man's daughter soon enough, dreading it, not wanting to add Hernandez to the equation of his personal dissonance.

When Poole had satisfied himself that Mirabelli was going to go over the roads slowly enough to check things out, watching his taillights weave around the dusky horizon, Poole walked down to the shack and told Hernandez he wanted him to start talking with all the fishermen and oil riggers along the beach, telling Hernandez that tomorrow was soon enough, after church, because he knew Hernandez would be going to Mass, especially now that his kid had been killed.

For some reason, Poole felt suddenly calm. He decided that he would walk down the waterline so he could take a closer look at the beach, the dunes, maybe scan the area with his flashlight just to see if somebody had left something lying around, although he thought that there was little chance of that because it was wild down there and the road was made with crushed hard coral and shell. As Poole walked, he could see bottles and cans everywhere in the dunes, and he could see how the humps of sand and sea grass had been leveled by three-wheelers and cycles, by guys in Jeeps who took off over the sand on weekends with their beer and boom boxes. Poole could see behind him that Hernandez had turned on an overhead light in the shack, by now not knowing what more to do, probably feeling badly about being all alone with a dead man.

It was after sunset and the mosquitoes were bad. Poole had a hard time keeping them off his neck. They were driving him crazy. He crossed the beach and went up into the dunes, shining his flashlight around while he walked. This place had once been a broad delta of the Sabine, where the river mushed-out into the sea, but what it was now was a sump, low and marshy, not very pleasant, though once it must have been filled with game. It was like all this peckerwood country, scraped over and left behind.

Poole climbed a hump of saw grass and spotted a house on Sabine Pass. It looked like it was made of stucco, standing on a rise above the river between the Clam Lake canal and culvert, which was navigable all the way to Walker Lake and the Intracoastal. The walking was hard work in the heat and Poole was sweating again inside his suit, feeling the gun belt tight around his waist where his skin was chafed. He felt like a stupid cowboy cop swinging a flashlight around in the half-dark, walking down a barren road. Then before he could see the stucco house again, he went down and up a hillock. When he got back to the top of a dune, he could see the house again, pink cracked stucco with a slab porch, sliding glass doors in back and a boat trailer in the driveway, just behind a pickup truck. There were slot windows near the roof, just like Mirabelli's house in Boomtown, prefab from hardware store kits, hauled in from someplace like Cleveland and planted on Sabine Pass. One side of the house, Poole could tell, was sloping already, downhill toward the beach, the other slipping into the estuary. It was coming apart in the middle, which wouldn't have happened if it had been built of cypress on stilts, the way the bubbas used to build on the Gulf before there were so many people.

Poole walked up the oil road and stood in the driveway of the stucco house, looking at the ocean, realizing that he could hear frogs croaking in the fresh water of the estuary. He looked at the estuary, bright nickel light on the water, and he thought to himself, Yes, these oil rigs are pumping two or three barrels a day now, maybe a little more, maybe not, and five or six hundred gallons of salt water a day along with the oil, which went back down the hole where it came from. So the sand was sinking, and the beach was eroding because of all the jetties, and the marshes were drying up as the salt came to the surface.

Poole walked across the dirt yard and tapped at the front door. He looked, but he couldn't find a bell, and so he knocked again softly and slapped some mosquitoes off his neck. He had his back turned when he heard the door open, and when he turned around, he was surprised to see an older woman with graying hair standing there, not Vietnamese as he had expected, but an Anglo with a nice face. Her face was wrinkled with character, as though she had gotten plenty of sun. She looked like a woman of laughter, too, but right now she just looked surprised, a little exhausted, and Poole knew he looked surprised, as well. They stood like two waiters who arrive at the swinging doors with full trays on their shoulders at the same time.

"I hope you're the police," she said.

Poole gave his name, explaining he was with the sheriff's office.

"I'm Adrienne Deveraux," she said. Poole probably looked perplexed, because she added quickly, "I live in one of the beach houses back there." She pointed back north toward the marina, from where Poole had come.

"I walked down," Poole said. "I didn't think anyone lived along that stretch."

"Just us," the woman said, "my husband and I."

She had stepped back into the house and Poole followed her, seeing the woman over his shoulder while she closed the door. Poole looked around and saw a slab patio directly across the living room, through sliding glass. The glass was partly open, but it was hot in the room, so close that Poole could hardly breathe. A fan on the kitchen floor was blowing hot air across the room. To his right, Poole noticed a hallway, which probably led to bedrooms. He was feeling heat-prickly, flashing on the citronella smell, which was strong in the room, and put off by the sound of the sand he was crunching under his shoes on the bare linoleum. Maybe it was a cultural reaction to the smell, the sand, and the hot air blowing along the floor, but whatever it was, he was a long way from blaming the dead Vietnamese for it.

Adrienne Deveraux was saying something. But Poole was busy noticing things, fixing himself on his surroundings as if he were a radar dish, locking in. There was an amplifier in one corner of the room and what he thought was a preamp next to it, and two guitars were piled around a Formica table in the kitchen. The table itself was covered with dirty dishes and ashtrays full of butts. It had the look of a welfare house, but what did that mean? What had Poole expected? You survive, hammered by facticity. There was nothing regular for these Vietnamese fishermen but need. It wasn't as if they were Pilgrims coming over on the *Mayflower*, sitting down one bright fall day with some friendly Indians, passing turkey around. Nothing was that simple anymore. Nowadays, you had to muscle up for everything, and if you didn't have any muscle, you didn't have anything. Even Poole felt that sometimes he didn't have muscle. And look where he was at. What would it be like for these people?

"Tran comes to see me . . ." Adrienne Deveraux was saying, her voice trailing off. Poole was looking at her now, taking his inventory, beginning to be impressed by the bones in her face. He couldn't guess her age, but thought she might be ten years older than Poole. She was telling Poole that the girl was in a back bedroom, pretty broken up still, but through crying, so she thought it might be okay to go on back. Poole nodded, noticing the woman's eyes, then took a long look at the kitchen, which was small and messy. Poole walked out the patio door and looked at the Gulf, where there were tankers and oil rigs, tugs lighted up like computer screens, palms in dim outline on the beach.

When he came back inside, he said, "How do you happen to be here, Mrs. Deveraux?"

"I told you," she said. "Tran came for me. She was down at the shack and came by my house on her way here. I told you, we're friends."

Poole bit his lip. He had been looking and not listening. He could tell he had dropped a notch in the woman's judgment, which was something he regretted.

"We're friends," she repeated, emphasizing the words so that Poole would hear and not ask again.

Poole was about to go back to the bedroom to talk with the girl named Tran when he asked Adrienne Deveraux if she would mind sticking around. He realized down deep that he had a mysterious empathy with the woman, an innate confidence in her he couldn't explain, which troubled him, because he thought it might be something sexual. She was trim and bony, done up in cotton pants with a rope belt, a blue ribbon around the crown of her hair. She looked something like his ex-wife. Maybe that was it, and Poole winced to think that he could still be so affected by the ghost of his Lisa Marie.

Adrienne Deveraux said, "Of course," as if it had been an expected request. But it helped Poole contract back into the flow, because he was beginning to experience the hooch again, the smell of citronella and fish sauce, and when he came back from the bedroom from talking with the girl Tran, he wanted to see something he could fix on that would be familiar.

The girl was down the hall in a bedroom. Poole found her there, sitting on a single bed in the heat, with only a ruffle of air coming through one of the slot windows up near the ceiling. Gray geese on cheap curtains, buff white walls with spackling, some cracks. Poole held out his badge and introduced himself, saying he was sorry but not speaking forcefully the way he knew he should.

4

Daddy John Lister had been elected three times by the voters of Jefferson County, and there was no telling when they would stop sending him back into office. Whether it was ignorance or plain sloth, Poole didn't know, but he did understand that Daddy John had burrowed his way inside like a tick and wasn't about to let go.

You could see him any day of the week, strutting around the courthouse in his western suit and Stetson, fat Lyndon Johnson jowls, all dolled up during the hottest part of the day when you'd think he'd be downstairs in the cafeteria having coffee and doughnuts, checking things with the county staff, chatting with the janitors, or upstairs, pumping hands in the clerk's office, where he knew everybody by name, along with their kids and grandkids. Daddy John had these people by the short hairs.

All in all, Daddy John passed around over a hundred jobs, and that was real muscle, especially in a town like Beaumont. Knowing first names, shaking a few hands in the hot mornings, passing around jobs and money.

Poole had gotten used to some of it. He understood the constant electioneering by the sheriff, how Daddy John treated the help like field slaves. Daddy John would run out to a crime scene and get his picture taken for TV or the newspaper, then drive back downtown to Beaumont and get on the phone and call around to see if there was any juice in the lemon. Whatever it was, some poor bastard gunned down at the Quick Trip, or maybe a woman raped down by the Waterworks Canal on the Neches, Daddy John would be there quick, say something patronizing, then get home in time to watch himself on Channel 6, see how he came off.

Poole didn't want to be like Daddy John at all. He wanted to deal with people the right way, but it was hard sometimes. That was how he was trying to deal with the Vietnamese girl now, the right way.

Tran stood when Poole came into the bedroom. He made her sit down, knowing that even in grief she would do something formalized. He touched her shoulder gently and smiled. Under the light of a table lamp near the bed, she looked very young, but pretty and nice, too, and Poole could tell that she had been crying terribly, big round eyes red and a runny nose. She was plump, her hair cut in a bowl around her head. Poole checked out the room, using his radar. Cheap modular shelving lined one wall, with family photos in frames on a plywood desk. It turned out Tran could speak good English. She wasn't self-conscious about it at all, but she did have an accent that made it hard for Poole at first, all the syllables run down into a flat line, exactly the opposite of what Vietnamese sounded like, which was wavy and cacophonous. He found himself trying to get a good bead on what she was saying, feeling awkward because there wasn't anywhere to sit down other than the bed, and he didn't want to sit there. He didn't want to tower over her, either, but that was how it ended up. So he paced the room in order to break the rhythm of the conversation.

"You found your father?" he asked.

Tran said she had been out for a walk. She had seen the back door of the shack ajar and had been curious. She'd gone inside and found her father. She said she lived with her husband, Danny, in a house farther north and she'd just come here to her father's house, hadn't found him home. Once or twice, Poole thought she was going to break out into keening. He could see it in her shoulders and it made him think of all the wailing he had seen in Asia. But she didn't; she just kept talking in a monotone. She said she didn't have a job, so she helped out wherever she could with the family, mending fishing nets and seines, doing the cooking, washing clothes, anything to earn money, like clerking during holidays at Sears. She wanted to go to business college in Port Arthur, now that she could speak English, and learn to be a secretary, maybe even learn computers, which was where she thought the jobs were. She thought it might be possible someday to start a restaurant.

Poole asked about her husband, Danny, and she told him that he came and went as he pleased, which wasn't the answer he particularly wanted to hear. Danny did some fishing or hung around Port Arthur looking for work. Then Tran said something Poole did understand. She said Danny was another refugee, *real boat people,* for the first time her voice tipping up the scale a bit, as if that set Danny apart somehow. Poole made a note of it but didn't press the point. She had met Danny hanging out at a fish restaurant in Port Arthur and they had gotten married. From the way she was acting, suddenly nervous, Poole decided that maybe Tran wasn't happy with Danny. Anyway, the family had been sharing food stamps, but Texas was cutting general assistance, and besides, the welfare people were very brusque, treating them like dirt, and so all of them tried to make money here and there, living out in the flats in houses nobody else wanted, FHA repossessions on the brine and oil flats, which was better than living in Beaumont projects, duplexes that were run-down. Tran said her own family were provincial Vietnamese, people who for generations had lived along the south Coast in weather that wasn't much different from Texas's, hotter, greener, with more fish and shrimp, clean water, a place everybody spoke her language.

Poole started thinking about the *Mayflower* again and white Pilgrims from England hanging on to the edge of a continent, hacking their way into the interior until they had found a good life and made their fortune. After that, other people started coming, hanging on to the edge of the continent, too. It was the hanging on part that impressed Poole about Tran. Here she was barely hanging on to the edge of a continent, clinging to the belly of something that was just about full already, buffalo shot to hell, forests cut down, a continent full of power plants, freeways, talk-show hosts. There were evangelists and truck-driving schools and advertising, too, information systems that had dulled existence to a blur of digital switches and financial transactions. This wasn't the Pilgrim shit anymore, sitting down to some turkey and corn. It wasn't Colonial Massachusetts and it wasn't the jealous God of our forefathers.

So, thought Poole, while Tran continued to talk, it looks like the old man was going to be left on the floor of the shack, metaphorically anyway, especially by Daddy John, because for him there wasn't going to be a TV camera following him around, and no newspaper stories. Frankly, Poole didn't know if he had the guts for this case, either, or whether he had the willpower to stick it out, what with all this hanging on to the belly of a continent. But he thought he would give it a try.

Poole asked Tran about her other family.

"My sister, Bhin," she said. "She lives here with her husband, Jerry." Tran pointed to a door across the hall. Poole took it to mean that the couple had a room, shared it with the old man in his house.

"Your mother?"

"She's dead. Long time ago in Vietnam."

"How long have you lived here?"

"Four year," Tran said. "From resettlement camp in Thailand."

"Where is your sister now?"

"Port Arthur, probably. With Jerry." She shrugged one shoulder, a gesture that indicated to Poole that perhaps she was ashamed that her sister wasn't here now that her father was dead.

"Donovan," Tran said when Poole asked his last name.

"And Jerry, what does he do?" Poole had masked his surprise, Jerry, an Anglo.

"He try to fish. That didn't work out so good. He does mechanic things. He's not working right now." Poole knew Tran was ashamed. She had looked away at the family pictures, big easy tears in her eyes.

That put the family somewhere else when the old man had died. Port Arthur, fishing maybe, Adrienne Deveraux down in her beach house. More and more, it was looking like the old man was fading out as a real thing. But something in Poole kept taking him back to the edge of the continent, these people hanging on by their fingernails, floating around like flotsam just inside the line where there were oil rigs and platforms, tugs and tankers, the palms with their fronds drooping in the poison wind. A vision was growing inside Poole, something intangible but real. He was imagining the old woman in the hooch up near Duc Tho. And when Poole had fully imagined her, he was surprised to find a stoicism of infinite capacity, not something that kept her from being afraid of helicopter gunships or mortars going over in the night, a hollow clunk and then a whine, but something that kept her coming down to the hooch day after day in the heat and the violent rain to sell her scavenged goods. It was the kind of thing that made suicide unthinkable.

Then Poole reached a dead end. He couldn't think of anything to say to Tran, but he was not going to start drilling her about her father right now. She had begun to cry again now that Poole was quiet. Poole tried to turn away. The girl was embarrassed, hiding her face in her arms while this stranger, and a cop, too, loomed over her with a notebook in his hand, speaking English with a Texas drawl. When she calmed down, Poole asked her about the gun, the new Colt, which was the one thing he really had to know about tonight. Tran told him she hadn't seen a gun before but that she knew her father had one, out on the boat or around the shack, because he needed it to kill shark and barracuda. There was a flute of silence before she added that maybe he needed it because some American shrimpers had attacked some Vietnamese in a restaurant in Port Arthur. Some Vietnamese houses had been ransacked, a few boats burned. One of her father's boats had been vandalized, but he had repaired it and continued to fish. He sounded like a tough old son of a bitch to Poole.

Poole remembered the whole situation. It was an ugly six months, with bubba fishermen hunting the Vietnamese night after night like possum, wanting to kick some ass because they thought they owned the ocean and all the shrimp in it. Poole hadn't been involved directly because it was a federal thing, but it was hard to miss, the atmosphere of violence, guys in dark glasses all over town. From Galveston to Biloxi to the Panhandle, established shrimpers were getting after the Vietnamese. Americans were pushing back at the people hanging on to the edge of the continent. The hell of it was that the real Gulf had been used up long ago by the oil companies, the developers, by the fishermen themselves, who killed dolphin and turtles, dredged channels, built jetties, and overfished. And now all of the sudden these guys were burning FHA houses on the dunes, punching holes in the hulls of Vietnamese shrimp boats. Poole knew how hard it was to get anything, to hold on to what you had. Poole sympathized, but damn! He wondered if the old Vietnamese down in the shack had been offed by some ugly bubba drunk on Lone Star.

Poole asked Tran if he could look around. The girl nodded but didn't say anything, all out of hope. Poole rummaged around the modular shelves, the single closet. There were some old clothes all laundered and some cheap shoes from Fabulous Footwear. He found a St. Christopher medal on the desk and it stopped him cold. *They're Catholics;* they have the same God we do, he thought. Then it hit him again, this time from a different angle, more metaphysical. Suicide, would that be something the old Vietnamese would do?

Poole reached the doorway in his tour around the room. There wasn't much to see. "Have you had trouble with the Anglo fishermen lately?" he asked.

"Yes, some," Tran said. "Last year, an old man named Teagarden put another hole in one of my father's two boats. He tried to sink it."

"Where did he keep the boats?"

"Down at the old marina." She gestured halfheartedly. Poole was ready to go into the other bedroom, so Tran got up, tried to stop crying. She was sniffling some, her chest heaving. She was wearing a clean white cotton blouse with a yellow halter over it, knee-length shorts with a cute wildflower pattern like Poole had seen college kids wear. These made Tran look frumpy, though. They didn't suit her at all, her dimpled knees, too chubby. Still, she carried herself damn well.

Poole felt as if some of the tension was draining away. He walked down the hallway toward the bathroom, looked inside, not trying to locate anything especially but feeling the place out with his eyes, making a point not to pry too much while Tran was standing behind him. It wasn't evidence he was after. It was too early for that kind of experience. He just wanted to look without making an official search. It was like finally getting your breath after a long time underwater, breaking the surface with the cool air on your face. Poole felt that way now because he didn't understand how an old Vietnamese with a handsome daughter, a Catholic, somebody who had come a long way, could walk into a fishing shack, put a gun to his brain, and blow himself into hell.

Poole walked back down the hallway and glanced into the other bedroom, the one shared by Bhin and Jerry. He was surprised, even in the dark, because he was sure he was looking at an ashtray full of marijuana roaches on the bed stand, a silver hash pipe, a water bed with a tie-dyed spread. There was another tie-dyed sheet on the wall, nailed there so it had split the stucco through to the lathe, making a crack that Poole thought was pretty sloppy. You could smell the syrupy dope aroma in the room, and Poole immediately thought about the guitars and amps in the living room, wondering what this had to do with Bhin and Jerry, if this was Jerry's bag, thinking it because Tran didn't look the type. Maybe there wasn't any type, but Poole thought it anyway, because he had begun to like Tran, liking her even though he knew nothing about her life.

Poole took a look at a chest of drawers, an open closet, the room just like the other one. He decided he wouldn't do more. He didn't have a warrant and he didn't want this to come up tonight, anyway. He would let the dope go for now. Poole wondered if Tran resented him going through the house or if she was too confused and grief-stricken to care, but it bothered him and so he turned around and tried to smile, touching Tran on the shoulder to guide her, a gesture she seemed to appreciate. And then they walked together to the front room.

Tran went straight to Adrienne Deveraux and fell into her arms. The older woman had been sitting on a couch and she got up and embraced Tran, who came up only to her neck. Poole stood with his hands on his hips, his spiral notebook in the palm of one hand, explaining to them both that the ambulance would be taking Nguyen Bao Do over to the hospital in Beaumont and that somebody would be riding along, this guy named Hernandez, who was okay; he would take care of things. He said the coroner would look at the body, but he didn't mention an autopsy. Poole said he would be in touch, that he'd like to talk with them in his office in more detail, but he knew now wasn't the time. Poole didn't see a telephone, so he thought Tran had probably made her call from Adrienne Deveraux's beach house. He said he'd help all he could, even with the funeral arrangements. All the while, Adrienne Deveraux had been brushing Tran's hair, looking at Poole with her eyes, telling him it was time to quit, doing it gently, with just a narrowing of expression in her marbled blue eyes.

"Did you touch anything in the shack?" Poole asked Tran.

"No, I didn't touch," she said.

"What do you think happened?"

She leaned away from Adrienne Deveraux, sniffling. "He didn't kill himself," she said. There was no anger in her voice, just a tone of resignation, like she wanted someone in authority to know, even if later the law forgot all about her father. It was a statement. It made a difference to the church. It made a difference to her.

Before Poole started for the front door, he made a couple of conscious decisions. He was going to do a good job, proceed with this investigation even if he had to break a few rules to do it. He knew Daddy John would fade this thing to black, but Poole decided he was going to light a candle. He was going to check out this gun thing, too. It struck him, something about a new Colt on the floor of the shack.

But right now he was tired and he thought he might buy a twelve-pack and drive up to Beaumont and park on Laurel Street and watch his house in the night, the one he didn't live in anymore.

5

They were standing outside in the dark. The ocean behind made lapping sounds on the sand.

Tran was leaning on Adrienne Deveraux, her arm around the older woman's waist, her head barely coming up to Adrienne Deveraux's neck. Poole was sweating heavily from being inside the closed house, from the night air, which had stopped moving. The wind was gone, and all that dope smell stayed in his clothes, along with the aroma of citronella.

Poole had lived all his life in Texas, most of it in Beaumont or Port Arthur, and he should have been accustomed to the late-summer weather, the sun like a rock in the sky, wet air like a blanket, a nightfall that made no difference to the heat, just making things black and hot instead of yellow and hot. The breeze would pick up in the early evening, coming off the ocean for a while, but even that would be hot and salt-choked, and then it would quit near eight and the air would sit down on you like heavy wool.

Poole had been up north once or twice in his life, extraditing prisoners, escorting them to other jurisdictions, and once in St. Paul, he had been stranded in a sudden summer thundershower, standing on a bridge over the Mississippi River. He had been walking around St. Paul like a tourist, admiring the city and its big trees. All of the sudden, the temperature dropped and lightning began to flash around him, jagged barks of it in the cloudy sky, while people in the park that fronted the riverbank ran for cover. But Poole had stayed there on the bridge, right in the middle, looking up at the rain as a downpour commenced. He couldn't believe how cool the wind was. The temperature had gone from eighty-five degrees in the shade to about fifty-five in just a few minutes, from being sunny and mild to dark and cool. He liked that, the suddenness of change, the wildness in the storm, which wasn't like storms along the Gulf; they came and went in summer, leaving the streets sizzling, hotter than before the rain. When it rained in Port Arthur during the summer, you stayed inside by the air conditioner and drank iced tea.

While they stood outside, he explained to Tran about police procedure, how the coroner system worked, and about his duty to write a report. Tran was listening, though, looking half-tranked out, as if she had taken something, a Valium, only all she had taken was a terrible shock. He told her he would like to talk to Bhin as soon as possible. He told her Hernandez would be checking out the neighborhood, that Mirabelli was already making a map. He said he'd like her to come to Beaumont and make a statement, that he wanted her to bring Danny, too, if that was okay. It could wait; it was getting late, and nobody was around, anyway. He still had a bad feeling about Daddy John, that he would black this case out.

Poole could hear a car bouncing over the oil roads, its lights appearing through the veil of dust, weaving over the sand hills in traces like rocket fire. He squinted and thought that maybe his eyes were really getting bad, but he knew from what he could see that the car was going too fast for the road. The suspension was making a terrible sound, and he could hear the car bottom out once or twice. Tran moved around so she could see the car, but she was still holding Adrienne Deveraux around the waist.

Adrienne Deveraux freed herself from Tran. She moved to where Poole was standing beside the pickup. "I'll give you a ride back to your car," she said.

"You own the pickup?" Poole asked.

Adrienne Deveraux parted her lips slightly as if she was beginning a smile, probably because Poole himself looked bemused. The pickup was a real antique, an old '54 Chevy painted blue. But then the woman turned her head and closed up, probably realizing the situation. Poole picked up on it and followed her mood, saying he'd like to hitch a ride if it was all right, that he'd been stupid to walk all this way in the dark. He was thinking that she might just be a woman who could help him, not that he wanted to use her, and he also thought that he had probably gained back the notch he had lost before. It was funny how he wanted to be on square one with Adrienne Deveraux.

Adrienne Deveraux had noticed the car, too. It was barreling over the oil roads through a tunnel of sand, bits of shell exploding away as it went, while behind the dunes the orange bulb of Port Arthur rose in the dark night. Just when Poole was sure the car would crash through a dune, roll right through the driveway and take them all out, it didn't. It screeched to a stop beside the pickup. He noticed Tran as she caught herself sneaking a look at Poole, like seeing yourself in the mirror trying to study yourself, a tangent of tangled intentions. He let it go and watched the car, an old yellow Charger with a black vinyl top that had been worn smooth by time, with rust under the door and wheel wells. Poole could smell burning oil under the hood.

A big kid who was obviously drunk got out of the driver's side. He had a gawky look about him and he smelled like beer and reefer. Poole had smelled that smell a million times. Even from where he was standing, fifteen feet from the guy, across the smoky hood of the Charger, the aroma was strong, sour grain and vomit-smell. Poole didn't like the scene right away, the disheveled kid with stringy red hair and bad skin, his hawk nose, the staggered pose he was striking on the concrete platform driveway, throwing himself off balance as he slammed the car door. He had expected music from a boom box or cassette, but when he walked around the pickup and checked the Charger, all he could see inside were two bucket seats in front, a stack of tools in back, the interior stripped down to metal. Poole really didn't want a close look at the car right then because he knew he would find some serious dope, not Mickey Mouse reefer, but maybe a line or two of coke, shit he couldn't ignore if he saw it.

What surprised Poole and contributed to his bad vibes was this picture of an Anglo from south Texas, this drip of shit you'd find along the south Port Arthur highway where there are strip bars and drive-in liquor stores and adult theaters. Poole didn't see where Jerry fit into the Vietnamese refugee puzzle. He was a loose end, like the .22 Colt lying beside Nguyen Bao Do, like redneck shrimpers putting holes in the old man's boat.

Tran was speaking Vietnamese, quick syllables that darted like tropical fish. Poole had been in country for two years and hadn't learned a single phrase of the language— about the same as all the other guys who went over there, nooky-nooky, you wanee fuckee, Chinese laundry talk, which wasn't much of an experience of another culture. He reminded himself that he had walked down to the hooch every Sunday for six months and had never learned how to say good afternoon to the old woman who ran the place. Maybe it would have made a difference.

Pretty soon, Tran emitted a high-pitched whine of anger and frustration as she talked to her sister, Bhin, who had gotten out of the Charger and was standing in the sand on the other side of the car with a shocked look on her face. Tran let go of Adrienne Deveraux and was going around and around her sister in the dark. Poole's vision was half-obscured, so he walked over and tried to look at the sisters. Jerry staggered away without saying a word. Poole could smell vomit on him for sure. It made him wonder about needle dope, which could make you sick if you took too much on top of alcohol. Jerry went through the front door of the house and Poole saw a light snap on in the back bedroom. He knew that Jerry would be lying there in the dark with one foot on the floor while the room spun.

If Poole thought things were getting stretched out of shape, he was sure of it when he caught a good look at Bhin. She was shorter than her sister, chubbier, and not as well-built. She had decked herself out in department store punk, black T-shirt with a Day-Glow and glitter rock band sequined in front, black pedal pushers so tight on her ass, you could see her crack. She had acne, too, bad enough to make her look too young to be taken seriously, even though Poole couldn't get a good feel for her right age. She didn't look exactly loaded to Poole, but she looked confused, which was natural, since her father was dead. As Poole watched, Bhin lifted her hands to her face and he saw that she was wearing black lace gloves without fingers. As he followed their movement, he got a good look at her eyes, which revealed dope confusion after all. Adrienne Deveraux came over to him where he was leaning against the Charger.

"Are you going to stay now?" she asked.

"It's late," Poole said. "This can wait. Tell Tran, would you mind?"

Adrienne Deveraux walked around the car and spoke with the sisters for a while as Poole trained back on Bhin, radar on the red fingernails and the henna-rinsed hair, a jet of it in front like on MTV. She looked like a Jap rock star, for God's sake. Still, the cultural thing was bothering Poole as he looked at her. Here she was, a Vietnamese refugee living in a stucco FHA repossession on the dunes south of Port Arthur, four years in the United States, her father still a traditional black-pajama fisherman. Now she shows up stoned on grass and who knows what, maybe quaaludes, from that glass-ball look in her eyes. Poole wondered about all of it, this Catholic family who probably took the church seriously, for years, getting into the ritual, all very French and very Vietnamese, a lacy religion. It was just the opposite of the way Bhin looked right now, slick and all fucked-up, sliding around on the surface of this new culture where all the crap was stored, which Poole could understand marginally. But he wondered how it had made her father feel.

Poole wondered if the old man could write, and suddenly he wanted to look around the house for a note. He hadn't asked about that, if there was a suicide note. What kept coming back to him was how unlikely he thought it was that a traditional man from provincial Vietnam, and a Catholic, a fisherman, a man with daughters barely grown and a dead wife in the old country, would put a bullet in his brain. Leave Tran alone. Maybe the old man was homesick, sure, having a hard time adjusting. But just now Poole didn't think suicide had been his way out.

Adrienne Deveraux had gotten in the pickup. Poole was going to suggest that they drive Tran back to her house, but it looked like she needed a lot more time with her sister. Both were crying as they walked down the path toward the front door, and when they went inside, Poole could hear the wailing as the door shut. It was bad, bringing him back to Vietnam, hell in a small place. He got inside the pickup beside Adrienne Deveraux, who had turned over the

Chevy's motor, idling it, then putting on the choke for a minute. Poole could see the ocean behind the house, which suddenly looked very bleak. The wind was blowing in the palms and tule grass, a steady click that seemed synchronous with the flashing lights out on the water.

"I want to talk to you," Adrienne Deveraux said, staring straight ahead through the windshield. It was as if she had set a trap in her mind and it had snapped shut. "It isn't my nature to blab."

"I didn't think it would be," Poole said.

Adrienne Deveraux took her hands off the steering wheel, one foot on the clutch, caught between gestures while Poole was silent. She bit her lip.

"Are you a serious man?" she asked. Poole must have looked empty. "I mean are you full of shit like most of the sheriff's office guys, or what?"

Poole laughed out loud, amazed at the words coming from the mouth of this very sophisticated-looking woman, and amazed, too, at how right-on it sounded, because he knew the sheriff's office men were certainly full of shit, if nothing else. Adrienne Deveraux stared at Poole. She kept staring until he told her he was a serious man. He knew what she meant.

Then she backed out of the drive and went over the back roads, north toward the marina. The heat had veiled everything so thickly that Poole could hardly breathe. He put his head outside the window to catch some breeze. In the cab, the woman's perfume was getting to Poole. This woman was in her fifties—what was Poole thinking of? They went over a hump of sand and down through dunes that gleamed like ceramic in the moonlight.

"I'm telling you this because I trust you," Adrienne Deveraux said. "I've grown very fond of Tran. I didn't know her father very well. His English was poor and he was very quiet. But I believe in the absolute dignity of these people. I respect them. I've learned a lot from them. If you can't accept that, Mr. Poole, then I've nothing more to say."

Any other time Poole would have been ready with an answer. He felt like a moron now, a mute. He watched some houses go by, wondering if one of them was Tran's place, if Danny had come home and where he had been all night. He could smell the swamp across the bay, the only thing that still smelled like the Gulf, hard tannic and real. Poole could see Adrienne Deveraux studying him in the rearview mirror, in the reflections on the windshield, a paper-thin image on glass, backdrop orange and black.

"I don't have a problem with that," Poole said.

"Then I'll tell you something. Bao Do didn't take his own life. I don't believe that for a single moment."

"Do you mind telling me why?" Poole asked.

"Bao was a hardworking fisherman," she said. "He seemed simple and generous and quiet. He loved Tran. He was trying to love Bhin. He was disturbed and discouraged. But he wasn't a suicide."

"I think he had a lot of trouble."

"Of course."

"You say he spoke English."

"Enough to be pleasant. We saw each other on the beach."

Poole knew he would get to it. "If he didn't kill himself, then who did? Who killed him, Mrs. Deveraux?"

They were approaching the fishing shack. Poole could see his Caprice nosed against a dune, the metal ablaze in the hazy moonlight. The shack was dark, which meant that Hernandez had gone back with the ambulance. Some lights were still on down in the marina bait store. Poole closed his eyes. He had been at it since early morning and he hadn't had much sleep the night before, and he didn't think he would sleep tonight, he never did. The long reflexive loneliness he usually felt on Saturday had drained away, maybe because of Adrienne Deveraux and maybe because he was going through something that had existential meaning, memories brought back by the aromas. It was possible he was going to have a foolish fantasy about the woman. It had been a long time since he had had a fantasy and he didn't think it would hurt. They pulled to a stop behind the Caprice. Everything was silent but the wash of ocean and wind in the palms.

"I don't know," she said.

"You don't blab," Poole said.

She sighed. She was having trouble. "I can tell you that house had become a nightmare for Bao Do. Bhin is going haywire, if you ask me. Jerry is quite worthless. He and Bao argued all the time, about money, about the noise and confusion. Especially about the marijuana, and who knows what else. Jerry and Bhin had been living somewhere else—I don't know where. But a few months ago, they came back to the house. Jerry was lazy, wouldn't work, just sat around playing the guitar and driving that car all over the place when the mood struck him. He would get drunk and scream at everybody. Jerry even argued with Tran and Danny. Danny hated Jerry. Maybe he thinks he has a claim on the house; maybe he was just jealous of Jerry. I don't know. Tran is too ashamed to talk very much about it. But it was terrible. Still, I don't think Bao Do killed himself."

"Hey, it's possible," Poole said. "Maybe he had seen enough anger and pain. Maybe he left it behind."

"The anger and pain, yes. He wouldn't leave Tran behind. I don't believe it."

"But maybe?"

Adrienne Deveraux gave it some thought. "No, I don't think even maybe," she said. "He bought two shrimp boats that nobody else wanted. He fixed them up. He worked and worked to get them back in the water. You should have seen him. He would work all day and into the evening. He spent his time at the shack, working on his seines, his equipment. His life was the sea, and I think it sustained him through all the bad times at home."

"All right," Poole said. "And there was Tran."

"And there was Tran. She's a jewel, Mr. Poole. They were very close."

"Anything else?" Poole asked.

"Yes there is," she said, training on Poole, turning her head slowly and locking onto him. She had her own radar, just like Poole's, maybe denser. "This morning, I saw him on the beach. He was very excited, upset; he could hardly calm down enough to speak. He wanted me to take him to Beaumont next week, Friday if possible. He didn't say why. I didn't know if I could do it. I'm down here on weekends usually." She dropped her hands from the steering wheel. "Do suicides make plans Mr. Poole?"

Poole thought about it. "Did he say what he was going to do in Beaumont?"

"No. I think he wanted Tran along. He doesn't drive; neither does Tran. If they go anywhere, they take the bus. They go with other Vietnamese who drive. I guess this was a special trip."

Poole caught a look in the woman's eye that glinted like tears forming. It was a shell shock that lapsed away and came back when it was quiet, like right now, in the dark with the ocean licking the sand. She blinked. Reality had hit.

"I'll speak with Tran," Poole said, noncommittal.

"You don't think he killed himself?"

Poole touched his own forehead, eyes closed. God, he was tired. It was crazy; his eyes burned. He thought he was too crazy and tired to give anyone such commitment.

"I don't know, Mrs. Deveraux," Poole said. He got out of the pickup and leaned against the door frame. He looked at Adrienne Deveraux through the open window. "He might have killed himself," Poole said. "But maybe some bubba killed him, one of those guys like Teagarden who punched holes in his boat. Maybe Jerry killed him when he was drinking. Maybe anything."

Adrienne Deveraux looked up. "Good night, Mr. Poole," she said.

He watched the pickup disappear down the oil road. The moon was high, brushing the sand and the surf like rolling silver branches. Poole decided that he would skip the twelve-pack and the all-night vigil on Laurel Street. He liked being up a notch with Adrienne Deveraux, if that's what was happening. He thought it might help his self-respect if he didn't drink beer and wallow in self-pity. Besides, now he was thinking about the old woman in the hooch, the one he hadn't spoken to. How he wished he had.

6

In the morning, Poole went out for biscuits and gravy. He drank some fresh orange juice and drove to a grocery and bought some real food to put in his refrigerator. Then he dropped by a sporting goods store and bought some fishing line and leader. When he got back to his apartment, he dug out his good spinning reel and cleaned it and put new line on his rod, then sat in the living room and ate a big lunch, watching football, an early preseason game with the Oilers.

He thought maybe he'd go down to Port Arthur and try to catch a redfish, take a run on the beach, go up by Adrienne Deveraux's house and check out the place. He had been bothered by something at the marina anyway, and this would be a good excuse to get him back into the flow of life, to spend a day near the water, soaking up some hot sun. He didn't need another Sunday night in front of the tube waiting for the sun to go down.

He decided to concentrate on his needs and forget about his desires. He wanted to fish again, to get in touch with the tug of the ocean down deep. If there was something else he needed, it would come clear later. But even if nothing came clear later, he knew he needed to find out what had happened to the old man, the Vietnamese who was being written off gradually.

Poole felt great, driving fast along the Port Arthur highway, out beyond the four-lane strip south of town, beyond the ring of shopping centers, out where there were scrub dunes and the first palm trees, cruising with the windows down in the Caprice and an oldies station playing loudly. The day was hot already, but that was okay with Poole, though he was anxious to hit the beach and leave the hot metal smell behind. He could tell the sky was going to burn and glaze over, but it wouldn't be so bad near the water. He could see the pine barrens way off in the distance. The pines looked dusted over, probably because it hadn't rained for a long time, too long for summer in south Texas, when it was supposed to rain a lot. There were usually big monsoon thunderstorms coming over the Gulf of California, then Mexico, swoons of low pressure over the water that set off fireworks, rookeries of cloud, sunset penetrating the big thunderheads, and then some lightning, followed by a steady downpour of wilting rain. Poole hadn't been into the pines or swamps for years, since he had gone out fishing as a kid, on those times when he came home from college in Denton. It was something he realized he missed, a portion of his real self that had disappeared.

There was almost no traffic, so he was free to gawk around, to try and gain a perspective on things instead of judging all the time, sizing things and people up, his consciousness of nonstop police work. He was driving and thinking about Jerry and Bhin, Tran, and Adrienne Deveraux, but it wasn't as if he was putting them under a light.

Poole was conserving their being without trying to put them on display.

All the way south, there were bars and strip joints; even on Sunday, you could spot a few cars in the parking lots, mostly pickups and motorcycles, beat-up jalopies owned by guys who couldn't make it home. The land all the way to the horizon was a flat compost of crushed shell and sand, fields of black cotton dirt, swaths of pine and saw grass. He could see stucco shacks back in the barrens, down hidden dirt lanes, old places dug back in the dunes. The farther south he went, the more he could smell the sea, the salt and the faint metallic brine, the wind languorous with its odor. For the first time since he had seen the old Vietnamese on the floor of the fishing shack, Poole was composing himself so that he could take stock of the whole scene at once, see things wide-angled, not just sudden flashes of Bhin and Jerry, pictures of the hooch triggering on and off in his mind.

The concrete highway and the gray-green pines and the white dunes had a cleansing effect on Poole and he was able to take himself back to the veranda, when he'd first arrived on the call, looking at the gas flame of the refinery with the tide dissolving into sheens of mud, the egrets poking in the flats, pelicans flying over the marina, settling onto pylons, some of them smacking the surface of the water.

He remembered being nervous, waiting for Daddy John with the feeling that he wanted to get it over with and buy some beer and go to Laurel Street and get drunk. And then something had happened. Without meditation, as sudden as lightning over the Gulf, the way it must have happened to Isaac Newton, the apple bonking him on the head, bingo, Poole recreated the sound and vision of the motorized dinghy chopping through the surf toward the marina, turning his head when the tone hit him, the high-modulated *putt-putt* of the boat riding through the waves and then the flick of the sun on binoculars and a figure trying to stand up in the dinghy, wavering as the boat dropped through a swell. Poole had turned and walked back to the edge of the shack, checking for tracks in the sand, and he remembered looking out at the marina again while he thought about the dead Vietnamese, just before he'd heard Daddy John driving up.

Just now, it was the wide angle that gave him a glimpse of the dinghy in his memory, a guy standing up and staring through his binoculars, which had glinted in the setting sun. Poole wondered why he was remembering this now. It was like a sliver under his fingernail, something harmless and irritating both. Maybe it would move if he let it alone.

Poole drove through the refinery district. He wished he had a convertible. He would put down the top and drink iced tea from a mason jar, maybe drive around the beach for an hour or two, down by Sea Rim Park and take a look at the mangrove, or what was left of it, or try to see the swamp from the estuary hill. When he hit the oil roads, he turned toward the ocean and clicked off the radio so he could hear the sea, like a rasp on soft wood, with a clear echo at the end.

He took a cutoff to the left instead of going right down to the beach to the fishing shack. He went up a hill of sand to where he could see the black jetty thrust into the ocean fifty yards or more, a board building next to it with a neon beer sign and a pier that fronted the jetty itself. Between the jetty and the ocean, there were some wharfs with vessels tied to their docks, mostly old sailboats that had seen better days, outboards, some shrimpers. This wasn't a fancy marina like the one in Galveston. It had always been a working marina. The sun was directly overhead, cracking down on the water. Poole was thirsty.

He parked in a glen of sand dunes and saw grass. There were some dewy clouds on the bowl of sky down by Mexico, three pink fingers and one white thumb. Poole was still feeling good, almost happy-go-lucky, except for his vision of the dinghy and the thought that the old Vietnamese was going to be written off.

With his rod and sack lunch, he walked down a path toward the marina and the jetty, looking forward to getting near the water with his lunch, spending a languid afternoon on the sea whether he caught anything or not, just to be in the heat and sun. He was wearing a straw hat and some old sneakers and a pair of cutoff shorts that were nearly worn out, held up by a rope belt he had bought on a trip to Matamoros. It was slightly affected, he knew, this look like a beach bum when he was really a divorced cop with a bad attitude, but he enjoyed the part he was playing.

Poole went down a hill choked by ice plant and then walked out on the platform. It wasn't a pier, just board planks laid on floating oil drums. He could hear hard rock coming from the bait store as he walked, and it jarred him a little because it wasn't the kind of day for hard rock in his mind; the music was too discordant. He didn't want any discord until Monday morning, which was discordant enough just thinking about, because he knew on Monday he'd be talking about his case, the old Vietnamese.

In the back of his mind was the dinghy. The dinghy wasn't discordant, because he didn't understand it at all. It was just there, a note slightly off-key. Poole watched the gulls diving around the jetty and the bait store, and he listened to the sounds they made as they buzzed for food, bait floating in the sea and the garbage, getting themselves tangled in line, setting up a racket. Then it occurred to Poole that maybe he needed a long vacation, some time to string out this good feeling for more than one day, not time in San Antonio, but something meaningful, three weeks in country he'd never seen, back in the woods or up in the mountains, someplace where he could stop focusing on himself long enough to get back to nature and play some piano.

Once Poole was inside the bait shop, it took him a minute or two to adjust to the light. It was a sharp contrast to the brilliant glare outside, a bright reflection off the water burning up through the glaze. He could hear the beer sign popping. He walked around for a while, carrying his broken-down rod, his sack lunch, looking at all the stuff on the shelves, wandering down the two aisles until he found a small bait cooler full of mussels and shrimp, bonito cut in sections. Out of the corner of his eye, Poole spotted a girl behind a counter up front. She was fingering a tape deck, her knees against her chin as if she might be sitting on a stool. She was wearing a man's white dress shirt with the sleeves rolled up. Poole kept looking at her, sneaking glances, and the more he looked, the more he thought she might be way out there in la-la land, her chin slack against her chest, eyes bugged out, but he couldn't be sure because so many people just looked that way now. Besides, he was used to a world where suspicion was natural. It led automatically to a bad conclusion. He wanted to give his cop nature a break, but he couldn't help studying her blond hair, unwashed and full of knots, the frayed fingernails she was chewing. Poole didn't know if she had looked up when he came in, if she knew he was in the place, but if she hadn't, that was strange. The bait shop was in motion and he could tell there was a tide on. The blonde turned up the music. It was bothering him so much, he wanted to get outside. It was like pain in his ear.

He found a jar of mussels and some chopped bonito and put them in a plastic sack. He wandered around a while longer, looking at the lures, picking out some lead weights he might need. He knew he was underequipped for real surf fishing, but he wanted to have a nice day in the sun, sit in the spray and dream. Catching a fish would be a bonus, and he would toss it back, anyway. Finally, he took his gear to the counter. The girl seemed to notice him at last, turning down the music reluctantly. Something made Poole want to grab the cassette and smash it on the floor, grind it up good with his sneaker.

Once, he read a newspaper story about a guy on a San Francisco bus who had grabbed a boom box from some dude and thrown it out the window and onto the sidewalk, where it had smashed into a million pieces. The other passengers began to applaud. Poole seemed to remember reading that the guy had paid for the boom box. He wanted silence; he paid for it. It crossed Poole's mind that the guy was a true hero. Maybe if the bait shop had been a public bus, Poole would have smashed the cassette deck and pulled out a fifty-dollar bill and laid it on the chick, grinning, walking out the door like Clint Eastwood. As it was, he tried not to think about the girl, a biker type, a tough kid who probably lived in an apartment in Port Arthur, sleeping around with all kinds of men, her life getting out of hand like the sprawl around Houston.

The girl bit her lip, itty-bitty style. She looked undernourished, almost skinny, with too-big breasts. She could have looked nice if she had cleaned herself up some, worn a bra. And then Poole thought, For God's sake, with you *sitting in your apartment talking to yourself until all hours of the night!*

The girl pushed the cassette away and tapped out some numbers on a digital cash register.

"How's the fishing?" Poole asked.

She finished what she was doing, ringing up his purchases, fumbling around in la-la land, getting the job done slowly.

"I'm sorry to say so, mister," she said, "but you ain't going to catch shit around this garbage dump."

Poole was sure she was ripped. Here it was noon on Sunday and she was running dry, her eyes red and scratchy and deep bags under them, too. She kept sliding her tongue along her upper lip for her cotton mouth, the way you get when you're doing coke: dry and breathless and superhuman.

Poole glanced behind the counter despite his pledge to

himself not to cop today. He saw some Dr. Pepper cans, Moon Pies, too. This girl, he thought, pure Port Arthur strip bar, coked and sugared up on Sunday morning, the kind of human slurry that runs out to sea and sits on the bottom and festers—human sludge. He wondered how she was getting the money to snort coke. She must be *some* dedicated chick. She must have let a whole raft of shit float away from her life in order to find her way this far.

Poole told her he was going out on the jetty to have some fun. She didn't respond when he asked her if anyone else had been out, if she knew what they had been using for bait. Poole pulled her up short when he asked her if she knew anybody who owned an orange motorized dinghy, if she had been working on Saturday evening and had heard it splashing around in the marina. It had been sundown.

Right away, he knew the girl had a problem. It was a subtle thing, but he had seen it plenty of times. It was like the viscera sitting right there on the surface of the skin, now that Poole had out his radar. He had watched guys sitting in the interrogation room with the wheels turning inside their heads so fast, you could see a thin stream of smoke coming out of their assholes. The girl was like that now, busting up in her confusion. Poole turned it up a click, asked her the name of the guy he had seen, if he docked the boat at the marina.

The girl did her best. She flustered at her fingernails and asked Poole why he wanted to know. He told her he wanted to rent the dinghy and take it out fishing. He thought it would be cheaper than taking a charter out of Galveston. "I'd like to go out for some dolphin," he said. Big smile.

"Nobody like that around here," she said. *Pump-pump,* Poole could almost hear her heart beat.

"You didn't see it yesterday?"

"I close up, mister. I go home and I don't see nothing."

Poole smiled again and paid for his bait and the weights.

She swallowed dry spit and then pulled out the cassette deck and turned up the music, shutting Poole out, getting on the defensive. Her hands had left wet marks on the counter. She was sweating heavily and there was a thin bead of it on her lip. Poole knew he could have gonged her good, rattled her cage, but he didn't. Maybe she was telling the truth, and besides, he didn't have any point in mind. It would be a hassle he might regret. Still, he was thinking, Blondie, the slightest tremor is going to set you off good, pull triggers in your brain.

Poole went outside and stood on the pier in full sun. He could feel the waves rolling under the planks, moving the barrels, and he stood that way looking up and down the beach, then on down the beach to where he thought Adrienne Deveraux might live with her husband. The sand was gleaming white in the afternoon and he could see the mangrove and the swamp with its cypress and pine.

Poole went out on the jetty, about two-thirds of the way to the end. The rocks were sharp and wet, and he almost fell getting there. He settled at a good place and threw his line into the swells. The seagulls began to wing around him, screaming, trying to get at his lunch and his bait sack. All the swells were coming in different colors, clumps of seaweed farther out. He was dazzled by the sun and the colors and the driving spray. Poole ate his lunch and drank some lukewarm iced tea from a can. He tried the bonito first and then the mussels, but he didn't catch anything.

7

Poole was acting like a kid, playing King Kong on the rocks while he eyed his rod and line in the swells where he had thrown it way out as far as he could. The line would jump and Poole would scamper over the rocks, but it would be the undertow and he would skitter back up on the jetty and look around again. He did this over and over until he finally slipped and put a rip in his knee, and then he just sat quietly and imagined getting a strike, the line quivering out in the swells, the sudden dip and the line murmur and Poole hurrying to set the drag while the line sang, then pulling up sharply to set the hook.

Ever since he had caught his first sea bass, one day out fishing with his dad, before his dad had gotten so sick and old, before the arthritis had crippled him, Poole had been excited by the thought of fish way down deep, Poole back on shore, the fish down below the water. As the afternoon went by, he began to wonder why he had given all this up, why this pleasure had deserted him with such finality. He wondered if this kind of pure sensibility deserted everybody in the same way, with the same blameless futility, or almost everybody.

During the afternoon, Poole spotted some Portuguese man-of-war beyond the swell line, floating like blue-green hubcaps where the seaweed was bunched. He picked up a flat rock and heaved it at the seaweed, trying to hit one of the jellied creatures, but harmlessly, knowing they were too far out, but heaving the rock anyway, just for the hell of it. Then, with the sun in his eyes and his pants soaked, he noticed how burned he was going to be, really piss-assed burned, sun brown going red, and he realized then the joy of fishing, the wonderment of the sea, which hadn't really abandoned him. It had been the other way around, like slamming a door on someone you love and respect, and only later, when you're unhappy or bitter, starting to rationalize that life did this to you, that life is to blame. Seeing it now with increased conviction, Poole understood that Lisa Marie hadn't left him; she hadn't walked out of the Laurel Street house. He was the one who had left the relationship, not Lisa Marie, but the idea that he'd left his true self, it floating somewhere beyond the rim of himself, was like the creatures he was watching beyond the rim of surf and swell, disembodied like hubcap things with tentacles that fell from translucent bodies, arms reaching nowhere.

Poole reeled in, thinking he should have bought some squid along with the bonito and mussels. He got off the jetty and walked back to his car and took off his pants and squeezed them as dry as he could, then rubbed some oil on his arms and his back, getting behind his knees, on top of his feet, too, which were turning ruby-colored. Then for a long time, he studied the marina store, wondering how the girl in la-la land was doing, if she had snorted more coke, or if she had cooled down finally, and if she had, what she was thinking about Poole. Probably nothing. Probably she was thinking nothing about him, but still Poole had something on his mind, like gum stuck to his shoe, annoying and persistent.

Now he was through with the wide-angle stuff and he was on a double track, watching the sky turn whey-colored from the heat, glazed and tired, some clouds building in the south while the sun broke the water into bright cubes, areas of color that walked on the surface, color growing bluer and bluer until his sight wandered to Sea Rim Park and the mangrove and the mush of Sabine Pass where the riverbed meandered into the ocean, spreading out like a fan. At the time, Poole was wondering what the girl's name was. Something cute, he'd bet.

Poole broke down his rod and put the bottle of mussels on the car seat and went down the beach. His sneakers were full of sand, drying off, hurting his feet. He had a pair of jean shorts on and they were full of sand, too. He could hear rock music loud now, but as he walked down the beach it faded as the sound of the surf and the click of the palms covered it over. The tide had come and gone and the beach was scoured clean. Poole could see sand dollars and bits of conch shell. The tide had left some seaweed in tangled clumps on the sand, and some of the hubcap creatures had floated in and were stranded on shore. He stopped and looked out into the Gulf, getting an odd, renascent feeling, and when he turned back, he saw the girl from la-la land standing on the marina pier with her head cocked lazily on one shoulder, like a pose, the girl seeming to watch Poole, though he was a long way down the beach. From that far, the girl looked like she had a good form, nice cupped hips, legs not too scrawny. Poole liked the way her hair was blowing in the breeze.

He zigzagged down the beach, picking up some shells, splashing into the surf, which was coming in tiny laps now, after the tide. Then he ran back into the sea dunes and the palmetto groves, pausing to look back at the girl from la-la land. She was still out on the boardwalk with her music on her arm, but she was looking at the ocean, too, not paying any attention to him. Poole followed the curve of the beach until he couldn't see his car anymore, until the jetty was just a black slash without structure. He was having déjà vu, an eerie premonition that went backward.

Poole was a mile down from the marina when it was obvious what he was doing. He sat down cross-legged in the sand and stared at an old-fashioned beach cabin constructed of pine and cypress, sheltered in a hillock of tule and palm. The cabin was surrounded by some spindly pines that weren't doing too well in the sand. He loved it at first sight. It had a screened front porch and hurricane windows with drop shutters. The more he looked at it, the more he became embarrassed, as if he had been caught telling fibs by his grandma, but still he couldn't keep his eyes off the cabin, wondering if this was her place, where Adrienne Deveraux lived with her husband. An immediate need to do something came over him in a panic, and he rigged his rod and reel for surf casting, putting on some new leader and a triangle set of lead weights, and he sat down in the sand and tried to feed some mussels onto the hook, the mussels too dried out to handle.

Evening was filtering in. The sun hadn't set, but it was going down behind the pine forests. It was growing dusky and the mosquitoes were coming out. Poole set his rod in the sand and splashed into the water, which was warm as a bath. He walked knee-deep into the surf and scouted the swells, then went back and tossed his rig as far into the surf as he could. The line sung just as he heard a screen door slam behind him and then the line snapped and he watched his lead weights and the mussels fly into the water. He swore under his breath just as the line whirled in to jam his reel. Poole felt silly, unable to imagine anything worse right now, sitting there in the sand with his rig in a shamble, his line snagged in the reel, his skin red as a beet.

Adrienne Deveraux walked down the beach. When she got to Poole, she stood with her feet in the water, looking at him as if it was the most normal thing on earth. Poole had turned to watch her walk, admiring her saunter, the flowered island skirt winding around her and her gray hair that had certainly once been black, the way it fed her eyes, which Poole liked very much. She was standing off a bit, silent, maybe amused, maybe just indulgent, but whatever it was, it had a warm tone. Poole thought he should say something, anything to show he knew how to behave.

"Fucking reel," he muttered.

"When did you last go fishing?" Adrienne Deveraux asked. She was standing off, wind ruffling her scarf.

Poole stood up, feeling foolish. He didn't know how to unsnag his line without cutting it or walking it up the beach toward the dunes like a novice. He didn't want to cut the line and he didn't want to walk up the dunes and he was cursing himself for getting into this ridiculous situation. After all, it had been years since he had rigged a surf-casting outfit, since he was eighteen. He grinned at the woman, apologizing for the word he'd used. She said she'd heard the word before. Poole knew then that he didn't know how to behave, or if there were rules he should be following so a person didn't have to hang his ass out every time he had a conversation. He doubted there were rules. Talking to Adrienne Deveraux wasn't going to be like talking to himself late at night. Talking to himself, he could scream whatever trash entered his head. But right now, he didn't know what he should say, so he sat in the warm sand with the woman gazing at him as twilight gathered around them both, lights twinkling on in the Gulf. Adrienne Deveraux finally asked him up to the porch for a drink and Poole said he'd like an iced tea, that he was parched and needed something cool.

Poole walked his line out of the water while Adrienne Deveraux went back to the cabin. While she was inside, he broke down his rod and cut out as much of the snag as he could with his pocketknife, trying to get everything done before she came back outside with the tea. He wished he had brought a leather bag for the reel, but he wiped it down with his shirt and stowed the rod and reel in some tule. Wet sand and bits of shell had worked into his pants. He could feel the chafe around his waist, against the sunburned skin. He went around the side of the cabin to the front and found the woman sitting on a porch step with two glasses of tea. He sat down next to her, feeling the breeze on his shirt, sensing the heat pouring from his skin, the hairs on his arms and hands turning white already. Adrienne Deveraux was sipping her tea with both hands cupped around the glass, and Poole suddenly felt a nearly inexplicable wave of tenderness rush over him. She handed him the tea. It tasted wonderful, cold and rich, with a hint of mint.

"Did you have any luck?" she asked.

She had made a tuck of her skirt between her legs, holding the tea in the cup, whisking at mosquitoes with a free hand. Poole thought there may have been some playful irony in her voice, but he didn't mind.

"I mean fishing luck," she added, definitely playful now.

"You never know about luck," Poole said.

"Oh really?" she said, raising an eyebrow.

"It takes a while to average out."

"Be honest with me, Mr. Poole," she said. "What are you doing down here?"

Poole thought about it. "I don't know," he said.

Then Poole astonished himself. He talked for about fifteen minutes. All that time, the color of the sky was dropping in register through orange haze to purple and then to violet, until long strands of sunshine had webbed the beach like filigree. The gulls and pelicans were flowing north, making noise, and there were terns in the wet sand, pecking for food. Poole told Adrienne Deveraux everything that came into his head, in a lunatic free association, about being a kid in Port Arthur, pretty poor, fishing on the jetty and coming home on hot days to sleep on the porch, away from the bugs and the heat. He told her about catching redfish, how his father sometimes grilled the fish over charcoal, out on the side lawn of their small house, and how his father would take him to the picture show in Beaumont. Poole told her about his time at the university, how he had been drafted, how he'd come home and had gotten married, how he had drifted into his job and his life.

Adrienne Deveraux got up once to fix more tea. She noticed the slash on his knee and asked him about it, telling him about some other things, about her husband. Poole told her about his divorce, his new apartment, how things in his life had seemed to weather away from him like limestone might weather away from rock but that he was beginning to realize that it was all more complicated than that. Adrienne Deveraux nodded at that and told Poole she had been married thirty-odd years, then corrected herself with a laugh. She hadn't meant *odd,* but so many years she couldn't keep track anymore. Poole felt mesmerized, indulging himself in the world outside for the first time in months. Some words kept coming back to him: *Are you full of shit, or what?* Poole listened, wanting to ask her more about her husband, but before he could make himself do it, they got around to it naturally. She told him her husband, Toby, was in Houston in a nursing home. He had worked all his life for AT&T, a wonderful father and loving husband, all the right stuff, then had suffered a terrible stroke last year. The cabin had been a vacation getaway during the years when they were raising their family, a place to come on the long, hot weekends of summer when Houston was so unbearable. She hoped Toby could return someday, but she doubted he could.

In time, the clouds over the Gulf took on pink under-coatings. Far away were thunderheads, like cauliflower with zinc tops. Adrienne Deveraux mentioned she was going back to Houston now. If Poole wanted to ask her anything, he should do it.

"I'd like to know about Jerry and Bhin," he said.

"The Do family were official refugees who came into the country through Thailand. Tran's mother is dead. She died sometime before. Tran is older, Bhin younger."

"This isn't what I want to know," Poole said.

"Then what do you want to know?" Adrienne Deve-raux had leaned back against the screen door, screwing up her eyes, looking into the last of the sunset. Poole noticed the wrinkled forehead, the years of expression.

"What do you think?"

She smiled, sadly, Poole thought. "A question within a question. Is that how it's going to be?"

"I'm sorry," he said. "I didn't have anything in mind when I came down here. I didn't know how it was going to be."

"All right," Adrienne Deveraux said, looking back at Poole, the breeze in her hair. "Tran was my friend. She *is* my friend, but I didn't see much of Bhin, just a few times on the beach riding in that stupid car of theirs. I saw almost nothing of Jerry. I heard about the goings-on."

"The goings-on?"

Adrienne Deveraux sighed, obviously hating this kind of tattling. "This cabin is only about five hundred yards from the Do house. You know that yourself." She gestured across the tule. "I take walks on the beach early in the morning, late at night when it's hot. You could always hear loud music from the Bao Do house all weekend, early in the morning, too. We've had a lot of things happening to the beach over the years, new people driving up and down on motorcycles, parties all night. But Bao Do was a quiet man, and I know from Tran that the situation with his son-in-law and daughter was almost unbearable for him. He was pained, but of course he would never turn away his daughter Bhin, no matter what she did. Bhin and Jerry got married and moved to Beaumont, I think, where Jerry had work as a mechanic. Then he lost his job, or quit—I don't know which. That was when they moved into the Bao Do house. I imagine Jerry had lots of rotten friends, and there were parties at the house. Jerry stopped looking for work and lived on welfare. There may have been more to it than that. I'm afraid there was a lot of resentment all around about the situation."

"Family arguments?"

"I'm afraid so."

"Was there violence? Did they mix it up?"

"I don't know. Tran didn't talk about that kind of thing very much. She expressed her displeasure with both Jerry and Bhin. She sided with her father. It was very upsetting to her." Adrienne Deveraux paused, drank some tea. "There were times when Tran looked so tired, it almost made me cry to look at her. Red eyes, bags under them. She was almost all her father had."

"Did you know Jerry and Bhin were doing dope?"

"I'm not surprised. That seems to be the hidden agenda these days. But Tran never told me that. Something like that, so personal, she would keep to herself. She was very proud. You know, in Vietnam these were very fine people, hardworking fishermen, good Catholics. It has to be very difficult to be here now, no language, no fish, no sense of family or community."

"But did Tran know about the dope? Where did it come from?"

"I'm not sure. I don't know where it came from. I don't know if Tran knows. Perhaps she does. I know she had fights with her sister about the music and the horrible people who came to the house at all hours of the day. I assume there was more going on. You have to."

"You know any of the people who went up to the house? Would you recognize them if you saw them again?"

"Oh, I doubt it," Adrienne Deveraux said.

"What about vehicles? You ever see any cars parked up by the house? Anything strike a chord with you?"

"Motorcycles," she said wistfully. "Lots of those. Sometimes people would just roar down the beach and stop at the house and then roar back."

"That bad?" Poole asked.

"Yes," she said. "Not all the time, but often enough. Maybe it's just because I come down on weekends."

Poole was building a picture of Jerry Donovan, an oil-town dropout, real punk, steel nuts in his pants and an attitude about women, hard and manipulative. He would be a guy who drank a lot of beer and did some reefer and wasted himself on coke and quaaludes whenever he got the chance. Poole could see Bao Do in his house, in one of the back bedrooms while strange bikers were making all kinds of outrageous noise, the guitars and the obscene laughter, Nguyen Bao Do holding on to the edge of a continent while a bunch of punks tried to knock him off.

Poole wondered if all this police work was dropping him a notch with Adrienne Deveraux, whether doing his job the way he had to do would turn her away. And if it did, what was the point anyway? Why did he care? He didn't know her at all; she didn't mean anything to him. And what probably mattered to her was her husband, her children, the past they had shared. Poole asked her if she had ever talked to the old man about personal things.

"I talked to him," she said.

"Did he say Jerry knocked him around? Threatened him?"

"I don't know, Mr. Poole." She had taken a matter-of-fact tone. "Mr. Bao Do didn't speak very much English. He would smile and say good morning, good evening. When we tried to chat, he was pleasant, but there was always some pain in his expression. I could tell he was suffering, because he spent a lot of nights down in the fishing shack alone when he should have been home. I felt terribly sorry for him. He would walk on the beach until the motorcycles scared him away. Sometimes he took out his boat for a few hours. But he was going just to be alone. There was never a decent catch to be had, no matter how hard he worked. Tran would come down to the fishing shack and they would visit. I'd see them on my walks. Both of them would be on the veranda, looking sad and lost. There was nothing I could do for them. I suppose things had gotten that terrible at the house."

"What about Danny?" Poole asked. He was hurrying, trying to get through with all of this, even though it was important, feeling as if he'd shot himself in the foot with Adrienne Deveraux, who probably thought he'd come down the beach just to pump her for information, when it wasn't like that at all.

"His name is Dhan Chuan Huan," she answered. "He's boat people. Tran met him in Port Arthur."

"What about their relationship?"

"I know Tran isn't happy. I don't know how much of it is what happens between Jerry and Bao Do. She doesn't talk much about Danny. Like I told you, she's a quiet girl with great pride. She talks about her dreams. I listen, drink tea with her. She uses my phone."

Poole put down his tea on the porch step. While Adrienne Deveraux went on talking, he watched an orange dinghy plow through the swells just beyond where the surf converged and rolled up. It was getting dark, but he could see the dinghy if he strained, the orange hull low in the water, spray erupting from the bow, a man in the stern by the outboard. Poole couldn't tell much from this distance, but it looked as if the man was wearing a ball cap over his long hair, maybe a black T-shirt. Adrienne Deveraux had stopped talking and he could hear the steady *putt-putt* of the engine chopping through the surf, Poole aware that the woman had tensed. He must have transmitted his feelings to her, because he was tense himself, his nerves suddenly taut.

"What is it?" Adrienne Deveraux asked. She was behind him now. Poole walked two steps into the sand.

"Do you recognize the dinghy?" he asked.

She said a halting no but looked along with him until the shape got hard to see going north toward the marina. Poole was aware of his own awareness, as if sheets of glass had been placed over his vision and were being removed one by one. When the dinghy was gone, he still had his awareness. He realized he was focusing so hard, he was scaring the woman. And then he knocked over his tea as he sat back down.

He could feel the muscles in his jaws. "They call him Danny," Poole said distractedly. He was trying to pick up the train of their conversation.

"Danny," she repeated.

Poole was buzzed now, forgetting all about his notch problem with Adrienne Deveraux. Now he was tuned to the girl at the marina bait store and he wanted targets for his radar. Right now, he had his beam on that pair of binoculars he had spotted from the veranda of the fishing shack, how they had flashed in the sun.

Adrienne Deveraux laid it out for Poole. "Danny Huan married Tran after what you'd call a whirlwind romance. They met at a restaurant. One of those places with billiards and some dominoes and steamed rice. Neither of them had a thing, just a little money Tran had saved from working at a Quick Trip and doing some sewing around town. They found a house on the dunes, a boarded-up shack that had been repossessed by the government. Danny tried his hand on the boat with Bao Do, but it didn't work out very well. He isn't a fisherman. Besides, there wasn't enough for Bao Do, let alone for two of them. Sometimes he took the boat out alone, perhaps to prove he could work, trying to impress, but that worked less well. I can't keep all the problems straight, but they had problems. When Bhin married Jerry, and then when that couple moved back into Bao Do's house, there were problems between Jerry and Danny. Danny resented him and resented the fact that an American bum was sponging off his father-in-law. He didn't have any use for Jerry, to put it mildly. Jerry hated Danny, but I have no idea why. Danny Huan is an angry young man. Danny Huan is an angry young man. Jerry is a bully, an idiot. The whole house is a mess."

"Danny Huan angry enough to kill?"

"Oh now . . ." she began.

"I mean, does he have a temper?"

"I'm sure I wouldn't know."

"He ever beat Tran?"

"I don't honestly think so."

It came as a surprise to Poole, but far away he could hear the *putt-putt* again. A hollow sound followed, the rubber hull bouncing on the surface of the water, *thump-thump*, the motor modulating as the waves rose and fell. Poole didn't say anything to Adrienne Deveraux. He just got up and ran down to the water's edge and sat down in the sand. He could see the purple-mottled line of seaweed bobbing up and down, heat lying on the water like gauze, beacon lights on the Gulf starring the horizon. Poole thought he could see the outline of a DEA balloon anchored to a cable. He was so tense and ready that he could hear the rustle of the tule far up in the dunes and he swore he could hear the pines swishing and the sand kicking through the saw grass.

Then the dinghy popped into his view above the swells, its orange hull tipped so that it was clear in the crystal evening light, plopping back with a thud so that he could see the bottom of the hull for an instant as it bounced, then tacked on through the swells, motor churning. The mosquitoes were bothering Poole, buzzing in his ears, but he didn't need to hear. That was because he could see the blond girl from la-la land sitting in the bow, one arm over the rubber hull, trailing her hand in the water, her head thrown back in the breeze, her blond hair blowing. The dinghy dropped from view again and Poole found himself staggering through shallow water, trying to see, until he was knee-deep and the salt was hurting his skinned knee. But he kept going, half-unconscious, until all he could think about was the bright circumference of the orange dinghy, luminous in the last shard of sun, and how he couldn't get a clear look. Then the dinghy was gone.

He came back to the beach where Adrienne Deveraux was waiting for him halfway. She was staring at a spot over his right shoulder where the dinghy had disappeared. Poole could still hear the *putt-putt* going away, carried on the breeze. The woman said nothing. Poole had been acting crazy and scary all at the same time. Here they had been talking about their lives, then about the old man Bao Do, and suddenly Poole had jumped up and splashed through the surf like a horse. Poole was on a downslope, looking up at Adrienne Deveraux.

"Do you know the girl in the marina store?" he asked.

"Janine," she said. "That's all I know."

"You don't go to the store?"

"Not anymore. I bring supplies from Houston. When I'm here on weekends, the place is crawling with bikers. It's too frightening a place for me to go."

"I don't blame you," Poole said, coming up the beach.

They walked to the porch steps together. A sultry breeze was coming off the water. Poole picked up the glass he had spilled and stood there, wanting to tell Adrienne Deveraux about the scene he had just witnessed, what it meant, if anything, but not quite focused enough to make sense. Besides, he was just about through with police business and he wanted to preserve something else with the

70

woman. He realized he was thinking on a double track again, all because he had gone fishing and had gotten sunburned.

"Did you ever see the girl Janine on the beach?"

"I don't think so," she said.

"Maybe at the fishing shack, near the Bao Do house? Could she have gone to one of the weekend parties at the house?"

"I don't know."

"Did Tran ever mention her?"

"Oh, I don't think so. No."

"I've got to go home," Poole said.

Adrienne Deveraux followed him up to the dunes. They stood in a palmetto glen, out of the wind.

"You don't think Bao Do killed himself, do you?" she asked, leaning away.

Poole wanted to say no. He wanted to tell her about the new Colt .22 and the lie the blonde had told about the dinghy. He wanted to take her into his confidence, something that had no place in the scheme of his business. Finally, he smiled, shrugged a shoulder—noncommittal.

She touched his arm lightly. "I'll be down next Friday about dark," she said. Poole moved away, just about to collect his rod and reel. He could feel his heart race.

"I could make some snapper." She paused. "If you'd be down on the jetty fishing . . ." Adrienne Deveraux was standing in the breeze with a glass of tea in her hand.

"That sounds fine," Poole said.

He went up the beach in the dark, wondering if this was the right way to behave.

8

After years on the job, Poole wasn't upset about how Jefferson County worked. It was as if the politics of south Texas were a dangerous atomic substance, having a half-life of thousands of years, radium you could store at the bottom of a rock cavern that would never stop glowing. Poole recalled the first Hispanic commissioner, and the first black, and he remembered running into the son of one on a county bridge that crossed a sump, Poole searching for a stolen car and this skinny kid sitting under the bridge drinking peach schnapps on a hot summer afternoon, eyes glazed, looking very stupid and happy and complacent, one of the county bridge inspectors. They had whiled away an hour together in conversation, Poole tired of his workday, wanting to shoot the breeze. That part of the politics, Poole didn't mind so much; where else was this skinny son of a bitch going to find a decent job in life?

That's what he was thinking on Monday morning as he drove on the freeway to Houston, the dull sun low on the NASA complex and a traffic copter flying over the packed cars. The first thing that morning, Poole had seen a memo from Lister in his duty box. The sheriff was kicking him out of the daily staff meeting, sending him over to state police headquarters to check a list of stolen oil field equipment against serial numbers maintained by the owners, all assembled on a master inventory of hundreds of items that had been stolen over the last couple of months. Daddy John probably had been strolling around the county courthouse already that morning, so Poole hadn't thought it worthwhile to do much but spend about ten minutes with the guy, trying to talk him into making a case on the Vietnamese. He didn't have a hassle or a heart-to-heart with the sheriff. He just made a short pitch and left the office. He tried to find Mirabelli and then looked around for Hernandez to see if they had anything to say, but he couldn't find them.

The thing with the old Vietnamese had been working on his mind all night, Poole sitting up late nursing his sunburn with baby oil and baking soda, taking a cool bath with the drapes drawn in the living room and the air conditioner set on low. He had sat in his chair in the living room, unable to stop thinking about the old man. And then he would flash on the girl Janine. Poole had a picture of her riding in the stern of the orange dinghy with her hand trailing in the water while the sun streaked across the sky, big purple clouds climbing in the far distance, over Mexico. Poole had gone to bed with this clear image in his head, lying there until way after midnight in his boxer shorts, feeling the air conditioning draw across his skin, which seemed to be smoldering on the inside, until he began to think about Adrienne Deveraux, imagining what it would be like to put his hands on her, all over her skin, what she might think, if that was any way to behave.

Whatever was at work on him, Poole had gone down to the courthouse early, feeling good even though he hadn't slept much. He had eaten a good breakfast of bacon and eggs and some fresh orange juice in the basement cafeteria. Then he looked at the morning paper, checking the local news to see what had gone down over the weekend. He noticed an obituary for the old man. It came across as something alien and strange, Nguyen Bao Do, fifty-nine, just a few years older than Adrienne Deveraux, an old man hanging on to the edge of the continent. It listed his daughters, Tran and Bhin, then other names from a foreign world that Poole seemed to be looking at through a window of remembrance. He realized that Tran must have called the papers on Sunday. It must have been something she had learned about living in America, the obituary and its relation to keeping someone alive who has slipped away, someone you love. Just reading the old man's name affected Poole. It was as if a piece of himself had flaked away, like the old woman in the hooch returning to his mind while he flew over the Pacific.

Something chill came over Poole at breakfast. He was sitting in the deserted cafeteria over coffee, putting himself back stateside only a few months, hanging around college bars in Denton, waiting to put everything aside and marry Lisa Marie and get on with his life in the world. He had gone up to San Antonio one day to see a guy he knew who was in the VA hospital there. It was a guy he had met in the service who had gotten shot up pretty badly, and Poole wanted to pay him a visit, just see how he was getting along. Poole had driven all that way one day and had found the huge hospital near downtown. Once inside, he became lost almost immediately, wandering around the halls as if in a mirrored fun house. Poole found a harried nurse and she helped him with his problem. He found the guy's room, but it turned out he had been released. There was nothing the army could do for the guy, so they gave him a wheelchair and turned him loose. Poole had brought along some paperback books and a transistor radio he had bought at Radio Shack. He couldn't remember what he'd done with the books and the radio, but he did remember feeling cheated. It was the empty room that got to him, yellow sunshine on the bed, the bare green walls.

After breakfast, Poole had gone upstairs and found his memorandum from Lister. He had his brief meeting with the sheriff and then he had gone looking for Mirabelli and Hernandez. And then he had gassed up the Caprice in the motor pool and had headed for Houston on a morning that was hot and hazy before 9:00 A.M. He would miss the squad meeting, miss the autopsy report on the old man, if there was one, the ballistics, everything, and it made Poole feel cheated, the way he had felt at the VA hospital in San Antonio.

It took Poole forty-five minutes to get through the freeway traffic into downtown Houston on the bypass and park in the underground garage of the headquarters, a black basaltic building on the edge of a hill overlooking the city. Poole was always amazed by the vision of Houston, how it seemed he could look right through all the buildings, as if the towers were radioactive spikes driven right down through the water table, aglow with an inner ferocity, like the power rods of a nuclear plant. When the towers were lighted by an evening sun, they took on an aspect of pure evil for Poole. You could taste the atmosphere of violence and total greed and he wasn't surprised that several recent Presidents had come from Texas or had made their fortunes here. Something in Houston touched a negative key in Poole, much more than along the Gulf Coast, and it wasn't just the heat or the shimmer of smog blanketing the city. It wasn't the bumper-to-bumper traffic and all the liquor stores, the trash in the streets and the garbage in the ship channels. It was something deep.

Poole worked in the property room, where it was stuffy

and dim. It wasn't even cool. He worked over lists of pump engines, pipe, expensive tool sets, beginning to sweat and feel gritty. He was matching lots of stuff from the master lists and he wondered if it would do any good, if he would wind up being a witness at trial, grilled by a lawyer about his chain of custody, trying to keep the facts straight, to keep from getting tripped up on a bullshit level. He didn't want to spend two weeks hanging around the hallway of the courthouse while lawyers argued, servicing the load of an already overloaded system. More and more, even working in the property room in Houston, his thought was being wedged between two tracks, the old Vietnamese and Adrienne Deveraux, the two linked in his mind somehow, not just by happenstance and place but by some metaphysical connection that Poole couldn't help but make into a duality.

One track fed the other. Poole was pretty sure the old man hadn't committed suicide. That was one track. And then when he thought about Adrienne Deveraux, he thought that somehow she might unlock the door to his own life. Maybe one door would lead to another, one key would open both doors. It didn't make sense to Poole, but it made more sense than cruising by Laurel Street and sitting up all night with his beer.

Poole finished making his notes and locked up the stolen equipment piece by piece. He wasn't due anywhere special. Once he was excused from the squad meeting, he was on his own so long as he could justify his time in the staff report he did every week. He rode the elevator up to seven and checked himself into the crime computer room, a fluorescent-lighted space with a screen bank along one wall and some printers underneath, all connected to the FBI data bank, the state court reporting system, prison administration, the Texas DMV, even Interpol and the DEA. Here it was, technology at your fingertips. Poole knew he could skin a suspect down as though he were a rabbit. Right here,

Poole had all the past history he could want, descriptions, aliases, addresses, associates, methods of operation, weapons preferred, even girlfriends and sex habits if you wanted to get down that low.

Poole pulled up a chair, feeling nervous. This duty made him feel funky and out of sorts. He knew these people weren't rabbits. They were men and women with real lives, but their futures were brightly embalmed on cathode screens. Poole punched in his first numbers, sitting down, looking out the window at the skyline of Houston behind the glass, noon haze thick.

Right away, he ran through Nguyen Bao Do, Tran, and Bhin but came up with nothing. It took about fifteen minutes for his basic input to run out over the country and come back blank. Then he ran through Janine, limiting his search to Texas so it wouldn't take so long, and he got back a page of small print, eighteen names and aliases, most of them from the DMV, assorted reports on driving records and arrests. Most of the names were associated with petty crimes, some cons on parole and the names of their supervisors. The one Poole wanted, he found at the bottom of page three, a Port Arthur address, probably no good anymore because it was two years old, but the same chick all right, five six and 111 pounds, brown hair and blue eyes. Poole knew that the blond hair had come from a bottle and that she was skinnier now because she was heavily into speed and coke, maybe even crack now that it was the drug of choice. This "Janine Bonner" clocked two temporary deprivation convictions in city court in Beaumont, which was shorthand for shoplifting; a suspended license for no insurance; and, right at the bottom of the page, standing out against the rest, a probated sentence for possession of marijuana, a city bust in municipal court.

It wasn't hard to match the two pictures: the girl behind the marina shop's counter listening to hard rock, her lips cracked, eyes pouched, undernourished on Moon Pies and

Dr. Pepper, and the green letters on the cathode screen. The two pictures were not that different, verisimilitude on a modern scale, the way people used to carry miniatures of their loved ones in a neck locket, only now Poole had an electronic picture of this girl Janine.

After that, Poole touched in Jerry Donovan. He sat back in his swivel chair and watched the print whine out, the DMV first because it was right at hand. The guy had been in some accidents, leaving the scene, suspended license. He touched in the state and found a robbery arrest in Beaumont, which had come to nothing, then two arrests for assault, same thing. Poole was thinking, For God's sake, this kid was twenty years old. It was him all right, six two, 145 pounds, red hair, guitar tattoo on his right shoulder. What Poole saw on the screen was a future all right, like predicting the weather. You make some mistakes, but pretty soon you could hit it right on the head. And Jerry Donovan was deeply into his future already, petty crime, violence, then something else that hadn't popped up yet on screen, but it was there, waiting to happen. Poole wondered if Jerry Donovan could get so out of whack that he would go down to the fishing shack and murder the old Vietnamese. He wondered if Jerry could do it high on crack, just because he was spaced out, or if he could do it in cold blood, that maybe he had some motive. He knew Jerry Donovan could do the old man, grease him, just because he was high and pissed off, for kicks.

Poole went outside and stood on the sidewalk in front of the headquarters building. He was directly above the city and he couldn't breathe the air. It was late afternoon and everything seemed to be burning, the office towers in clusters, the girdered arrangement of freeways, helicopters overhead, deep tremors of noise from all the traffic. Poole was thinking back to yesterday on the jetty, how he had almost forgotten that this whole nightmare existed, how that was one of the benefits of being on the edge of the continent. He felt as if he had been dreaming for five years, since Lisa Marie had left the Laurel Street house. And just then, Poole wondered if he was looking at one of the office buildings where Lisa Marie was sitting behind a desk, and what she might be doing.

Poole hurried to the Caprice. He thought if he drove quickly, he could avoid the heavy rush-hour traffic through town. He was beyond the underpass, on his way to Beaumont, when he realized he was leaving town, that once he might have tried running Adrienne Deveraux through the computer just to be scientific, to see how she looked in cathode ray green, all lighted up. But now he knew: That was no way to behave.

9

Poole was making his report, sitting in a cubicle in the squad room. He wrote down what was going through his head, all his theories, but what was behind everything was his *plan,* how he knew he needed to do something before the old man faded away completely. Leaning back, he discovered that he hated the cubicle, the swivel chair and the gray metal desk, and he was finding it hard to concentrate on the report. He tried to imagine himself composing music instead, something to keep him focused while he worked. It was late afternoon and he was dead tired. He'd been out all morning on Fannet Boulevard with a policewoman from Beaumont, talking to a clerk from a Hardee's who had been kidnapped and brutalized, had the shit scared out of her, not raped, just taken out into the scrabble countryside and put through a ringer by a couple of punks.

They had talked to the woman, and then at the hospital, after the doctors had fixed her up, Poole and the police- woman had sat around a sterile recovery room trying to get her to tell them the facts, the woman sobbing so hard, she couldn't speak. That had taken most of the morning and the policewoman had done most of the work while Poole stood off to one side, making notes, trying not to stare, not to make the victim feel worse than she did already.

Right now, Poole was in another world himself. He was nearly alone in the squad room, with just two or three secretaries up in the front partition, banging away on their typewriters, phones ringing once in a while, and the elec- tronic background blending into the seamless background of everything else. Poole had come directly from the hospi- tal to the police lab in the basement, trying to find out the results of the ballistics tests on the gun found beside the old Vietnamese in the shack. He couldn't bring himself to be- lieve it was suicide. Still, after thinking about it for two days, he was thinking in terms of some terrible family quar- rel, a sudden death at the end and someone running away. He was thinking about redneck shrimpers, real bubbas, guys who'd hate the Vietnamese for hanging on to the edge of their own continent. One thing Poole knew was that Jerry fit his bill, a redneck bubba, somebody crazy with a hard-on for drugs and rock and roll. Poole was thinking all this because he had no way to rationalize an old Vietnamese fisherman with two daughters walking down to his shack and pulling the trigger on himself.

There was something *uncultural* about it. It didn't make sense to Poole that this tough old guy would wade through all the horror of the war, then through the dirt and filth of the refugee camp in Thailand, then come across the Pacific on a cramped cargo plane like a load of fertilizer, existing on Red Cross food, bussed down to Beaumont, then set free in a strange world where everybody was hostile and suspicious, and then give it all up like an adolescent kid in the suburbs. Something Adrienne Deveraux had said to Poole came back to him. What had she said exactly? Bao Do had wanted her to take him to Beaumont, wanted Tran to go along maybe, which was a thing he didn't do very often, if ever. The old man didn't have a car, didn't even have a telephone in his house. Poole figured he bought his food at the Vietnamese markets in Port Arthur, his fishing gear and gas on the bay, maybe over in Louisiana, along the Intracoastal, where everything was cheaper. Maybe Tran knew what her father had wanted to do in Beaumont.

Still, Poole needed a plan. Then, down in the lab room that morning, he had discovered that there wasn't a work order on the gun that killed the old man. It hadn't slipped through the cracks; they weren't late with the order. It just wasn't going to happen, period. Poole talked to a guy named Covington who ran the property room in the lab, and he found out the gun had been backed out of line and was going upstairs to the evidence room, where it would gather dust. Covington said they weren't going to make a case. Poole got him to dig the gun out of the back room, and when he looked at it, it surprised him because there weren't any serial numbers on the barrel. You always make a case, Poole knew, unless the district attorney or the sheriff say otherwise. He stood for a long time in the cool air of the basement while Covington put away the gun. That was when Poole hurried upstairs and got the call to go down to Fannet Boulevard.

And then before he got back from the hospital, he heard that some city cops had busted two guys driving a stolen tan Cordoba in Beaumont. The two guys had been drinking beer in the car, weaving around, and they were both in jail, three floors down from the squad room. They were eighteen years old and had robbed the Hardee's for some cash, taken the woman out in the bush to make her scream. Maybe now they'd have to stand up in court and say out loud that they had done it, maybe explain why, if they could, and the woman was going to have to tell it again, with everybody listening, looking at her as if she was a freak.

When he heard some detectives come back to the squad room, Poole left for the coroner's office. Even when they told him that the body had been released and no autopsy was scheduled, Poole acted calm. He was beginning to see things now; there were going to be no surprises. The old man was slipping away; he could see him going, going, gone. Poole tried to telephone the coroner, but there was nobody in the office. The fact that there was no autopsy scheduled was a bigger deal than the gun. You could always drag the gun down to the lab, but once the old Vietnamese was in the ground, he would be gone forever. All Poole wanted to know was whether there had been a real discussion between the sheriff and the district attorney or if they'd chatted over cigars and iced tea way up on the top floor of the courthouse.

Poole stood out in the hall, thinking about endings. The old Vietnamese was ending. The century was ending. It looked as if the whales were ending, too. There were millions of ways to end things, some natural, some not so natural. There were mysterious and ineffable ends, like the way Lisa Marie had walked out of the Laurel Street house, without a word, her clothes gone from the closets—hell, the coffeepot could have been on the stove with hot coffee in it. These endings had a riddle at their core, an existential side. Then Poole remembered his buddy, the one with no legs who had disappeared from the VA hospital in San Antonio, how he had ceased to exist for Poole, how Poole had resented it, which wasn't how he felt about Lisa Marie. It was as if his buddy's disappearance contained a hidden message for Poole, if only he could decode it. Oh, all these messages for Poole, the old Vietnamese, Lisa Marie—blip, the radar screen goes blank and two hundred people go down in a rough sea; an old woman disappears from a hooch near Duc Tho.

Snap—Poole broke the lead in his pencil. The music in his head stopped and he realized that the report he had been writing was actually a political document and that he had been advocating a position instead of reporting the facts the way he had been taught. He felt all wrung out in his clothes, as if they were surgical garb and he had spent all day over the table, sewing up holes in flesh. Here he had been composing music, when what he was supposed to be doing was writing a report. He had started a long essay on Jerry, how the slimeball had been drunk on the night of the old man's death, putting in some shit about marijuana in the house, how Jerry had fought with the old man and had a record for assault and robbery, observations Poole knew were pure fantasy.

When the pencil broke, Poole was adding a section about the old man's boat, how it had been vandalized by bubba shrimpers—as if it was a fact in the case; as if it meant shit to Daddy John or anybody else. Maybe it was Poole's unconscious that stopped flowing, but he knew he didn't have any hard evidence. He didn't know anything about anything. All he knew was that the old man was dead and there were no witnesses. He knew he was moralizing, writing music in his head, sitting there in his clothes that had started to chafe him. He checked the clock, realizing there would be a late afternoon vespers for Bao Do at the Catholic church in Beaumont.

Poole called dispatch and asked them to get both Mirabelli and Hernandez in touch. He said he would meet them out on the highway for dinner at a rib joint they all knew. Poole had some time to kill, so he went over to the public library and fussed around in the newspaper files for stories on the shrimper war, back when the fishermen were beating up Vietnamese in bars, burning some of their boats. There had been a lot of nighttime shooting, rough times up and down the coast. When the feds came to town, it got quiet, but there was still a lot of anger.

Down in the library basement, it was musty and cold. Poole felt the sweat evaporate off him as he sat there in the clear white light, running across names that repeated like themes. But there was a special one, a guy named Everett Teagarden who owned a good-sized shrimp fleet, maybe five or six boats that brought in a fair catch in good times, enough to make a decent living. It was a name he'd heard Tran mention, too. One night, Everett had tossed a can of gasoline through a fish restaurant's door. The thing hadn't caused any damage. It just fizzled on the floor with a burning rag in the spout while dozens of terrified Vietnamese made for the doors and windows. Good old Everett was brought downtown by some local cops and kept for a few hours, but nothing came of it, and the feds didn't get their hands on him. It was an easy time for Everett, as well as for other men from over in Cameron, Louisiana, who had started a fistfight in a local bar. Poole studied the newspaper history of the redneck wars and wondered what kind of dent five or six Vietnamese fishing families could put in the shrimp catch around Port Arthur. He thought that the dent had been made already, by oil companies, by the dredgers working up and down the canals and beaches. Hell, everything was silting in, and developers were filling the swamps. It looked to Poole as if the shrimpers were lashing out at the first helpless things they found—Vietnamese, Mung, Cambodians. It used to be Mexicans, and before that, blacks.

Poole went upstairs. Outside, the daylight had settled over everything like a fine mist. It was weather that seeped inside and rotted you out, until you thought you were full of holes. Poole shivered as he stood standing there in his dry clothes on the steps, fingering the list of names he had made from the newspapers, Everett Teagarden right at the top. He thought he might be acting silly by trying to make something out of this, but he was also angry and disappointed at how there wasn't going to be an autopsy, how the gun order had been canceled, how Daddy John was ignoring Poole.

Traffic was beginning to circle out of downtown. Everybody was heading for the freeway, the suburbs in the creosote wilderness. Poole put his notebook in his coat pocket and went over to the motor pool and drove the Caprice down to the rib place on the Port Arthur highway. He found a booth in back, all by himself, under a ceiling fan. He ordered some iced tea, barbecue pork, and dirty rice. He sat drinking the iced tea when it came, waiting for the food, watching out the window while the sun went down in the west over the low dunes and the green pines. The waitress brought his pork and rice and he began to eat it slowly with some hot sauce until he saw Mirabelli pull into the parking lot in his new Nissan Centra, the red car with black stripes, a custom fin on the back.

Now, Mirabelli was definitely in fashion; Poole could see that. Custom everything, including the fin. He was wearing a blue dress shirt and a red power tie, a clean suit that had been recently pressed. He had on a gold chain, too, like Don Johnson on *Miami Vice*, looking as fresh as if he'd just gotten out of the shower. Poole wondered how he did it in the heat.

Mirabelli sat down and they traded small talk until Mirabelli ordered some tea. He sat in the booth, tapping the Formica with his pen until the tea came. Then he drank some of it as he looked out the window. Poole knew he wanted to go home. Mirabelli said he hadn't heard much about the old guy in the shack, that he'd been out on a robbery detail in the county, working with some Louisiana cops who had come over to schmooze, to get after these punks who were doing gas stations in Texas, and then going back home to Louisiana at night. Mirabelli said he'd been to the squad meeting, and he figured the old Vietnamese had greased himself. That was Daddy John's line, anyway.

Poole tried to sound casual. "You get anywhere on the map thing?" Mirabelli told Poole he had made a good map of the oil roads that crisscrossed the dunes, all the way from the shack to the highway leading to Port Arthur, showing Poole how he had noted the houses with the names on the mailboxes when he could find them. There were lots of Vietnamese names. Poole had to hand it to Mirabelli. He had done a good job. But then, Mirabelli was pretty new on the force and hadn't had time to get cynical about these tasks. He wasn't to the stage of sitting under a bridge drinking peach schnapps.

"You doing your report?" Mirabelli asked, plainly hoping the paperwork would fall on Poole.

"Such that it is," Poole said.

Mirabelli had heard about the woman from the Hardee's on Fannet Boulevard and he wanted to know about it. Poole studied Mirabelli's map while he talked shop, nodding his head once in a while. Poole found Everett Teagarden's place on the map, a house edged up against one side of the bay, where the Sabine widened before it drained into the Gulf. It was about two miles from the shack. Maybe it was close enough that Everett couldn't forget about the Vietnamese, seeing them all the time, down at the beach, in their fishing boats. Poole wondered what kind of memory Teagarden had.

"What about this Teagarden place?" Poole asked.

"Old guy in an undershirt, halfway lit up on Stroh's." Mirabelli spread his hands into the safe sign of an umpire, saying, "Zip . . . hadn't heard anything, didn't know anything, didn't give a shit about the gook." Mirabelli was tapping his pen again. Poole knew he wanted out of the rib joint, probably wondering why Poole was wasting his time like this, because nobody heard a shot that afternoon. Nobody had seen anybody.

"He said he didn't give a shit about the gook?"

Mirabelli looked up. "That's what he said."

"You say it was a Vietnamese?"

"Yeah, I think so," Mirabelli said.

"Anybody at the house with him?"

"Oh shit," Mirabelli said, smiling. "I took a peek inside and the place was a mess. It looks like this guy lives alone, eats out of the toilet, hasn't done a lick of work in years. You know the guy. Old bubba going down."

"Yeah, I know," Poole said. "I appreciate the help."

Mirabelli stood. He looked very pleased, grinning, adjusting his tie. Poole thanked him again as he was going away, explaining that he would wait around for Hernandez and wrap this thing up, write the report. Mirabelli could go home to his kids.

Poole nursed his tea. He watched Mirabelli hop into the Nissan and head back to town. Everything outside was being covered by the sunset like a coat of paint. Poole could see the neon signs on the bars down the highway, some dim light from the doorway of a strip joint. It reminded him of those faraway evenings, all the shredded sunlight in the oaks, long shadows in the dusty lanes, when his father would come home from work, the same sun, the way his father used to drag himself through it as if he was paralyzed, as if the sun itself were a radiant muck and he was stuck in it.

Poole saw a blue-gray Caprice pull up and park, Hernandez getting out, stretching. He was holding his suit coat over one arm. He looked tired, the underarms of his dress shirt pitted out, one big sweat stain on the chest. He seemed dusty all over, his pants, his black hair, as if he had been out in a bean field somewhere, digging. Hernandez was short and stubby-looking, a permanently somber expression on his face. He walked inside the rib joint and caught Poole's eye, smiled, and came back and sat down in the booth. Poole waited while he ordered some tea with lemon. They chatted for about fifteen minutes, work talk and some stuff about the Astros. Hernandez didn't want any food; he had to go home. Poole smiled, thought about ordering some cherry pie, then thought about how fat he felt, how he had ballooned to nearly two hundred. Poole watched Hernandez, knowing the guy wanted to go home to his wife. Then he wondered what it was like when Hernandez went home. They had lost one of their kids; what could they talk about? Hernandez started talking about the staff meeting, about how shitty his Caprice was running, how he thought maybe his spark plug wires were shot and the carburetor, too. He couldn't chase a kid down the street on a trike. It ran that bad.

Poole had a mouthful of beans. "I guess you're wondering why I called you all here for this meeting?"

"I guess you could say that," Hernandez replied.

"It's about the Vietnamese fisherman. Guy we found in the fishing shack down on Port Arthur beach."

Hernandez looked a little surprised, but he said he knew. After all, he'd ridden home with the dead guy in an ambulance. He said he didn't mind the ride so much, but he'd wished there had been some company; it was a bad way to spend a Saturday night. He guessed the Vietnamese felt the same way. Kind of lonely for both of them. Poole sat listening to Hernandez telling how he hadn't found anything in the shack except the gun, and it was in a plastic sack. No fibers, not even any fingerprints. Poole found himself wanting a smoke, a cold beer. Hernandez drained his tea and ordered another one. Lonely, Poole thought, looking out at the scrub dunes, the sun gone, just purple shades and the lights in the shacks twinkling on.

"There won't be a case on the Vietnamese," Poole said.

"I get that impression."

"No autopsy, no ballistics."

"I didn't know that," Hernandez said. He looked interested. He was squeezing lemon into his iced tea. Poole detected a trace of thought in his expression, something beyond being hot and wanting to go home.

"I had a short chat with Daddy," Poole said.

Hernandez looked at Poole. "It is not-so-holy," he said. A gentle dreamy look now. "To take one's life." He was probably thinking about his boy, Poole thought. The poor kid who didn't look both ways. Some kid you read about in the newspapers, only it was Hernandez's kid, and Hernandez was sitting across from Poole in the booth. Poole admired his suffering, how he had ridden all the way to Beaumont with the old Vietnamese and hadn't complained.

"Maybe he didn't," Poole said.

Hernandez licked his lips. Poole could see how tired he was, the creased forehead, little crabs at the corner of his eyes, gray in the hair. Poole wondered if he would have any more children, how old his wife was, if they had talked about it late at night, lying there in bed next to each other.

"What is on your mind, Tom?"

Poole collected himself and told Hernandez everything. He told him about the gun, the new .22 Colt, about Jerry Donovan being drunk, the family jealousy, all the arguments and the heavy drug parties at the house, how *uncultural* it was because the old man was a Catholic, a fisherman, and he had two daughters. Poole said it didn't add up. He even mentioned Everett Teagarden, the bubba war, the old bubba living just two miles from the shack. Hernandez nodded and said he remembered the bubba wars.

"What is it you're going to do?" Hernandez asked.

"I'm in charge of this investigation."

"There isn't any investigation."

"I say there is. I'm going over to see Daddy John. I'm going to saw through the bars."

"Good luck," Hernandez said, smiling faintly. Hernandez knew where they were headed, and Poole could see it wasn't easy for him.

"I want you with me," Poole said.

Hernandez sighed, put one hand over his mouth, his elbow on the table. "Just give it to me," he said.

"The old man didn't kill himself," Poole said.

"You don't know that," Hernandez said.

"Right now, I don't know anything. But I know maybe Jerry Donovan did the old man. Maybe Everett Teagarden did the old man. For some reason, I can't let the old man down."

"Meanwhile, Daddy takes strips off my hide." Hernandez had screwed up his face, eyes all narrow. "Man, I need my job, can't you see that?"

"I will cover your ass. You won't lose any hide."

"Man, if I could only believe that."

"I give you my word," Poole said, leaning over.

Looking away, out the window at the purple sky, Hernandez said, "You go see Daddy John. Call me."

Hernandez moved, but Poole caught his wrist. "I want to watch the Teagarden house. It's up on the curve of the bay, where the river goes into the Gulf. You know it. You can't miss it. We can sit across the lagoon in a grove of oaks. Hell, there's already a picnic table there, a roadside park. Just sit down, eat some grapes. See what goes down in the bubba's house. It would be fun."

"Jesus and Mary." Hernandez laughed. "What kind of fun you think is fun? You like hip surgery? Fun like that? You like biting heads off lizards?"

"I'm serious," said Poole.

"I know what you're doing," Hernandez said, looking out the window again where the sky had filmed over to orange. It was a Gulf sunset with billowy clouds, coral-toned, caps in bright silver. There was a flight of grackles in some oaks. Hernandez watched them settle.

"We take turns watching the house. I'll do it all day. I just need some relief in the evenings so I can get some rest. We give it a few days. If nothing happens, we give it up. No harm, no foul. We just watch Everett Teagarden after I give him a little upset to think about. Maybe he does nothing. Maybe he does something. We do it for the old Vietnamese. Right now, I think a bubba killed the old man, Jerry, maybe Everett. You want a thing like that to disappear?"

"No, of course not," Hernandez said, disgusted.

"Daddy John won't find out." Hernandez was shaking his head. "Somebody sees us in the park, we're just shucking around in the shade on a hot day. Hey, I won't say anything."

Hernandez got up and put on his suit coat. He laid a dollar on the table, some change for the waitress. "Call me," he said. "Tell me how it turns out with Daddy."

Poole watched Hernandez leave the rib joint and get in his Caprice. It was a pretty night, the red taillights going down the road in the pale twilight. There was a Dr. Pepper truck heading south. Poole couldn't imagine where it was going at this time. But it made him lonely all the same.

Suddenly, Poole wanted to go to vespers for the old Vietnamese. Here he was on a dual track again, wanting to say a prayer for the old man, wanting to stake out Everett Teagarden, too. On the way outside to his car, Poole knew he needed to get a different job and leave this Gulf town. He wanted to start unlearning the things he had been taught to think. He wanted to learn how to behave.

10

Poole left the rib joint and plunged into near twilight. Beyond the dunes, the west was washed in orange. Flakes of cloud had broken off, floating in from shore with the prevailing breeze. He stood in front of a plate-glass window that had a border of neon, looking out across the crushed coral-and-sand parking lot, the white dust turning pale blue mixed with orange. He had expected to be exhilarated by now, getting this off his chest with Hernandez and knowing he was going over to Daddy John's to saw through the bars.

Instead, Poole felt riddled by mood. He had broken into a light sweat after the air conditioning in the joint, his face flushed from the hot sauce. Just two minutes into the parking lot scene and his suit was soaked through. There wasn't much traffic on the highway, just the sound of the breeze clicking through the palms, particles of dust and sand in the air, biting against the cars, all the pine trees along an irrigation canal leaning into the wind. A few snowy egrets were poking around in the canal and a magpie had found a road squirrel and was picking it over in between cars. A diesel roared by and the magpie jumped aside, into the ditch. It was a beautiful scene with the orange sky pierced by dark jolts of blue where the clouds spiked through to the horizon, a neon glow on the coral-shell earth.

Poole stood there for a while, trying to organize himself for Daddy John. He needed to be forceful now, even dogmatic on some level, if that's what it took, and he knew it would because he'd be up against a five- or six-minute window where he'd have to say his piece and make himself understood, then the window would close. If nothing happened in that time, the old fisherman would really be gone, and Poole would, perhaps, go home to his apartment above the mall and have a beer and write off the fisherman.

He got into his Caprice and rolled down the windows, trying to get some air. His mind was working like a camera shutter now. He could see Adrienne Deveraux with lines at the corners of her eyes, how nice she looked, her brown skin, a few freckles. Then he would blink out, click, and she would be gone and there was Daddy John in Poole's eye, the fat guy wiping down his glasses in the stifling heat of the shack while Poole stood paralyzed in the doorway. Daddy John with a half smile, Poole thinking, What is this shit?

Poole decided to drive about forty-five miles an hour all the way to Beaumont to tease out his moods, not wanting to show at Daddy John's with the heavy aroma of nerves around him. He wanted to be cold on this thing, remembering how condescendingly Daddy John had treated him when Poole had read his report. Inside his anxiety, Poole knew there was a core of anger, like the bulb of blood inside a syringe. He wanted rid of it if only for fifteen minutes. He wanted an absolute diffidence going for him as he drove around Daddy John's circular drive, the one lined by prize azaleas, the red-painted Negro statue with a ring in its nose.

Poole followed the curve of bay northeast. There were still saw grass pastures south, full of egrets and cattle, but north, Poole could see in the dim twilight plumes of exhaust from the gas plants and refineries. Every once in a while, he would shutter-stop to another scene of something long ago, a shred of memory that had him driving south on the highway when he was maybe seventeen years old, going down to the jetty to fish or take in a ball game at Port Arthur. Everything seemed different in his mind and he wondered if this was a different country from the one it had been, if it had changed, or if it was only his intense desire for immutability that made things seem so screwed up now, open pastures changing into Burger Kings, trees sheared away for parking lots, all of life cabled and rigged and figured into a financial scheme. Then Poole hit the suburbs of Beaumont, watching as the stucco boxes came into view, rows of them, then the fast-food places, the Quick Trips and 7-Elevens.

Poole worked through downtown Beaumont, which was nearly deserted until he hit a diagonal parkway in a nice part of town where older houses were shaded by oaks and big magnolias. He turned into the circular drive and parked behind a tan LTD with a custom kit. It seemed to him that there were a lot of cars parked up and down the block, and he noticed that all the lights in Daddy John's house were lighted. Right then, he felt his nerve slip, and he wanted to drive away, across town to his apartment, and get a cold Dixie out of the fridge and watch the evening die. He would have been more comfortable in his old skin, lying around on the couch in his boxer shorts while the AC squirted rarefied air on him. But he walked around some azaleas, knocked on the door, then rang the bell.

He thought he could hear mariachi music. He waited and rang the bell again.

The woman said, "Oh," when she answered the door, taking a step back, surprised. She was a small-boned woman with rinsed white hair tinged blue, tight curls around her head, rouged cheeks. She was trying to place Poole, looking up at him as if he should have been familiar but wasn't. Behind her the room was bathed in a copper glow, kitchen on the right, separated from the rest of the living room by a bar and stools, lots of knickknacks on the walls, braided rugs, a dull ranch split-level feel that made it hard to penetrate through the levels to grasp the significance of anything. Poole told the woman who he was before she said anything, what he wanted, that he needed a few minutes of the sheriff's time. He almost apologized but moved inside instead without being asked, remembering his pledge to himself to get something done, not just drift around and go home, hop away like a rabbit.

Poole stood in the doorway, ramrod straight, while the woman went back through the dining room, a hallway, out some glass doors in the back of the house. He waited, trying to bite down his anxiety, get at its core, until he saw Daddy John come through the glass doors, pulling the doors shut behind him while he looked at Poole with curiosity. Poole heard the doors *snick* closed, one deep draught of mariachi music just before, Daddy John getting a sour look all of the sudden, just inside. Lights were flickering on the glass as if an old 16-mm reel was being played just beyond Poole's line of vision. Then Poole got a good look at Daddy John as he advanced across the distance. The sheriff was almost snickering. Daddy was wearing blue bermuda shorts, Nike running shoes and black socks, a white campesino shirt buttoned to the tip of his breastbone. He had a can of Dixie in his hand.

"I'm surprised to see you, Poole," Lister said, not asking Poole inside, but not unfriendly, either, standing about five feet across the room, one arm on the breakfast bar.

Poole slid inside, as if Lister wouldn't notice what he was doing. Daddy John wiped sweat from his forehead.

"I've got to talk to you," Poole said. Lister walked around Poole and shut the door. Suddenly, Poole heard a swell of music, and he understood the cars now, some kind of cookout, Mexican theme.

"I'm busy now," Lister said. "Can't this wait?"

"No, it can't wait," Poole said. Lister walked back around Poole, stood leaning against the bar, beer in his left hand, very relaxed but tensing up a bit as time passed.

"All right," he said, smiling.

"It's about the Vietnamese fisherman."

"What about him?"

Poole took a good look at Lister. He could see Lister wasn't ready to focus yet with his half-amused grin and sweaty red face, still not down from his backyard party. Poole hated the fact that Lister was half a head taller and Poole had to look up to catch his eye. It was a man thing, hard to define.

Poole said he thought the fisherman had been murdered. He said he thought the investigation should be reopened, should be pushed hard, Poole putting a lot of tone in his voice, not urgent, but heartfelt, with an edge of anger. He said he thought there were a lot of loose ends but that they might be tied up with some police work. That was why he was here; he wanted the goddamn police to do a little police work for a change. "Hey," Poole said, "we ought to be doing police work. We're police, aren't we?"

"We've been through this, Tom boy," Lister said, drinking some beer, guiding himself on a course between anger and relaxation. "I've got some people out in the backyard. They expect me to show them some fun." Lister glanced back to the glass doors. "You understand what I'm saying?"

Well, Poole could hear the window sliding closed already. This was where he needed to take up the slack, start sawing on the bars.

"Bullshit," Poole said harshly. Scary, scary. "I mean this is fucking bullshit." You could have cut the silence with a blowtorch. Here they were, standing in Lister's front room, where copper kettles hung on the kitchen wall, and Poole imagined himself going by the saw grass pastures just half an hour before, the same places he'd bicycled past as a kid, only now the camera shutter had dropped on a fat guy in bermuda shorts who had a scowl, real bad, real bad, real bad.

"What was that?" Lister said, disbelieving.

Poole was looking over his shoulder, watching the glass door slide open as Darnell Lister pushed through, catching Poole's eye. Poole just waited as Darnell came through the dining room, got up to his father, and stood there, slightly confused, probably wondering what the hell all this silence meant.

Father and son stood together, separated by about four feet, Darnell a junior version, meatier and short, jet black hair in a crew cut. It looked as if Darnell had just come to the party from work, because he was wearing a white dress shirt, a loose tie. He looked about three Dixies into a fine evening, with some enchiladas, barbecue pork sandwiches, maybe a little bourbon and poker later on when things got smoky. Poole could see father and son up at Rice Stadium, sitting in fifty-yard-line seats on a warm autumn afternoon, drinking bourbon from a flask, watching the Owls lose to TCU. It made Poole wonder where it would all end, the fathers and sons, the fast-food joints, and if there was a way to disconnect both the gene pool and history, to let nature take over again.

Poole took a deep breath. There were some things he wanted to say; he didn't know what function Darnell would have in the scene.

Poole said, "There are five or six things we should be

doing." He had gathered his thoughts now. On the drive up the Port Arthur highway, he had made up a nice speech, but he had forgotten it. One thing he knew, it hadn't started with the word *bullshit*. Darnell went to the refrigerator and got a beer. He was standing across the breakfast bar, looking at Poole as if he was trying to place the face.

"We've been through this," Lister said flatly. Darnell snapped open the beer.

"A guy named Jerry Donovan is the son-in-law. He's an Anglo who does dope, throws big parties in the old man's house out on the estuary. They hated each other . . . well, maybe Donovan hated the old man. I've seen this Donovan drunk. He looks like a punk to me, the kind who might kill his father-in-law."

"The fishhead?" Darnell said from the kitchen. Out of the blue, just a thing to say to lighten this up, have a little joke on the Vietnamese.

"Just trash talk," Poole muttered. "You remember the bubba wars?" Poole asked, going ahead. "Well, an old bubba named Everett Teagarden lives about a mile from the fisherman. Up by the lagoon, Sabine marsh. He blames the Vietnamese for all the fishing problems. This is another guy who might get drunk and kill, walk over to the fishing shack and off a Vietnamese fisherman."

Darnell had leaned his elbows on the bar, shiny-faced, probably still thinking about the "trash talk" comment, how to get an edge into the conversation.

"I told you before, goddamn it," Lister said, "and I think you've gone a little abstract in the head. Why don't you go home and get some sleep?" Lister tapped his beer can on the bar. "I mean, you talk like you're all tangled up. I ain't heard you like this before. I'm going to give you the benefit of the doubt. And I've got considerable doubt about you, son."

Poole had heard this double-talk many times. He wanted to strangle Lister, pull his tongue out of his head, let him have a look at the offender, right now. "You've got a gun in evidence that hasn't been examined, identified, nothing. You've got a bullet in the floor of the shack that hasn't been recovered. No ballistics even, for Christ's sake. What the fuck makes you think I should go home and get some sleep? We've been asleep for two days on this case."

Jesus, there had been a moment when Poole thought he might crack a boyish smile, ask for a beer, one for the ride home, give Daddy John the impression he had stepped in dog shit, and go on about his business. But now there was something impassable between the two. Poole had a ringing in his ears.

"The old man was shot in the *left* temple," Poole said finally, after the silence had gone on long enough. "Doesn't that strike you as odd?"

Darnell laughed, a really perfect cackle that gave the impression of a man who'd just heard a dirty joke. "Is this old boy one of your people?" Darnell asked. Lister smiled and looked at his son wistfully, then nodded. They had a mutual drink of beer, looking at Poole as if he were damaged goods.

"There isn't any autopsy scheduled," Poole said.

Lister smiled again, more nervously, though. "Now what the hell would that do?" he asked.

"It's how it looks," Poole said.

"And how does it look?" Lister asked.

"Yes, how does it look?" Darnell added.

"I'm talking to you," Poole said, looking at Lister now. Poole was scared, talking shit to the man's son, too.

"That's enough shit," Lister said.

Poole heard a dog bark. There was an Irish setter climbing the glass doors, paws on the panes, tail wagging. Somebody dragged him away, but he came back. That's fine, Poole was thinking, Daddy John Lister, dog lover, friend to man, and here was Poole crapping on the guy in his own home.

"How does it look?" Darnell said angrily. "And I'm talking to you."

Poole wondered what Hernandez would think if he could be here. Poole said, "The old fisherman wanted to come up to Beaumont to see the sheriff this week. Maybe somebody had threatened him."

"Who told you that?" Lister asked. The pink tip of Darnell's tongue had slipped out of his mouth. It was a gesture that transfixed Poole, made him uneasy.

"One of the neighbors," Poole said.

"Aside from all that," Lister said, "I don't like you talking shit to me."

"Do the ballistics," Poole snapped. "Talk to Donovan and Teagarden. These guys, we can scare. Conduct an autopsy. For God's sake, I think that's what should be done. I'm talking about police work here. I'm talking about how we should go about our business."

"You have a lot of opinions," Darnell said, leaning over the breakfast bar, pink tongue snaking out.

"That's right," Poole said to Darnell. "They came over me this week. I thought you should hear them."

"You do what you're told," Lister said, raising his voice finally.

"This is important to me," Poole replied. A moment passed, then Poole realized the absurdity of what he'd just said. It would be crazy trying to tell Lister about the hooch, all those funky mornings he'd spent sitting on sandbags while the Asian sky colored up, all the rainstorms through the blue-gray trees, how the monkeys sounded during a firefight.

"Goddamn, boy!" Lister shouted. The fabric had split, and it came as a shock to Poole, Lister suddenly very red in the face, spilling his beer on the counter. "You ain't listening. I said you do what you're told. I been through this with the district attorney. There ain't no fucking case now. And there won't be a case. The slope killed himself. And now I got two judges and half a dozen lawyers in the backyard and they got a mind to eat some food, drink some beer. That ought to mean something to you, Tom boy." Lister looked at Darnell, then back to Poole. "Let me tell you something," he said quietly. "This country don't belong to them people. It never goddamn will. It belongs to you and me. That old man killed himself and there ain't anything you can do about it. You ought to let a thing like this rest."

Poole said, "Everett Teagarden tossed a can of gasoline inside a Vietnamese bar two or three years ago. He and his friends vandalized Vietnamese fishing boats about the same time." Poole was watching the father and son stare at him in disbelief. They looked like they were watching a dog on the freeway during rush hour.

"Cool down, Tom," Lister said. They were sinking into a frozen place now, hate down there, a skein of revenge Poole didn't understand. "And I want you to get out of my house."

"The gun is another thing," Poole said. Poole guessed he'd been inside for about five minutes now and already it felt as if it were raining smoke here, some heavy industrial glue. "The fisherman didn't own a weapon like the one that killed him. He might have had an old one to shoot barracuda. That's all."

"I ain't debating you, Tom," Lister said.

How do you engage someone like this, Poole thought?

"You want me to put him out?" Darnell said.

"Oh shit," Lister said. "Tom's still on the team, ain't you, Tom?"

"Let me lean on Donovan and Teagarden," Poole said.

"That ain't team play," Lister growled.

"Jesus Christ, Daddy," Darnell interrupted just before Lister finished, halfway through his thought before Lister picked up his Dixie and drank some beer.

Lister smiled, not too sincere. "I understand you, Tom," he said, about to soft-soap Poole. Poole had seen it before at the courthouse. Lister had a flair for it. "You being in Vietnam and all, you probably seen those people a lot. Maybe you feel like you owe them something. Maybe you feel guilty about it, Tom. That ain't nothing to be ashamed of, even if it is stupider than cow shit."

Poole felt like screaming. Here Daddy John had almost seen through to the real motives behind Poole, but at the last second he'd veered off, mashed everything out of shape.

"It isn't like that," Poole said dully.

"And I know your wife ran off," Lister said.

Poole could detect the shift in tone. Lister was amused and having fun. "It would make anybody crazy, a pretty wife like that fucking some other old boy, then taking off to Houston, going out at night. But I'm surprised how you're carrying on about it. You're divorced now, right?" Lister had walked over and was standing just across from Poole, a wicked grin on his face.

"This isn't about me," Poole lied.

"I'll put him out," Darnell said.

Lister reached over and touched his son's arm. God, it was good cop and bad cop now, and Lister was running the old number on Poole. And here was a county commissioner going to kick Poole's ass down the steps, put him out. Something inside Poole accepted this jump shift in the mood, the tilt toward violence. He could feel his physical response and it was okay. He thought for once he might really get inside the mood now that it had become visceral. It made his head swim momentarily, then he straightened out and things were clearer. He was running on hate now, just shooting the blood in the syringe, doping himself up on it. He thought if Darnell put his hands on him, he might touch one off on the guy's jaw. It would be worth it.

"Poole is leaving," Lister said. "Ain't you, Tom boy?"

Poole was so wired, he couldn't think. His fantasies were nearly unbearable, so loud that he could hear Darnell's nose pop in his imagination. Something parted Poole from where he'd been before, torn between his two moods, and suddenly he felt severed from his new skin. He was operating down at the zoo level, where instinct reigned and reason was left behind. He could picture himself pounding Darnell's face. And Darnell was probably boiling inside, too. That was the hell of the thing, the syncopation of structured emotion that was all bad, something that could involve two people so much that they killed for it. Poole thought to himself that it was better than late-night television for sure; there the violence remained inward, dropped deeper and deeper until you just had to make a call to the Confession Line, a 900 number in New Jersey, where a recording was waiting for your call.

"I want to know," Poole said, trying to look as if he was going to go, "if you'll open the investigation, let me do some police work."

"You just ain't got the team spirit," Lister said, shoving forward, eyeing his son, keeping him off.

Poole opened the door, trying to get some perspective on the scene.

"Don't come in for two or three weeks," Lister said. "I don't want to see your face. You need a rest, anyway. And if you show up around the courthouse, I'll take away your job. Now, I want you to think about that and let me know if you can play on my team. Give it three weeks, why don't you."

"This isn't a team decision," Poole said. "It has nothing to do with Vietnam, nothing to do with my goddamn ex-wife." At this point, he found himself outside on the stoop. He caught the scent of the azaleas, the thick night air full of moisture and barbecue smoke. He was standing on the porch, alone with his fantasies. This is stupid, Poole thought, so goddamn stupid. Lister backed away into the house. It was as if they had crossed into separate mirrors.

Darnell came out the door and stood on the porch, just above Poole. There was smoke in the sky behind the house, a shred of gray ash rising into the moonlight, and Poole was wondering what was inside Darnell's head. Was he having exactly the same fantasies as Poole? Wasn't it funny, Poole thought, how these two grown men were having overlapping fantasies, teenage fantasies at that. But Poole was still transfigured by the violence. He felt as if he was sharing Daddy John's ignorance, and it made him vaguely ashamed. At any rate, he wasn't sharing the craziness, the bigotry.

Poole was on the walk, surrounded by azalea bushes. Darnell closed the door. It looked as though he wanted to come down the steps and was thinking it over, but something stopped him.

"If I had time," Darnell said, "I'd kick the shit out of you."

"You're really grotesque," Poole said, smiling. He thought this might get Darnell in his face fast, but it didn't.

"You don't have a job," Darnell said.

"My life is over," Poole replied. It was kind of fun, this sandlot insult game, Poole walking slowly down the path, back turned.

"Fuck you!" Darnell said, trying to keep his voice down, desperate to get it out, though. "We'll get it on sometime."

Darnell, his arms folded, was still on the porch when Poole drove around the circular driveway. Poole was feeling the effects of his shock now, a little shaky in the hands. He hadn't known how wired he was and it came as a surprise that he'd just been inside the sheriff's house for five minutes, giving him shit. Now he was falling apart.

Poole reached steady state by the time he got to the wayside park above Teagarden's house, above the lagoon and the ragged Sabine marsh. He sat down on a park bench, looking down at Teagarden's stucco place, where there were lights on in the kitchen even though it was late. The lagoon spread around back in a dog-leg shape, tapering inland to the marshes. Poole felt prickly in his clothes, washed out, all the moisture in the air wringing through him. The moon was laying down a silver patina on the water, and Poole could see the line of palms along the beach, the dunes down by Adrienne Deveraux's cabin, and he could hear the wind tipping through the pines, clicking the palm fronds. It was a relief to have the nerves in his neck stop twitching, his knees stop shaking. He sat there for a long time, until he was completely calm, until the lights went out in Teagarden's kitchen.

11

Poole was standing just inside the doors to St. Mark's, the big Catholic church downtown. He felt haunted, as if an icy shroud had dropped over him. He was tired, too, from staying up half the night watching the Teagarden house, sitting in his car in a grove of oaks high above the lagoon, where he could see almost everything—the driveway, the house, the slice of water going away in the darkness. Now he was at the church, which covered a whole corner, the rectory down the block, a parking lot. The main thing running through his mind, after Daddy John and Darnell, after the forced layoff, his vacation, was how much being in a church meant, how the smell and the organ music affected him. For one thing, it was nice to be inside away from the broken ozone smell of the summer air and into the candle wax and cool stone. For another thing, he sensed some stress draining away as he listened to the ethereal music.

He didn't recognize the organ piece. It was baroque, but not the Buxtehude or Bach that he loved. It was a nice melody, though, and it reminded him of his talent, the one for the piano that he had forsaken. It wasn't special music, but it was good to hear it being played, and Poole found himself following the technical flow of the simple chord structures.

He walked around the pews to the side of the church, past the font, around decks of burning candles that had a tawny smell like port wine, sneaking looks at the inner recesses, where there were plaster saints. He hadn't been in a Catholic church in a long time, or any church for that matter, since his marriage to Lisa Marie in a chapel on campus in Denton. Poole had been a music student after his time in the army. He wanted to be a musician, but he knew he might not have the talent. He thought he would be satisfied to teach, maybe in high school. It was a desire he'd had since he was a kid.

For a week or two after Poole had married, after a short honeymoon in New Orleans, he considered studying the Catholic faith. He thought it might please his wife and her folks, that they would all be partners in something special, in prayer and salvation. He thought his conversion might solidify their mutual relationships, but the feeling died in the months to come and he worked his way back into his music, studying jazz with a fine arts ensemble, playing around town in pizza parlors and at frat parties.

Pretty soon, Poole knew he had fooled himself. He couldn't find faith the way you find a pet in the newspapers. You don't snap your fingers and begin to worship some fearful God. But now Poole was drawn to the music. The instrument was beautiful. It was on a stone pedestal and a bald man was playing it in the light of a single bulb above the keyboard. There were a dozen or so people in the church, most of them Vietnamese, as well as one or two other parishioners. Poole saw Adrienne Deveraux all by herself on the other side, wearing a black suit and a white silk scarf on her head.

A priest walked to the altar. He was looking down into the open coffin, saying something low over it, and then Poole heard the sound of crying, probably from Tran, whom he could see only from behind, her head down and her shoulders moving slightly. He felt guilty right then. He was thinking ahead to Friday night, wondering what was going to happen, if he would know how to behave. Adrienne Deveraux was looking right at the priest, who was leading the prayers.

Poole counted the noses. There was Jerry Donovan, wearing scruffy slacks and a white dress shirt. He wondered, looking at him nod, if he was stoned, if he would come to the funeral high on reefer, if he thought it would be cool to be stoned in church. Poole had experienced worse, guys high on acid or PCP while the mortars roared overhead, guys listening to Jimi Hendrix while they fired their weapons, wearing earphones in the first full-tilt rock-and-roll war in history. During those times, all Poole had been was scared. And now, here was Jerry Donovan, nodding out at the funeral.

Poole moved over to a pew and sat down. He spotted Bhin, who was wearing a pleated black-and-green-plaid skirt, a white blouse, and a thin black sweater. She looked like a Catholic schoolgirl in uniform. She was crying, too, chewing on her lip, biting her knuckles. Jerry was sitting down the row from her, like none of this was happening for him, which was why Poole thought maybe he was tripping. Poole stared at the guy. He was making little quaking movements with his head. For a minute, Poole wanted to take him outside and shake him, put him straight to the scene. He kept thinking that when he was through with Everett Teagarden, if he ever was, he would start in on Jerry Donovan.

Tran and Bhin were sitting together, but Poole didn't

spot Danny Huan right away. It puzzled him, this guy. He did see a well-muscled man with a dark complexion down the row from Tran. He had a thin mustache and well-formed high cheekbones. Poole thought he was about twenty-five years old. He made him about five ten. Poole kept looking around, but the man was the only other young Vietnamese in the church, so maybe he was Danny Huan. Still, something wasn't quite right about the way he looked. It was the way he was sitting off, very cool and aloof. Poole put it in his memory bank for later.

The rest of them were old people, a couple who looked Cambodian, all of them scattered in groups of two and three. It looked as if this was part of the refugee community, old folks from the country, peasants, all of them hanging on to the edge of the continent. For a minute, Poole felt like a spy with a camera, taking pictures of their grief. It was worse than that, because down deep Poole was still thinking more about Adrienne Deveraux than about anything else, and it bothered him.

Poole bowed his head and tried to pray. He said a few words of the Lord's Prayer, but it was more an unspooling of his feelings than anything else, and then he was done with it and was looking at the old Vietnamese with his waxy yellow face, the shower of lilies on the coffin, the old man's suit ink blue against the white silk lining. There was a plug in the old man's head, smoothed over by undertaker's makeup, some hair plastered over that, but you could still see the wound above the ear. It had the unreal look of doll repair or cracked porcelain. Thinking about it, Poole realized the bullet was still in the floor of the shack. It wouldn't go into the earth with the old man.

An altar boy was lighting more candles. The priest was finished, working his way behind the boy as he lighted the candles, both of them moving slowly. Tran and Bhin stood up and walked to the coffin to say good-bye to their father. They were making a terrible noise that Poole recognized from Vietnam, from the war. It made his muscles react; it was that immediate. Jerry was still sitting, his head bobbing. Just then, the music stopped and Poole watched the muscular Vietnamese man get up and walk to the coffin and touch the wood and then walk away down the aisle and go outside. Some sunshine sliced down the aisle and Poole could hear the city outside, a hush as the door shut. Adrienne Deveraux was still, and then their eyes met across the church and Poole saw the blue of them. She must have driven all the way down from Houston just for vespers. Poole admired her for doing that, for honoring the dead father of her friend. *Are you a serious man or what, Mr. Poole? Are you full of shit?* Poole realized that this woman was a time bomb ticking away in his life.

Poole twisted out of his seat and walked down the side aisle. The music began again and he stopped to listen, but he was near the entrance and all he could hear was the sound of a city bus stopping in front. When he got outside, he was immediately aware of the enormous heat and the thick white clouds on the horizon, some black on top, storm clouds. He was standing high above the sidewalk and he could see the ugly courthouse down the street and a slab of freeway with evening traffic going by. Down at the bottom of the steps was the muscular Vietnamese, who had lighted a cigarette and was smoking it in a distracted way.

Poole walked down the steps. He was nervous, feeling like an outsider, which he was. He wanted to be in control, come on strong with Danny Huan, put the guy on the defensive, as if he was a goon in the squad room, a position that would give Poole leverage. Sometimes guys came unraveled and spilled their guts in positions like that. But now, it was Poole who was confused and nervous, made so by the experience of the church.

Danny Huan was dressed in shiny gray slacks and a cutoff sweatshirt. He had one foot on a step, holding his cigarette between a thumb and forefinger, glancing up at Poole, who was standing just above him, watching the city bus pull away from its stop. And then Poole zeroed in on it, that clean look on Danny Huan's face and the heavy-lidded brown eyes, the high cheekbones, and the skin that had a chocolate-milk cast. Poole knew he was looking at a GI kid whose black father had left him alone in Vietnam, who probably didn't know he was alive, if he ever thought about it in the first place. This accounted for Danny Huan's large stature, so unlike most Vietnamese, and for the glazed fluid expression on his face, his muscles, his dark mustache. And it probably accounted for his wistfulness, too, an outcast in every sense of the word, even among the mourners united by grief and faith. Here was a guy with nowhere to hide, and Poole wondered what it was like for him, hanging on to the edge of a continent. Still, he had an immediate respect for his position. It made Poole feel even more out of control, just when he needed to get tough.

Huan registered Poole's stare, looked him in the eye. Poole needed some props—a mask maybe, something to give him an advantage.

"You Danny Huan?" Poole heard himself ask.

Huan nodded imperceptibly. He was already alert, way beyond being herded anyplace. Poole stepped down to street level. "I'm Tom Poole," he said. "I'm with the sheriff's office."

"Tran mentioned you," Huan said, not smiling, not really anything. It was Huan who had the mask. "Did you come to pay your respects?"

"Yes and no," Poole blurted stupidly. He was fumbling the ball, trying to think of something to say. And what he had said seemed awkward and ridiculous, but it was what he really meant, if only he could explain himself. For a minute, he toyed with the idea of giving in to the situation and expressing his regret, but there was nothing to gain, and he was too far in to change now. He stood there and the only thing happening was that some pigeons were scuttling around, scooting up in the bus exhaust while the sun blazed away on the glass office buildings down the street. "I didn't come around to make a scene. Nothing superstrange like that."

"That's good," Huan said.

They were caught up in something now, shapes at war with the heat.

"So, you think Bao Do killed himself?" There, Poole had done it, shredded the vague territory he'd staked out for himself. Danny Huan seemed to be working it over, even with his unblinking gaze directed at Poole. There was something happening in the void, like light moving through space. Poole watched the guy take a drag from his smoke.

"I don't know," Huan said flatly. "What the hell do you think?"

Now Poole felt more solid. This was not a novice being kicked around the squad room.

"Hey, I don't know, either," Poole said. "But I don't think so." Poole thought he detected a glimmer of surprise in Huan's face, something smooth that waved through and seemed to center in his eyes. He thought it might be a good tactic to force a fast shift and pass through a number of levels of bullshit and see how the scene played, also see if the shift let him off the moral hook he felt as if he was on. He was hoping Danny Huan would let down his hair, get it on good. But the guy crushed his cigarette with a shoe, lighted another, and looked away at the street. There were only so many ways Poole knew to play the scene: buddy-buddy, hard-assed, dumb, accusatory. Poole ran through them all before long, just standing there. "I thought you might be able to help me out. I mean, you knew the old man pretty well."

"Yeah, sure," Huan said. It was like a yawn, only less exaggerated. "Help you out."

They weren't looking at one another. They were having a conversation in a vacuum.

"Well, yeah. Help me out. Tell me what it was like. I mean, seeing that the old man let Jerry live in his house. You didn't like that shit, did you?" It seemed to Poole he had gotten Huan's attention. You'd think they were pals the way they were smiling at each another.

"You really have a way with people," Huan said.

"It's my best trait."

"You got a *bad* trait you'd like to tell me about? Maybe we could discuss it. Get you some counseling."

"I told you, I'm not into a strange scene. Get together with my ex-wife. She'll tell you about my bad traits."

"So, what is it, man?" The cigarette was burning down in Huan's fingers.

"All right," Poole said. "Would you tell me where you were last Saturday afternoon?" This got Danny Huan's attention. He ripped a quick smile and took it back, standing there shaking his head.

"In the Port," Huan mumbled. "Hanging out."

"What does that mean?"

"It means I was in the Port. It means I was hanging out."

"You get home late?"

"Very late."

Poole began to chat. He told Danny Huan the whole story from his own point of view, one of the tricks of the trade. You tell the guy everything but leave out some of the details, hoping the guy might tell you something you've left out, shit he shouldn't know, couldn't know unless he was on the spot. In which case, you had the guy wired up to another kind of conversation. Poole left out the part about the new .22 Colt. He left out seeing Jerry Donovan drunk at the house that night. He told Danny Huan he wondered where Jerry had been that afternoon, too, shifting the spotlight so that Huan would open up. Danny Huan said he'd been at a billiard club, The Sung, all afternoon, into the night. He said he didn't have anywhere else to go. That was the meaning of hanging out.

Poole took out his notebook—another trick. "You got anybody to speak for you, Danny? Somebody who knows you were in the club all afternoon?"

"This guy Ki who owns the place," Huan said.

"This is just the way it is," Poole said, writing the name in his notebook. You could spook people with a pencil and paper. "You clear out the underbrush and see what's under it. That's all this is." Huan looked away, unconvinced.

"I know how it is," Huan said.

"You take out the fishing boat anymore?" Poole asked. Now he was quick-pitching the guy, hoping maybe the bat would be off his shoulder. It was part of the game.

"It's a hard living."

"The answer is no? Yes?"

"Nobody takes out the boat."

"Bao Do does—or did."

Huan closed his eyes just briefly. It was a tired gesture. Poole knew how he felt. "Bao Do was an old man. He had these dreams, you know?"

"You have personal trouble with him?"

"No, I didn't have trouble with him."

"They say you did."

"Shit," Huan muttered. He was looking back up the steps, just a quick glance. "Who says that? Was it Bhin?"

"Pretty much everybody," Poole said. Poole had used the line for years.

"Yeah, well everybody is wrong."

"You have trouble with Jerry?"

Another city bus was coming down the street in black clouds of diesel, scattering pigeons. Danny Huan stared at Poole while the birds spiraled away. Poole thought the palm trees downtown looked napalm-singed.

"Everybody has trouble with Jerry," Huan said. He

smiled big. "You said you talked with everybody. Just ask them about Jerry."

"Bao Do have trouble with Jerry?"

"No shit," Huan said.

"You think Jerry killed him?"

"I couldn't say."

"You think those two argued about dope?" Poole put away his notebook. That part of the game was over. Now he was into the inspiring confidence phase. Servant of the people. It was funny: Here he was on vacation, still shoveling the same shit. "Maybe Jerry had friends who trashed the house. Something real ugly like that."

Poole hoped he'd get a flash of hate from Huan, something he could sink his teeth into. But he wanted to keep a tight rein on things, not wanting to drift into an abstract region where anything could happen, where nothing mattered.

"The whole scene was dog shit," Huan said.

"You know a girl named Janine?"

"Don't know her."

"You know why Bao Do would want to go to Beaumont?"

"No, did he?"

Poole ignored the question. Answering questions was not on Poole's agenda.

"Did Bao Do own a gun?"

"He had a gun," Huan said. Poole nodded as if he was expecting more, another trick of the trade. "All right, man," Huan said. "I took the boat out sometimes. Me and the old man didn't get along very well. There was a gun on the boat for shark. I hated Jerry Donovan, but not for what you think. You want to make some notes, fucking go ahead."

Poole could feel some of the air go out of Danny Huan. Here they were, offense and defense. Poole had marched down the field, got right up to the goal line. He didn't go over, but maybe he had kicked a field goal.

Poole said, "You know a guy named Everett Teagarden?" In the back of his mind, Poole could see Hernandez in the oak grove, looking down at the bubba's house. What was he seeing? Was he even there?

"Chief of the bubbas," Huan said.

"That all?"

"Just a name to me, nothing else."

Poole decided to draw some more blood, just a little, then he would quit. "So now you own the boat, the old man's house, everything."

Danny Huan came close to the edge, just where Poole wanted him. He put his hands in his pockets and got that distracted look again, as if his modem had dropped off the receiver. Poole was dimly aware that the church doors had opened and a slight degree of coolness had drifted down. There were people coming down, too, Tran and Bhin, Jerry Donovan behind them, some more Vietnamese in the vestibule.

The mourners passed by, very near Poole. All the sensuality of being in church had left him and now he was recording these people passing, noting their ages, how some needed help going down the steep stone steps, how Tran came down and touched Danny Huan on the shoulder very gently before going on down the sidewalk with her sister. Adrienne Deveraux walked down the stairs alone. Poole was taking in the elegance of her gait, her slimness, and her marbled blue eyes. He had punched into a richly philosophic fantasy—one he trusted fully—having to do with the woman's skin. Danny Huan had gone and Adrienne Deveraux went by without saying anything. Then Poole was alone in front of the church, thinking about Hernandez in the oak grove. He thought he might rattle up Everett after a couple of days if nothing was happening. After that, he would move on to Jerry and Danny Huan. Hell, he was on vacation and he had the time.

Pretty soon, he started having a fantasy about Adrienne Deveraux again. It was a dream he trusted, because he knew it was unlikely to be betrayed.

12

Poole was on the porch. He could see Hernandez in the oak grove, way up on a hill across the lagoon. The guy was sitting at a picnic table, eating grapes.

As soon as Everett Teagarden opened the door, Poole felt like a fool. He was wearing a Smith & Wesson on his jeans belt and a badge clipped to his shirt so that when the old man slid open the door, he would get a healthy look at Poole, a big hog on his belt and a badge on his shirt. For sure, a look of surprise came over the old man's face, but it gave Poole no pleasure as he stood back on the flagstone porch near some busted patio furniture, worn-out stuff that had never been any good, now gone rusty in the salt air. Everett Teagarden stared at Poole through a narrow slit in his pinched eyes. Those eyes, Poole thought, are the sick eyes of a cat, yellowed and wet, sunk back in skin that had stretched tightly over the sockets. The old man looked as if he would be dead soon, or was already on his way to the grave, while this tough sheriff played mind games with him. The skin was tight around his mouth, too, which gave his whole face a skeletal mold.

The late sun was making powdery confections on the bay where the bulk of the light seemed to have precise weight, a patina of color, maroon and orange, and way across the water a ball of reflected sun on the surface. Poole could see all the way across the bay to some handsome palms on the shoreline and the gulls and terns jumping diagonals in the sky, gray pines in the background.

Before he had pounded on the door, Poole had walked up the driveway, pausing to study the water and the board pier jutting out, thinking how he'd run Everett Teagarden through the crime computer, registering some bullshit traffic things, a few Coast Guard violations, fishing fines—no life jackets, no licenses—but nothing Poole could tell the future from, nothing on the cathode tube that might divine whether the old man was crazy enough to kill Bao Do. He and Hernandez had been watching the house for a couple of days, and now Poole had decided to come out here and check it out, see if he could spook the old man, run some plays on him like he'd done to Danny Huan. Poole would come back later, watch all night if he had to, see if the old man did anything. Then he'd move on to Jerry.

What he had been looking at on his walk wasn't a bay anymore, not really, just a sumped estuary where the Sabine River spread out, tule marsh on one side and mud flats on the other, the bay drying up from drought and overuse. The vast cypress stands were now just brown patches where some egrets poked around. There were some shorebirds in the marsh, not brilliant white, but sullied. Poole remembered the old days, seeing flocks of birds as a kid, but then he thought he was probably idealizing the situation. Then he began to feel sorry for both the birds and Everett

Teagarden, because they were both dying breeds, speci-
mens that the culture had bypassed. He looked at the
stucco house. He could imagine it with new paint, the
oleanders and bougainvillea in bloom and the shrimp boats
putting out from the piers, the birds climbing in a pearl sky.
But it wasn't that way anymore, and Poole thought it might
be an excuse for the old man to kill somebody. Maybe there
was the sense of a lost paradise that Teagarden had known
and now he was blaming the loss on the Vietnamese.

Poole had strapped on his gun at the car so that he
would look official and scary. But now that seemed paltry,
because the old man was already scared and half dead, looking at Poole through his narrow, sick cat eyes. Poole saw
the limestone-colored hair plastered back on his head. It
looked as if it was full of dust or excelsior, a remnant of
industrial fluff, and it made Poole uneasy.

Crap, Poole nearly muttered aloud, sublimating in himself a deeper anger, transferring it over to Teagarden, who
had already broken an uneasy grin, as if he was fixing himself for whatever was coming. Poole had made the old guy
into an object, which was one of the tricks of the trade
Poole didn't like much anymore. He thought he didn't have
any business doing this to the old man, turning him into an
alien, but in that instant, Poole knew he was transferring his
frustration with Daddy John to the old man. He'd had a
bad time with Daddy John, and Everett Teagarden was getting the brunt of his frustration.

Walking up from his car beside the lagoon, Poole had
thought all the way back to Monday, when he'd gone down
to see the sheriff, just popped in to talk about the case. That
day, Daddy John had been behind his oak desk, his big
belly propped on top, Poole's report already in front of
him. They had finished their conversation in about two
minutes, Daddy John clearing a frog from his throat, then
asking Poole what the hell kind of report was this, full of
bullshit theory, then asking Poole what he had been doing

in Houston when he should have been matching records on stolen pipe. Poole made it short, asking Daddy John to open the case on the Vietnamese, at least dig the bullet out of the shack's floor. Daddy John had produced a yowling yawn, looking at Poole with incredible contempt and boredom, not even bothering to engage Poole in a debate. Lister had said, "This is a goddamn waste of department time, buddy boy."

It had been thrown back on Poole right then, that simply, and not during the big argument. Lister had made Poole seem as if he had been asleep on the job. For a minute, Poole had thought he would try to persuade Daddy John about the *uncultural* circumstances, how it couldn't be suicide, but then he'd realized that was just the territory Daddy John didn't want to traverse. So Poole told Daddy John that nobody had ever found an old .22 that Bao Do was supposed to own and that it seemed unlikely that the new Colt belonged to a Vietnamese fisherman. If they could find another gun, they would have a case, wouldn't they? Then Poole had asked Daddy John for a favor, had asked him if he could have another few days so he could play a hunch. He said it didn't matter that he didn't have a witness or a clear motive, even if there were some shrimpers who hated Vietnamese and there had been family quarrels. What Poole had were opinions and feelings, which wasn't enough to open a case, but maybe enough to spend some time on.

Daddy John had said he'd talked to the district attorney and the coroner. Everybody agreed there wasn't any probable cause, not even what the district attorney called a reasonable suspicion, which was considerably less. Poole didn't even have time to sit down. He knew it wouldn't take long, so why waste his energy? "I appreciate your interest, Tom," Daddy John had said, humoring Poole, leaning back in his chair and fiddling with his cigar, which was another way Daddy John handled his detectives before he kicked them in the ass. It all made a stark contrast to their conversation the next day when Poole had something, when Daddy John had just kicked Poole's ass, no fatherly bullshit at all.

That day, he had thought about Janine Bonner. She appeared like an afterimage when you've had too much sun, carrying her just behind the eyeballs. He thought about putting in for some vacation time, maybe going on a camping trip or looking for a new apartment. He thought about a place with lots of windows, where he could sit and think. And now it turned out he was on leave; he had gotten his vacation, but he wasn't going camping. He was scaring Everett Teagarden, sitting up all night watching the guy's house.

But the old man looked so frail. He was wearing a sweat-stained undershirt and some unbelted cotton pants, sneakers without laces. Now that he had opened the door all the way, Poole could see how really sick the old fisherman looked, with his sunken ribs and bony arms, the points of his elbows visible, loose flesh on his biceps. Poole identified himself in the official way while the old man began to sag against the door frame, as if it was all that was holding him from a fall. Poole almost backed off, but right then he tried one of his tricks. He told the old man that the department was holding a .22 Colt that had been stolen and asked the guy if he owned one like that, if it was his, if it was missing. It was pretty dull stuff, trying to slicker this old man, or confuse him like this, and Poole's heart wasn't in it. The old man stood in the door as if he hadn't heard a thing, but pretty soon a grimace passed his face and Poole knew that his gears were turning. Poole had the old man's attention and that was something.

"The hell," Teagarden growled. "I've got lots of guns. I wouldn't know what's missing and what's not. I ain't paid any attention."

Poole decided he'd do a magic act. He was going to use

both hands, get the guy watching one hand while the other was doing the trick. "You hear about the Vietnamese fisherman got killed last week? Down by the marina?"

Poole was fixed on Teagarden's white false teeth. Teagarden had opened his mouth as if he needed air, and Poole heard his tortured gasp of breathing. He was a long time pushing away from the door before he caught his wind, a rotten-egg aroma on his clothes, until Poole thought he could smell the guy's soul. The old man used an arm to balance against the frame and looked away over Poole to the lagoon. Poole was afraid he was going to see Hernandez.

"That old gook?" Teagarden said slowly, Poole thinking it was the kind of phrase to be followed by a spit. "He was one of them ruining our fishing."

"He was killed with a gun like yours."

"*Like* mine," Teagarden said. "What the hell is that supposed to mean?" Here was Poole trading questions with the old man. It was outside the path. The old man was supposed to look at the Smith & Wesson and the badge and roll over and play dead.

"You know who stole yours?"

Poole was still trying magic, the part where you keep one hand working like crazy while you fuck the guy with the other. Poole was sticking to his story about the gun theft while playing with the idea that it had been used to kill Bao Do, all pure romance. He was trying to pull rabbits out of a hat while Teagarden stood in the doorway, a crooked man with a bowed back, his eyes screwed down, really trying to concentrate now that he knew this was a performance and he was totally involved. Poole had been pulling the magician shit for years, but mostly down in the tank, where you could really make people spin.

"Hell, I don't have no gun like that," Teagarden said.

"You don't *know?*" Poole acting surprised. "I'm getting confused here, Mr. Teagarden. First you say you don't know if you have a gun like that, now you say you don't.

124

I'd like to know which it is, because somebody killed the Vietnamese down at the marina. That's only about two miles from here. I'd just like to know." Poole creased a nice big smile.

Teagarden had puffed up like a bantam rooster. Poole knew the pose well, which told him the guy was both confused and scared, because even if he didn't own a gun like that, he wasn't sure now himself. Teagarden had decided to protect himself at any cost. But it was getting hard for him to know what was the best way to go. Then Poole began to wonder if the guy really lived in this ramshackle house all alone; maybe he had a son, some business partners, someone who might have done the job for him. Teagarden began to mumble about the marina, asking Poole if anyone had said anything about him, wanting to know who was telling tales. Poole started to back away, eyeing the house, then he asked Teagarden to give him a call when he found out about the gun, because it would be nice to know. Poole was thinking he'd come back later tonight and relieve Hernandez, after he'd gone to see Adrienne Deveraux, maybe sit up all night and watch the house. He'd just sit and see if anyone came and went, write down some tag numbers. Then he'd move on to Jerry Donovan in a day or so if nothing happened. He was on vacation, what the hell. There was one thing Poole couldn't control, and it came up right away.

"I might just talk to old John Lister myself," Teagarden said. He was showing Poole his nice white teeth. The guy had some menace about him, for sure. If the old man called Daddy John, Poole's vacation might get kind of permanent.

Poole had parked one level below the driveway, on a terrace beside the dirt road that went around the bay. He walked down to his car and put the Smith & Wesson and his badge in the trunk, then got inside the Caprice. He sat in the twilight for a long time, looking at the record he'd brought along, a Brahms piano piece he'd bought in a music store in the mall across from his apartment. He wasn't sure why he'd bought the record. He had considered taking some wine to Adrienne Deveraux to have with the grilled fish, but he had found himself pacing nervously around his apartment like a schoolboy, tilting the windmill of his fantasy. The more he thought about taking some wine, the sillier he felt, seeing himself showing up with the bottle under his arm as if he was on a date, which he didn't know if he was or not. He wanted to be calm, but he wasn't. He wanted to look like he knew what he was doing, but he didn't. To him a bottle of wine was a talisman with all kinds of sexual connotations. Poole hadn't bought anyone a gift in a long time, which clouded his thinking even more, and then he had found himself standing in the mall, surrounded by people. Some kids were skateboarding. Old people hiked briskly in the flourescent glare.

At that point, Poole became his real self. He found Melody Land and went inside the store, despite the rap music blasting from speakers hanging from the four corners of the shop. Everything was strange to him, the CDs, posters of heavy-metal bands on the walls, all the tapes. He found a bin of classical records in a far corner of the store, records nobody wanted. He picked out the Brahms and paid for it. A seventeen-year-old kid with purple hair stood behind the counter. He tried to make change, looking to the digital cash register for help. The coins Poole gave him could have been magic beans to the kid. He didn't seem to understand the transaction.

Once outside the mall, Poole had snapped on his badge and Smith & Wesson. The record made him nostalgic for his days as a music student, but the weight of the gun brought him back. He knew he hadn't been all that talented, but he was competent, and he might have been a good teacher for someone who did have talent. He stood in the mall parking lot with the gun on his hip and the record in his hands, these two tracks of his life, and suddenly he felt the physical bifurcation of his existence, a gulf between what he was and what he might have been, maybe could be still if he had the courage. He wanted to show Adrienne Deveraux part of himself anyway, the real part, and he wanted to show part of it to Everett Teagarden, too: Brahms and Smith & Wesson.

Driving down to the old man's house, he'd tried to think about this gulf. It was as if the art of love and the act of violence were inseparable in his nature, the one running right into the other. One was the record he was taking to Adrienne Deveraux. The other was the kick Poole got from carrying a loaded gun.

13

Poole was dog-tired. He had been up most of the night for two nights watching Teagarden's house, snacking on grapes while he sat at the picnic table above the lagoon, mosquitoes eating him alive while he waited for something to happen. Some vacation, and now Poole knew Hernandez was up there while he rattled the old man. The two days were shot, the old man going in and out, doing some fishing in the lagoon, getting drunk every night on his porch, looking at the bay, where the night went swimming silently around and around. Maybe nothing *would* happen. Maybe Poole would have to get off Teagarden and move on to Jerry Donovan, but it had been a long two days, no shit.

The last thing Poole wanted was to spend all evening telling Adrienne Deveraux about his marriage, to rhapsodize about Lisa Marie, how the whole episode still had a power over him, with heat and motion both, but here he was standing on her porch with a cold beer in his hand and talking about it nonstop, telling about the last silent years and the fights, which had seemed uncontrollable currents in an ocean.

Every once in a while, Poole would catch himself in midsentence and stop, look out at the water, where night had fallen, and feel embarrassed, as if perhaps Adrienne Deveraux would believe he still loved his wife, that he wanted her again, that he was spending too much time thinking about her when he should be thinking about something else. Poole would be quiet for a while and then start talking again, as if someone else had control of his mind, the voices of his marriage shaping themselves in the water, dark diamond shapes on the surface from oil rigs and platforms, a mess of past intentions welling inside him that he couldn't control. He was afraid Adrienne Deveraux was only tolerating him, or worse, thinking him a fool.

Like a sap, Poole told her about his wedding, repeating the details about seeing Lisa Marie's father's eyes, how they had bored into him insectlike, these piercing things going into his brain as if it were a boll of cotton. Goddamn, he even talked about the piano, how Lisa Marie would sit for hours in their Denton apartment, listening while Poole practiced. The place had been so small that she had nowhere to go while he played, just back to the bedroom, which was partitioned from the living room. Worse yet, Poole receded further back in time, recalling his honeymoon in New Orleans, how he and Lisa Marie had driven an old VW bus across the river to someplace about twenty miles south of the city where there wasn't any more town, just miles of bayou and swamp, the moon racing in and out of the clouds and a dark rich silence in the plantation houses they passed, the forms of the houses like monoliths through the cypress stands, until it had begun to rain, a drenching summer rain that pounded down from the clouds in flat drops. They had stopped the bus and run around in the rain like kids until Poole caught Lisa Marie and held her down on the wet ground, where they made love as rain roared around them, until the whole Gulf seemed as if it had risen like a specter, ocean inverted and the sky beneath, where smoke obscured the moon.

Adrienne Deveraux was grilling redfish over charcoal. She had wrapped the fillets in foil with lemon wedges, added paprika and hot sauce. Poole could smell the fish, the hard iron aroma of the sea, the richness of the cypress wood of the Adirondack chairs. The cabin he was in was a contrast to his normal environment with its everydayness of vinyl and glass, gray-vectored freeways, the fiberglass space of his apartment.

But in the cabin, there were knots in the cypress floor planks, on the walls, and Poole began to study the wood the way he might study a piece of music. While the fish cooked, Adrienne Deveraux mixed a green salad in a crystal bowl. She poured herself a glass of white wine, sometimes watching Poole with her blue eyes.

Because Poole couldn't stop himself, he didn't even try. He talked about the past five years, the glide into rancor, boredom with his job, and worse, concern about its moral dimension, how unhappiness enveloped his life like kudzu, how he was unable to sleep. He didn't tell the woman he'd been up the better part of two nights watching the Teagarden house, but he told her about his last few weeks with Lisa Marie, the loud and angry fights that trailed into huge fits of silent invective, Poole building his gripes, Lisa Marie abjectly impregnable, unwilling to compromise, until they both had become bored and fractious and irrational.

Poole followed the woman out to the porch. Adrienne Deveraux said something while she unwrapped the fish, putting it over the grill to sizzle for a minute or two, and Poole came back to where he really was, which was on the screened porch, watching her.

Earlier, Poole had been up on the Port Arthur highway where it intersected the dirt road that ran to Everett Teagarden's place, the sun low on the horizon, sifting through the palms, the sea like a watercolor. He had been feeling sorry for the old man because the guy looked just like his father had looked during his last years, worn out and hollow, as if something had collapsed inside him. When he had driven to the bottom of the dirt road below the bay, Poole saw the marina with the shrimp boats tied to the docks, but no orange dinghy, just the shape of the bait store and the black jetty in the water, a neon beer sign spitting shadows onto the water. The oil roads were spread to his right in the dunes, clumps of sea grass, and a flat plane all the way to Bao Do's house above the estuary running to the swamp. Right then, he saw a bonfire on the beach and a group of people drinking beer in the firelight, and he heard boombox music roaring in the night while some punks on motorcycles did wheelies on the beach, their Harleys throwing up sand, the sound of the engines covering up the wave action.

Poole stopped, got out of the car, and put his gun in the trunk. Carrying his Brahms record, he decided that later that night he would look for the fisherman's gun. Tran said she knew her father owned a weapon, something for the shark and barracuda, something all fishermen needed out on the ocean. Now it really bore in on Poole that he should be looking for the gun instead of dicking around with reports, watching Teagarden's house all night, asking Hernandez to do Poole a favor. He even felt that scaring Everett Teagarden had been a waste of time, even though it had been fun. Maybe Everett Teagarden had killed Bao Do, but watching the house wasn't going to do any good. Poole had to have a fact that would get him off the dime.

Right then, looking at the bonfire against the ocean, motorcycles roaring around on the sand, Poole had decided that he would nose around the shrimp boat when he had the chance, maybe before he relieved Hernandez, when the beach party had shut down. Maybe he would go around to Tran's house and look for the gun, too. If he could find the gun, he wouldn't have the killer, but he would have proved Bao Do wasn't a suicide. Poole had looked around the fishing shack, so he knew it wasn't there, and he had asked Hernandez about it briefly. Hernandez hadn't found a rusty gun when he'd made an inventory, after Poole had gone to Bao Do's house the night he was found dead. There wasn't a gun now, and there might not be, but it was a place to go before giving up on Teagarden.

After Poole parked his car, he walked down the beach in his canvas boaters, feeling a little fat and self-conscious. He was sweating under his clothes, not sure if it was the humid night or his nervousness that was making him feel this way, suspecting it had to do with Adrienne Deveraux and his own inability to come to terms with what he was really doing. One of the motorcycles went by fast, making Poole think he had been buzzed on purpose, and he watched a kid with long blond hair zoom along near the waterline, getting on the throttle pretty hard. The sound was like a line of howitzer fire and it bothered Poole. He felt sorry for Adrienne Deveraux having to put up with this kind of shit every weekend when she was down here trying to get away from it all at the family cabin. Here was a punk tooling down the beach as if he thought the whole earth was Disneyland, something organized solely to give him pleasure. Poole hoped the punk would come along again, and then he didn't, because he knew he would lose his temper and go after the kid and then his evening with Adrienne Deveraux would be ruined, so he hustled down the beach, away from the waterline, until he saw the kid pass by and throw a beer can into the waves. Poole watched the can bounce in the water with neon shining on it.

Poole could see the woman on her porch. Was she ten years older than he was? Probably, but she was standing behind the wire mesh door in a cotton sleeveless blouse over a cantina dress of pleated green that hung to her ankles. She opened the screen and smiled at Poole. She was barefoot, which made Poole happy, and she had pulled her hair back with a ribbon. She looked elegant and relaxed, almost unapproachable, and then Poole realized it wasn't just that she was so much older than he was, it was that he was feeling terribly young and inexperienced. But looking at her now in the dim evening light, there with the dusty moonlight over her shoulder, she looked older all right, with her hair not quite gray, her arms loose and her face lined. Poole was admiring the fact that she wore no makeup, except maybe a wisp of lipstick. She gazed at him from her intelligent eyes. Poole held out his Brahms album. Then like a dope, he gave it to her as he stood on the bottom stair, holding it out, not even saying good evening.

"How very thoughtful," she said.

"I bought it from a kid with purple spiked hair."

"There is a lot of that going around," she said, taking Poole gently by the arm, leading him up the steps. "I have an old portable phonograph inside. Nothing special, I'm afraid, not even stereo."

"It isn't much of a recording," Poole said. He was feeling he should explain his gift, or himself, as if they were things that needed explaining. He was so out of touch with people. That was when he took a cold beer from Adrienne Deveraux and started remembering out loud his days at the university, studying music, his marriage, telling the woman that Brahms was his special favorite, that he had thought about bringing wine but that it didn't seem right, and so he'd gone to the mall and searched a bin of classical records, coming across this piano piece.

Adrienne Deveraux showed him around the cabin. It was small and compact. She carried the record as they went through the two big rooms, one with a corner kitchen, one long room in back where there were two beds and a hurricane window with the shutters propped open by wood struts. Poole could see a stretch of dune outside, tule grass and palmettos whipping in the wind. That was when he noticed the wood smell, the cypress planks and the pine dowels, an old brass bed with a patch quilt coverlet, some bookshelves and pictures of the family, four little girls with big smiles and braces. Poole imagined how it had been during those years of Adrienne Deveraux's youth, her husband reading out on the porch with a beer, the girls playing out on the beach, all the long days gliding wistfully into the evening and the light speckled on the water while she cooked fish in the oven, did some black-eyed peas with bacon, all of them coming inside at dinnertime, tired from their day, sunburned, ready to shower and go to bed. It gave Poole a sense of peace, this imagining someone else's past, as if it had happened to him and he was recapturing it while the woman poured him another beer and sent him out to the porch.

Now, though, Poole could hear a boom box down the beach and the sound of cycles. It made him hate the future, which was already here, the awful combustion of modern life. He walked idly around the porch, picking up an old *Life* magazine, leafing through a *Reader's Digest* while Adrienne Deveraux told him she had put the place up for sale in the fall, hoping she could find a buyer, because she didn't want the place torn down and something new built of steel and glass in its place. She was a little concerned because these beach kids were tearing everything up, wasting things, and who would want a vacation house that wasn't quiet?

Poole still had most of his Corona in a glass as it became fully night outside. He felt like a simpleton when Adrienne Deveraux walked to the porch and began to talk about herself, telling him how she had been a French teacher at the university level, then substituted in a high school, finally leaving the profession altogether to raise her daughters. Even though the girls had been a handful, she and her husband had traveled widely, through the Loire valley, the Piedmont, even to Latin America on business. She visited her daughters often in the lake country of upstate New York, though one lived still in Houston and helped take care of Toby. Poole was impressed, not with the facts but with the way she laid them out, as if she had lived *in* her life and not *through* it, the way so many people did. Poole realized he had been concentrating on the doubts and failures of his life, that it made a terrible contrast to Adrienne Deveraux, and as they stood on the porch together, in the dark with the ocean lapping on the sand, Poole knew he was learning things from the woman, little things about how to behave.

They ate on the porch. Poole had a glass of wine, enjoying the fish and the salad, which was full of artichoke hearts and cherry tomatoes. Adrienne Deveraux had put on the Brahms and Poole talked about his love of the piano, maybe the one thing he lived in and not through. They had to put up with some motorcycle noise and boom-box music from down the beach, but Poole made it through, feeling himself more relaxed after two glasses of Chardonnay. It had been a long time since he had really noticed the air, its texture, how it was full of subtle tones, the gulls bouncing over the water, Brahms, the sand sheening as the water hit it, the water going back out. It soothed him tremendously, something he had been a long time without. He thought he detected a slight blush on Adrienne Deveraux. Maybe it was the wine, maybe just pleasure, but he was happy with it, no question about it.

Pretty soon, they had brandy—still on the porch, standing just inside the door, looking out at the night together. It took Poole some time, but he finally did something incomprehensible. He stepped behind the woman and put down his glass of brandy and placed two hands lightly on her back, up near her shoulders. He closed his eyes and was gripped by terror, until his heart became so frail and disorganized that he thought it would jump out of his body altogether. But then she moved back into him, her shoulders tracing the arc of her relaxation as she continued to talk. He thought his soul would shatter, and he was certain that Adrienne Deveraux could feel him quake, his chest heaving as he tried to breathe and speak, breathe again, his imponderable feelings made explicit. He was having a surface event, something that was happening entirely on his skin. But he wasn't thinking about it; he was having it, and was inside it, and suddenly he was talking about fishing and being a cop and living alone, and he felt the self-pity drain away, Adrienne Deveraux listening quietly, moving her hips against him until he could feel her back, legs, and the cup of skin beneath her waist.

Poole thought it must be late. The motorcycle noise had stopped.

Adrienne Deveraux turned. "Give me five minutes, will you?" she said, standing so close that Poole brushed her face with his chin.

Poole nodded and she went into the back room, where the beds were, closing the door softly. He strained to hear something, but there wasn't anything except the sound of the waves and the *clump-bump* of a tanker going north to New Orleans. Poole could see the glimmer of a bonfire by the marina and the black edge of the jetty in the sea, and he was amazed at himself and his fantasy, the one he had trusted so completely, which he still trusted, so that now it was transforming itself into another thing entirely.

A singular peace settled on Poole. It was like a new skin, like being in church, a sensuality that layered itself just so that it could be peeled deliciously. When Poole went into the room where she was, he found her standing in one corner, surrounded by an ocean breeze. She had on a black negligee. Poole managed to sit on the bed and place his hands on her legs under the silk, then move his hands until he felt the hair between her legs. He put his head on her stomach.

It was funny, but he started to remember things then. Odd assortments of images came to him: One summer afternoon when he was at Boy Scout camp and had suffered such a terrible bout of homesickness that he was physically ill and had to be sent home; one night in the hills outside of Austin when he and Lisa Marie were camping and Poole heard his first coyote howl. He remembered the first dog he had owned, a half-breed German shepherd his dad put down because its hip was bad, the way he had cried when his dad took the dog away in the car, knowing what was happening even though he was only five.

Poole found himself beside Adrienne Deveraux on the bed, and then all of the sudden she was lying down on her back and he was half-kneeling between her legs, the woman's feet on the floor, Poole suffering a wild and engulfing fright, as if he were falling, or flying, he didn't know which, a sensation of pure wonderment and terror at the same time, a foolish gut-churning joy, saying he was sorry for God knows what, both of them giggling. And then Poole was inside her. He came wildly and too soon, embarrassed and happy at his uncontrollability, whispering his regrets, feeling the muscles shredded in his body.

He was lying on the bed. "Everything is fine, Tom Poole," she said. "Don't worry and don't think. Have absolute faith in this single moment."

He was beyond the simplicities of speech, there on the bed with his leg over her leg, her head on his shoulder. He could feel her hip, her hair on his face. An imponderability came over him again, but he felt he was closer to it now, as if it was a puzzle he might one day solve, and that it had something to do with the way Adrienne Deveraux had closed the circle on her life, how it had ceased to be a succession of moments, was now an absolute encased in a single moment. Poole knew then that he was involved entirely in a struggle against those things that had no consequence. He dozed, comforted beyond measure.

When he woke, he felt completely refreshed, like a person who had been hypnotized, the cone of his being waltzing in moonlight, wading in tule grass. He could hear the wind in the palms and he took in all the smells of Adrienne Deveraux, the cypress planks in the floor, the heavy hint of wine in the air, the broken clove aroma of sex. He came inside her again, more slowly, but still unabashed, and then he slept, for how long, he didn't know. When he woke again, the woman was asleep beside him. He lay there for a long time feeling overwhelmed and then he dressed himself in the dark and sat on the bed, holding her hand, feeling as grateful as a schoolboy or an orphan. Poole kissed her cheek.

Outside, Poole walked up the beach under a canopy of stars. Near the marina, the bonfire had gone out completely, just a smolder now. The motorcycle punks were gone, probably up to Port Arthur to the strip joints, where they could drink until morning, then stand around in parking lots along the highway snorting coke, smoking reefer, downing the last of their cheap red wine. Poole wondered if his Caprice was okay on the dune and he walked up to check it out. Then he walked back down to the marina boardwalk and out to the last row of boats moored to the pier. There were two shrimpers, one with a tiny cabin. Poole was sure it belonged to Bao Do, because it had a good-sized hold and a large gas tank, a boat that could keep you out for a week or more. The other boat was worn out, something like what Danny Huan might use, with a makeshift cabin built of plywood, a shallower draft.

Poole hopped onto the big boat. He poked around the cabin and found some maps, shining his flashlight around carefully. It held the usual stuff, packing cases, but no gun. Below, the hold looked nearly empty, a few gas cans, some nets and seines, two rusty bunks with no mattresses. Poole wasn't surprised by what he was finding, a rusted-out hunk of junk, some gasoline, empty bunks, packing crates, but he was disappointed because he really wanted to take the old Vietnamese off the list of the missing in action, get him back in the grip of his world even if it was only for Tran, or himself. He sensed that if he wasn't able to do it, he would feel it for a long time.

The other boat was moving in the water, so light it rode the swells. From the way the sea was roughing up, Poole estimated that the tide was coming back in. A few waves banged against the jetty rock, spray going up like black glitter. Poole got on board and found five or six drawers in the makeshift cabin. He went through them one by one so he wouldn't miss anything. He found more maps and charts, some flares that looked serviceable, a first-aid kit, regular fishing gear. He could smell diesel, so he knew the boat had been run out recently. Poole climbed down into the hold, going down the steep stairs.

What he saw down there was bad: bread box–sized packages in brown paper tied with twine. Poole sat down on his haunches and looked at the packages resting on pallets out of the inch-deep salt water. He knew he was looking at kilos of reefer, seven hundred dollars a pound, maybe a thousand when it got to the streets of Houston, then twenty thousand in ounces up north. Poole sat there in the dark damning Danny Huan at first, thinking, You fucker. Poole used his pocketknife to scar one of the packages, and the dope was there all right, probably Jamaican. Poole backed up the stairs and checked the charts again. They were mostly of the Clam Lake area, inland from the sea, and Poole knew that no shrimper would go inland to Clam Lake or anywhere near there, because there was nothing to catch there, just smallmouth bass, sucker fish, and lots of little perch. It was not a commercial fishery, anyway.

Poole didn't know what to do. Here he had been looking for one thing, the old man's gun, and he had found another, but still he wondered if it connected to the old Vietnamese and why he was killed. Perhaps the old man had found the stuff on the boat and was going to Beaumont to the sheriff. It made Poole doubt his theory about Everett Teagarden, but then he thought maybe there was a place for him, too. It all depended on so many things. Poole knew that it was time to call off the surveillance of the Teagarden house. He would go up and eat a grape with Hernandez and shoot the shit about this. Maybe Hernandez would have an idea.

He could just sit around and wait to see who came for the boat, Danny Huan probably, maybe Jerry Donovan, Everett Teagarden. What the shit, maybe all three.

Poole walked up to his Caprice. The wind was blowing hard and there was some lightning over the Gulf. It hadn't rained for a long time, but it smelled like it might.

14

More than anything, Poole needed a rainstorm. He had
conjured a vivid monsoon riding up the Mexican sierra,
down in Monterey, then gaining up over the Gulf until
there was a ceiling of cumulus about thirty thousand feet in
the air, purple-and-gold clouds that would gush raindrops,
beat down on the saw grass, the kind of storm that would
crash against the coast, fill up the irrigation ditches, put a
crease in the heat and boredom.

He walked up the pier under cover of the rocks and
reached the thumb of the jetty, when he began to think of
rain and smell it in his imagination. Then he walked up to
the Caprice and got his gun from the trunk. He sat on the
hood, his feet touching the bumper, staring out at the Gulf,
trying to hear the rain advancing across the open ocean, but
all he could hear was the steady *thump-bump* of oil tankers,

the bleat of oil derricks, waves slicking against the sand. It seemed to him a storm would be a fine fulcrum, a way to push himself across the accelerating gap between his mood and real events. Then he thought about Adrienne Deveraux.

Damn, damn it to hell, Poole whispered. He hadn't finished enjoying the woman. He could sense her skin on his; he could still smell her in his clothes, his hair. And here was all that dope in the Vietnamese shrimper, Poole not knowing quite what he was going to do with it, especially since his blowup with Daddy John. It wasn't fair how life could tear things from under you, even if you were half-expecting it.

Poole tried to think while he waited. He was trying to make connections between the dope and someone unknown, another between Teagarden and Jerry, then all the way back to the Vietnamese fisherman. These names kept rinsing through his mind, Danny Huan, Teagarden, Jerry Donovan. They were motifs of something he was trying to compose, but he didn't know what it might be. Even so, he felt relaxed in his canvas pants and boaters, his gun in a shoulder holster. If nothing else, Poole decided he could drive up to the wayside park and relieve Hernandez. After all, the guy had been up most of the night for three nights doing Poole a favor. Maybe Poole would walk to the Teagarden place and really get in his face late at night when Teagarden was tired and drunk, maybe even lay it on him about the dope. Perhaps if Teagarden was drunk on Dixie, it would make him confused enough to talk. Poole had no business doing it, even thinking about it, but that was the part about breaking away. It was almost enough to make him smile.

Pretty soon, Poole backed the Caprice onto the oil road and drove up the windward side of the bay on a secondary road that paralleled the highway. It was a pretty night, very hot, and because of the moon, shapes appeared in outline.

He could see the curve of the bay almost to Louisiana in some places. It was only a few minutes to a state road loop that went past Teagarden's place out on the Sabine lagoon. From below, Poole could see Hernandez's car parked in a grove of oaks. Poole pulled uphill and parked behind it, off the dirt part of the trail. He had a clear view of the stucco house, the front drive, the reverse L shape of the structure and part of the stone patio in back. All the lights in the house were on. Hernandez was sitting on the picnic bench with binoculars and a sack of grapes.

"You're late for the gig," he said. Poole sat down beside him, smiled. "Have a grape," Hernandez said.

Poole said he was sorry. He popped a grape into his mouth and studied the stucco house. Hernandez had on jean shorts and a white fishnet tank top. He mentioned to Poole that it was after one o'clock. It didn't sound testy to Poole, just matter-of-fact.

"Anything happening?" Poole asked.

"Quiet as death," Hernandez said. Then Hernandez opened a spiral notebook, flipped through a few empty pages of blue-lined paper, damp from being in his pocket. "This is the list of cars that came and went this afternoon—since about five o'clock." Hernandez held out the notebook. He munched some grapes, looking tired.

Poole sighed and tried to think what these three wasted days might have meant. "Nobody," he said stupidly, just to fill in a space until he could think of something to say to Hernandez, who was sitting in a pair of jean shorts on a picnic bench at one o'clock in the morning. "I'm about to switch tactics," Poole said.

"You going to eat pineapples now?" Hernandez said.

Poole laughed. "No, I'm serious," he said.

"My wife will appreciate it," Hernandez said, putting the notebook back in his pocket.

Poole was trying to decide if he should tell Hernandez about the dope. If it had been Mirabelli, he was sure he would have let it go. And if things had been different, if he hadn't had a row with Daddy John, Poole thought he might have told the guy. But now he thought he would just tell Hernandez to go home, forget the whole thing. It was getting out of hand now, with the dope. When Poole had called Hernandez after the Daddy John scene, he had asked for three days. Now the time was up, and Poole didn't think he could ask Hernandez for any more time. If he was going to switch tactics, he was going to leave Hernandez out. Poole would be on his own. Right now, that sounded like a good idea. As things were, somebody might get hurt, and Poole didn't want it to be a guy with a wife and family.

"So, what have we seen this week?"

Hernandez took a grape. "Teagarden's brother-in-law drives over once in a while. Shoots the breeze, drinks a beer, goes home. Teagarden goes out for beer and cigarettes. Teagarden comes home, drinks the beer, smokes the cigarettes. Mailman delivers the mail at four o'clock. Sometimes he's late. Teagarden talks to him for a while. At sundown, the guy starts to drink beer. Stays out on the patio until late, goes to bed."

Hernandez had stretched his legs. Poole tried looking at the stucco house through the binoculars. It made a lonely impression, out there on a shelf of coral land above the lagoon.

"It isn't much of a life," Hernandez said.

"I think I know how he feels."

"How's that?" Hernandez asked.

"He had a life. He thinks somebody took it away from him. He can't come to terms."

Hernandez was looking at Poole now, listening. "Yeah, I guess so," he said. He was folding his grapes in Saran Wrap, getting ready to go. "Hey," he said, "I spent some time with the case records." Poole looked at Hernandez with surprise. "You're right," Hernandez went on. "They should be doing more with this. I don't see how the fisher-

144

man did it to himself." Poole handed back the binoculars. Hernandez had a peculiar expression. "You're right," he said.

"About what?" Poole asked.

"I mean, it stinks—this case."

"That's what I told Daddy John." Poole smiled. The two were sharing something now. "Those were my exact words."

"Well, you were right."

"I can add it to my resumé," Poole said.

"You think you're finished?"

"No doubt about it. Matter of time."

"You going to walk away?"

Explanations were something else again for Poole. If he tried to explain, he thought the filament of understanding connecting himself to Hernandez might break. Walking away from something was not a thing men like Poole and Hernandez did, not something they understood readily. Poole remembered the day he'd come home to an empty house, realizing that Lisa Marie had walked away, how he had been staggered by the finality of it, how he was un-reconciled.

"I don't know if you'd call it walking away," Poole said. Hernandez was watching Poole now, not moving. Poole wanted him to stay and talk a while. Maybe it would rain and they could sit in the Caprice and watch the storm. Poole wanted to ask him about his kid, the one who got hit by a car. "Maybe I can walk *into* something if I'm lucky."

"Yeah, maybe so," Hernandez said. After a while, he said, "You think Teagarden killed the old fisherman?"

"I don't know," Poole replied.

"You ever find a gun?"

"No," Poole said, "not yet."

"Hey, if it exists, it is probably at the bottom of that lagoon. You'll never find it."

Poole had to admit that. He took the binoculars and

studied the stucco house. It looked shabby now, broken tile roof, cracked windows, all the patio stones misplaced. There was even a split in the porch concrete where the mud flank of the lagoon had shifted down, sinking. And the oleanders that lined the drive were dying, tough as they were.

"Sort of makes you sick," Hernandez said while Poole was still observing the house.

"How's that?" Poole asked.

"Place like that going to shit."

"Yeah, for sure," Poole said. He felt sorry for the old bubba whose world was fading out, seeping into the ocean while he held on to the edge of the continent. Not feeling young anymore, seeing his fishing grounds deplete. Not knowing what the hell was happening.

"One thing," Hernandez said. Poole looked over at him. "The bubba is up late. He's usually in bed by this time."

"How's that?"

"Three nights now I've been watching. He's usually asleep by midnight. He must be having himself a big night with the Dixie."

"I guess so," Poole said.

"It's strange, is all," Hernandez said.

"Well, I'm going down."

Hernandez looked strange. "You feeling crazy? Just a crazy Friday night, why not barge into some guy's house about one o'clock in the morning?"

"Something like that," Poole said. He was thinking about dope in brown paper.

"I'll tag along," Hernandez said suddenly.

"You don't need the grief."

"Nobody needs grief," Hernandez said. "I just want to go."

"Daddy John will eat you alive if he finds out."

Hernandez grinned. "You're walking away from it,

right?" Poole nodded. "So, when you're gone, I blame everything on you. Say you made me do it, that I had no idea what I was getting myself into. I shit on you. You'll be gone, anyway."

"I can handle this, Arthur," Poole said, realizing he'd used the man's first name.

"Sure, I know you can, Tom," Hernandez said. "But you could use backup, too. It's late. You might scare the old bubba. You can use me—you know that yourself."

Poole shrugged, suit-yourself style. He didn't want Hernandez along, but what could he say?

"Besides," Hernandez said, "I have a bad feeling. The old bubba should be in bed by now. You don't know, he might be in a bad mood."

Poole said okay. If that's the way Hernandez wanted it, then it would be okay. They decided to walk. It was only about two hundred yards down the dirt road to the main highway, another twenty yards to the front of the house from there. They could cut off part of it if they went down the shale hillside from the park.

The lagoon was noisy with frogs. There in the pale moonlight, the water had taken on a transparency that Poole couldn't keep his eyes off of. He was thinking about Adrienne Deveraux, too, trying to keep her out of his mind, failing, thinking about her skin, the silk negligee against her thigh, how she smelled in bed as the wind tilted through the hurricane window. He found himself trailing Hernandez by ten paces, hurrying to catch up.

When they got to the front door, Poole peered through a pane of glass that bordered it. Through the louvers, he could see the outlines of furniture, chairs, a disarray. He knew the patio was around in back, above the lagoon. Poole didn't know whether he should knock, barge right in, or what. He didn't want to surprise Teagarden, but he didn't want to be polite, either. Hernandez had gone partway around the side of the house where the ell broke away, to just about where the patio would start. He was standing on an incline above the lagoon, watching Poole. Then Poole opened the door and looked inside, where he could see wicker furniture, the stained linoleum floors, a big ceiling fan circling. He closed the door and walked over to Hernandez.

"Nothing?" he asked.

"The guy is probably around back," Poole said.

"So, let's go."

Hernandez took two steps, stopped, then touched Poole's right arm. It looked to Poole as if the old bubba was sitting in a lawn chair above the lagoon, an end table next to him, on it a glass of beer and a radio. The radio was playing cowboy music. The lagoon spread around the house, going out of sight toward the ocean. There the dunes began, the Sabine marsh. When they got over to the old man, they saw he was wearing an undershirt and boxer shorts. He looked frail to Poole, as if he were made from twigs and might blow away in a breeze. There was an aroma Poole thought could be the lagoon.

Hernandez was on one knee. "*Jesús, María,*" he whispered.

Poole felt the abysmal tug of something at his mind. He had pulled his Smith & Wesson and was trying to take his eyes off the old bubba. Back in the crook of the ell, it was very bright, the kitchen lights on, throwing spears onto the patio. Hernandez touched a finger to the old man's wrist.

"Stay quiet," Poole whispered. He walked to the patio doors and looked inside. He could see the whole front of the house, maybe part of a bedroom in back, and part of the ell. Poole walked back.

"Dead," Hernandez said, standing up.

Now that Poole looked, he could see the old man's chin resting on his chest, one flip-flop off his foot, resting on coral shell. This bubba looked so peaceful, sitting on his own ground, gazing out at the lagoon in the moonlight.

There was a blue hole at the base of his neck, a thin flap of skin, a crease. Hernandez walked a circle around the lawn chair and looked up at the wayside park. Poole had holstered his gun. It had all come down and was done.

"What now?" Hernandez asked, walking back to Poole, looking down at the old bubba.

Poole wasn't sure, so he drifted away, back to the break in the ell, where the lagoon wound below the house. The lagoon became a neck of shallow water meandering toward the ocean. Metallic-looking white dunes, some palm trees, a few old cars heaped like garbage out in the middle distance.

"No cars tonight?" Poole called over.

Hernandez shrugged him off. Nobody had driven up the driveway. It hadn't happened like that. "We going to call this thing in, or what?" Hernandez asked.

Poole said they wouldn't call it in, glancing over at Hernandez for support, not really expecting any. He thought they should let the old man sit all night, staring out at the lagoon. When morning came, his brother-in-law would find him, maybe the mailman later. Whatever, it would be soon enough. Poole didn't think it would alter the flow, because they weren't going to run out and catch the killer right now, anyway. Now Poole knew Teagarden hadn't killed the Vietnamese, and that was enough. "He'll be found in the morning," Poole told Hernandez.

"We ought to do something," Hernandez said.

"Go home, get some sleep."

"There's this picture in my head," Hernandez replied dreamily, as if he wasn't addressing Poole.

Hernandez walked over to the bank where the lagoon began, standing in the moonlight, his arm extended. He made a sweeping gesture. "He came in from behind, from the lagoon on the ocean side." It was a meditation Hernandez was sharing with Poole, the vigil of his personal thoughts. "He came up the bank and onto the patio, being real quiet. The old bubba was drunk, listening to the radio.

This cat came up and put a bullet in the bubba's head. The old bubba didn't hear anything. He was here and then he was gone." Hernandez looked over at Poole, who had walked back from the patio, both men in the half shadows of the house.

"Yeah, that's about it," Poole said.

"The question is, why?"

"And who," Poole added.

"Yeah, that, too," Hernandez muttered. "I swear I didn't hear anything, didn't see anything." Hernandez was staring at Poole, his eyes narrowed. He wanted Poole to know he hadn't been asleep at the wheel. Poole understood and said it was okay, that there was no problem. "So, we let him sit here?" Hernandez asked again, obviously bothered.

"Tomorrow is soon enough for Everett," Poole said.

"Yeah, I suppose," Hernandez answered.

They both went around the house and walked back up the hill to the wayside park. It was a dusty night with gusty wind, and the oaks were creaking. Poole said good night to Hernandez, told him to take it easy. He could tell Hernandez was terribly bothered by the scene, but Poole couldn't do anything about that now. He just told the guy to get some rest, try to forget the pictures if he could. If there was anything to be done, Poole would do it; it was a promise. They shook hands, Hernandez saying, "Hey, I hope you walk into some luck."

Poole watched Hernandez drive downhill, then disappear up the Port Arthur highway, taillights flickering across the lagoon and edging through the dunes. Poole sat at the picnic table for a while, thinking about luck. He had heard a lot about luck in Vietnam. It had been a constant source of conversation, and now he knew why. Poole was going to walk away all right, but not just yet. Luck was like a maze. It had crazy angles. But luck or no luck, you had to walk away if you wanted to find out how it would play.

15

Poole sat slumped in his chair, looking out the plate-glass window at the sun coming up over the mall across the street from his apartment, a gray JCPenney blocking out some of it, the acres of parking lot turning pink, a few cars on the freeway, *whizz, whizz.* Poole wasn't drunk on beer, though, not even tired, focused now without hatred or regret, trying to come to terms with his true feelings and how he had made love to Adrienne Deveraux, how nice it had all been, how he had gone down to the shrimp boats looking for a .22 pistol and had found twenty thousand dollars' worth of Jamaican dope, knowing he had to do something about that eventually, even if it hurt Tran terribly, because what choice did he have?

The thought of Everett Teagarden came back to Poole, how he had been sitting in a lawn chair, looking out at the arm of lagoon, green water under an emergent moon, the guy relaxed and having a good time, only he had a hole in the back of his neck. Poole couldn't get out of his mind how natural he looked, how any minute he might wake up in the morning and wave to the water-skiers.

While it was still dark, Poole had sat down in his chair, naked except for his boxer shorts and the wet boaters, remembering Adrienne Deveraux, taking some deep breaths to calm himself. He had a feeling of pride about the woman, to know he could still love someone he admired, having forgotten how nice that could be. He got over the feeling soon and began to think about Everett, trying to puzzle together in his head all the pieces he had, and then the sun came up over the mall and Poole made himself some coffee and sat down to drink it and think about Nguyen Bao Do, taking himself back to last Saturday afternoon.

All he could see in his head was Danny Huan, a big muscular guy standing in his cut-off sweatshirt on the church steps, appearing wistful or glum—Poole couldn't say which—how the guy hadn't given Poole a single inch despite the fact that Poole was a white cop and it was his country and he knew some good tricks. Poole couldn't read Danny Huan's face as he thought he had read Everett Teagarden's, as he thought he could read Jerry Donovan's, Bhin's even. Huan's wasn't a thin rice-paper face blushing up on a cathode tube. He couldn't tell from looking at Danny Huan if he was a stoner or a thief or what, or if he had killed Nguyen Bao Do. It didn't matter much now that Everett Teagarden was dead. The equation was getting too long for the blackboard. Maybe Poole would have to get another blackboard.

Poole trusted Tran, though, mostly because Adrienne Deveraux seemed to trust her, but also because he liked her face and how she had handled herself that night at the house when Poole had gone to her room. But if Poole trusted Tran, what did that do to his picture of Danny Huan? Perhaps Danny Huan had tried his best to become a fisherman, couldn't hack it, and had gone sour. Who could blame him? If it was Danny Huan's dope on the boat, there would be a motive to kill Bao Do. But you had to stretch to find a place for Everett. Poole wondered if Danny Huan knew enough about navigation to get himself around on the ocean to deliver dope? Just now, he couldn't see Jerry or Danny running dope without a partner. Shit, Poole thought, none of this is going anywhere.

Poole was sure of one thing. It would take two guys to run dope on the shrimper, and there would need to be a contact somewhere along the coast, in the inlets and swamps, the ragged mangrove down the beach, where there were lots of places to hide. It wasn't hard for Poole to envision Everett Teagarden dropping down to the marina, visiting Jerry or Danny, these kids with a dope connection, him a fisherman with sea skills, both of them making some money selling grass, picking it up from a Honduran freighter out at sea, taking it back to the marina in the morning and sailing it down somewhere to drop it off. Someplace like Clam Lake, which would explain the inland charts on the boat. Weird, going inland in a shrimp boat, but it might work. It didn't matter, neither Danny nor Jerry could pull off an operation like that alone. Nobody could.

Poole used to know the country inland from the beach, deep-holed swamps with cypress trees and scrawny pines and lots of undergrowth in black water. He could not see these guys, whoever they were, chugging down to Galveston Bay with a hold full of marijuana, finding a place to dock, off-loading the shit. That was how Poole decided Danny Huan was the one going inland with the dope. Maybe he took out Everett Teagarden just so he wouldn't have to split the take. Maybe he had learned enough about shrimpers so he thought he could handle it alone, thought, Why split the take? This would be a very ruthless guy if that was it.

Poole thought a lot about Everett Teagarden. It made sense that the old Vietnamese was killed for something he had known and was going to tell. That was where Teagarden came in, since it was hard for Poole to see Danny Huan greasing his own father-in-law. Teagarden was a guy who hated Vietnamese anyway, for their imagined destruction of the fishing grounds, because they were foreign and looked different, hung together and talked funny. Everett was a Texan who wouldn't mind pulling the trigger on Nguyen Bao Do, and after it was done, what did Danny Huan do? Hell, Poole thought, maybe Danny Huan killed Teagarden for revenge, and dope wasn't involved. Maybe it was Jerry who killed both of them. Maybe they were not connected. Poole went around and around. But he kept coming back to the dope. What cop wouldn't?

Then Jerry Donovan came into Poole's head and the equation really expanded. Jerry was an obvious asshole, driving around in his gutted Charger, drinking beer and snorting coke, puking his guts. Poole could see the cathode-tube future right on Jerry's face, his acne skin and hawk nose and the greasy red hair around his shoulder, bones poking through his T-shirt. It was as if the guy was a career-track candidate for state prison, but somehow Poole still couldn't see big-time dealing in Jerry's future. For one thing, he was too gone into the stuff itself to step back and handle it the way you needed to if you were going to buy and sell dope. Poole had never seen a dealer who had anything but disregard for his customers. Poole could see Jerry doing two years for a stickup pretty soon, then doing it again and doing three, and then by the time he was forty, the kid might do some real hard time in El Reno or Leavenworth, but by then he wouldn't have a future anymore because he'd be in the place for twenty or thirty, the kind of guy who was a bad citizen and good prisoner. He'd be a part of the population and nothing more.

Still, maybe he had just gotten his start and was still wet behind the ears. Poole could see a partner on the scene for Jerry Donovan. It could be somebody outside, or maybe Teagarden, but probably Teagarden, because somebody outside would stand out. But it would have to be somebody who knew the swamps, somebody with connections. And then it occurred to Poole that he might be thinking entirely wrong, that maybe Danny Huan and Jerry were the guys, together, this horrible trick of fate played on the old fisherman, his sons-in-law both dope pushers. And when he found out, they killed him for it so they would have the boats and the house and a good business on the side. That didn't account for Everett Teagarden, but right now, nothing did. Poole found this last thought hard to believe, but he kept it on his list, just to be complete.

Poole scrambled some eggs, microwaved leftover grits with hot sauce, them messed them together on his plate and covered the mess with syrup. The sun had come over the JCPenney and it was getting hot already, even though he was in his undershorts and the AC was on low. Poole sat with his eggs and grits at the kitchen table in the nook, realizing he had a problem on another level. Last night, he'd had no business being on the shrimp boats, looking around the decks and cabins, then down in the hold. There was no case being made on the Vietnamese, so he shouldn't have been looking for the gun. And he shouldn't have been in the Teagarden house, either. He had no way to justify himself and his action as a cop, no criminal case, no obvious felony, no contraband in plain sight. All he could do was wait and read the papers, see who found Teagarden and what the sheriff would do then.

Poole showered and dressed in slacks and a blue sport shirt. He was feeling good for a guy with no sleep, maybe two hours of naps with Adrienne Deveraux, eggs and grits in his belly, and a corpse on his mind. He had a crick in his back and his eyes hurt, he didn't know what to do about the reefer, but he felt okay, going down to the parking lot to get the Caprice and move uptown.

When he arrived at the post office, he parked in the employee section behind the building. Poole was looking for a generic Buick and he found it, the car completely featureless, with bench seats and plastic hubs, an antenna on the trunk. Downtown was very still, beginning to heat up with a haze in the air, but when Poole went around front, he found the inside of the Federal Building cool, almost sterile. He went down a flight of stairs and found the DEA office at the end of a hallway. Poole had been down here a couple of times, not lately, though, and he had been on one local roundup for TV, a circus show where the local politicians find some money just before elections and go around breaking down doors with the cameras rolling, big klieg lights and everybody dressed up in orange flak jackets, a SWAT team for the occasion, the kind of Mickey Mouse shit you couldn't avoid now and then. He remembered a guy named D. J. Donald, who had seemed okay to Poole, a guy who might be able to help Poole with his current problems.

The DEA office was in a partitioned area that should have been for storage and probably once had been. It had a high ceiling and gray walls with a green stripe, some dying plants and a coffee machine, that's it. Poole kind of liked the place, even if it was bleak and underground. It had the look of a bomb shelter. D. J. Donald was sitting behind a metal desk and looking up at Poole, probably wondering what the hell Poole wanted this early in the morning, smiling, though, very sympathetic-looking.

D.J. looked as if he could still sink some hoops, maybe grab a dozen rebounds and weave one of them downcourt once in a while, even though he looked his age, tired, with pouches under his eyes. He was a guy who would always be skinny, and strong, too, no matter what he ate. But the weight was a tricky thing that way, because D.J. probably went over two hundred pounds standing six five. He had been talking on the phone when Poole came in and Poole could tell D.J. couldn't quite place him but still knew he'd seen him around, knew that he was probably a cop. He was impressed with the size of the guy's hands, wrapped around the phone almost twice. Poole could see the hands going up to the glass strong and he remembered once when the DEA had gone on a circus bust how D.J. had pushed Daddy John out of the way when the sheriff was trying to get his picture on TV, hog the show, D.J. pushing the sheriff and the cameraman back together, instant rage on Daddy John's face as he and the cameraman fell back into some bushes. Poole didn't necessarily like all the guys at DEA. There were some great assholes and pricks on board; the informants and finks were the worst. But D.J. was very straight and thorough, and he had courage and integrity, which impressed Poole just the way it had impressed him in Adrienne Deveraux. He milled around outside the door while D.J. finished on the phone.

"Tell me, brother," Donald said, a great big smile on his face, "is this business or pleasure?"

Poole told D.J. his name. He could see the guy remembered him now, relaxed. "Business," Poole said. They shook hands, Poole even more impressed now that he felt the grip.

"Now, why did I think so?" Donald said. He poured himself some coffee in a Santa Claus cup and poured some for Poole in a Styrofoam one, shooting the shit, letting the phone ring to a dead stop. He was telling Poole he was going to referee Junior College ball in winter to keep in some kind of shape, see if he could keep up with the kids, up and down the court. He told Poole he had two kids himself but that they weren't old enough to play organized ball yet. He said he'd rather see his kids grow up happy and disorganized. "Maybe they'll go to law school," Donald said, smiling slyly now, sharing his distaste for lawyers with Poole, saying he'd rather his kids shoot dice in the street than go to law school.

It wasn't as if Poole didn't know what Donald had been doing for the past few years, working his ass off in this cramped basement office with a staff of two or three, two phones, a budget of maybe $300,000 a year, if that much. And one doper from Houston, a small-timer, did that kind of business in two weeks. It was worse than that. Donald would get fired if he drove his generic car down to the beach for an afternoon with the kids, but you could bet the government's Drug Czar stepped out of the shower every morning right into a huge black Lincoln Continental, his shoes never touching pavement. Donald was shooting some more shit while Poole looked at the photographs of his wife and kids, a nice-looking family. Poole envied the guy. They were drinking their coffee when the phone rang again, Donald staring now, running out of juice, but Poole noticed he didn't answer the phone. Then Poole asked him about the old Vietnamese, Nguyen Bao Do, who had been found dead about a week ago near the Port Arthur marina. Donald said he hadn't heard. Should he have heard?

Poole told him all about the old man. Poole left some things out, his conjectures, because he wanted Donald to see a clear picture, unclouded by opinion.

"How does D. J. Donald fit into this scene?" Donald asked when Poole had finished.

"Between you and me," Poole said, deadpan now.

D.J. sat back in his metal chair, a serious expression on his face. Poole thought his face was entirely remarkable, the color of campfire smoke, dark gray eyes with black pouches underneath. Poole was thinking he had come to the right place, whether it was instinct or experience, he didn't care, but he felt good sitting here shooting the shit with the DEA guy, then getting down to business with no bullshit, feeling he could be straight with Donald, that the guy wouldn't freeze him out no matter what happened. Maybe it was that Poole remembered that first big circus bust, charging into a crack house down on Freeman Street in Beaumont, a very hard place, how he'd seen Donald dressed in orange flak, a pump shotgun under one arm, Daddy John behind a car across the street, Poole only backup, not part of the action then. Poole had been scared, no doubt about it. The whole scene had been surreal, as though it was happening only on videotape, a deep blue curve of light on a diskette, and it had made Poole feel liquid inside. Under the scan and piercing screams of other men behind him, Donald had gone onto the porch. Poole had heard the door splinter as Donald hit it with his shoulder. In Vietnam, Poole had been a medic assistant and he was used to hearing the action, seeing the blood, but the bust was something different; it seemed so personal, not like incoming fire, which had a high smoky whine. It was like D. J. Donald versus whatever was on the other side of that door. And the bust had gone down, leaving Poole feeling methed-out, wired so bad, he needed two or three beers just to stop shaking.

Poole told D.J. how he'd gone looking for the old fisherman's .22 Colt, how it was a way to put the Vietnamese back into a rapidly darkening picture. He was doing a negative search, he said, just for some peace of mind.

"Man, you say a *negative* search. Now I've heard it all. You're going to have to explain that one." D.J. broke into a jive laugh.

"I wasn't searching so much as satisfying myself something wasn't there." Poole smiled. Donald was smiling, too.

Donald almost laughed, holding a hand over his mouth, his eyes dancing. "You know, a negative search. It has a nice ring to it," Donald said.

"Yes," Poole said.

"Yeah, it do," Donald said. "Yes, sir, Your Honor, sir, this here was a negative search, yes, sir. We have to make up some new rules, maybe change the Constitution on account of this here negative search."

Poole let it go for a while. "Well, I didn't find the gun," he said. "But I found two hundred pounds of Jamaican grass in the hold of one of the shrimpers down at the marina."

Donald tipped back in his chair, concentrating now, ignoring the phone, which had been ringing again, six rings, then a silence, the gray hum of the post office basement, the waxed shine on the floor, some kind of dust and oil smell in the ventilator system, circulated and hushed.

"What you found, man," Donald said. He made a web with his fingers, thinking it over. "That's fine Poole, but I'll tell you something. If you took a real good look someday, you'd probably see about two hundred pounds of *seeds* on the courthouse floor right here in Beaumont. Things is fucking bad, you know? I'm talking seeds now. You got to convince me this is worth my time." Donald leaned over the desk, tapping his Santa Claus cup on the metal. "Hey, I'm serious. It's not that I'm too good for this bust. It's a busy war."

"War is war," Poole said, half-grinning. "You count the bodies where you find them."

"You say." Donald laughed, leaning back.

"You interested?" Poole asked.

"Just so you know," Donald said. "I know what kind of problem you got here, Poole."

"You know about half," Poole said flatly. Donald leaned up again, asking Poole to tell the other half. Poole told D.J. he'd tried to saw through the bars with Daddy John but that the guy wasn't going to make a case on the Vietnamese. Then he told D.J. about his hard-on for Everett Teagarden, how he'd been sitting down on the guy, why he'd been doing it, how they'd come down from their perch last night and found the old bubba in a lawn chair with a faraway look in his eyes.

"Man, oh man," Donald said. "You can't take this negative search of yours back to your outfit. Our old buddy John Lister would have your ass, black-and-blue. I mean, you need a way to turn this negative search of yours around. Am I right?"

Poole said he was right. He also said he didn't have a clue as to who might have done Everett Teagarden. Donald thought about it, then asked Poole if there was a connection between the dope and Everett. Poole honestly didn't know. He went over the points he'd thought about, but it didn't make much sense. "I'd say the clock is running out on the old Vietnamese," Poole concluded.

"I can see that, Tom," Donald said. "One thing is, dope is always a connecter. It is the Super Glue of life, let me tell you that." Donald got some more coffee and sat down again. "You think they're going to find Everett pretty soon?" Donald asked.

Poole was thankful he didn't say anything about the fact that he had walked away from a dead body, just left the old guy, this bubba, sitting there in a white lawn chair with a blue hole in his neck.

"Pretty soon," Poole said. "But I'm concerned."

"I can understand your concern, Tom. I really can."

"Thank you, D.J."

They were having official fun and everything was working the way Poole had hoped it would. He wanted D.J. to know that he took the Vietnamese fisherman's death very seriously, that he didn't know how the old bubba fit in, that he wasn't a cowboy running around throwing ropes over everything in sight, looking for newspaper space. Just the opposite, in fact. He wasn't into roughing people up, pointing guns around. He needed help and he wanted to be equal to the task. It was that simple.

Donald got up and sat on the edge of his desk, looking at a wall map of the whole bay region in blue and red and white, with Port Arthur at the center, Beaumont northwest,

161

the Intracoastal Waterway down to Galveston, over to Cameron, Louisiana, the swamps and dunes in between. Then Donald stuck a red pin beside the south bay, where the marina was, where the seashore road went along the beach. "Your old Vietnamese found here, right?" To himself, thinking out loud, Poole not saying anything, just letting the DEA cop do his thing. That's what Poole had come for, anyway. "The shrimp boat full of reefer"—sticking a pin in the map—"then the old bubba found dead, the house on the estuary." D.J. was standing in front of the map now, looking at it with his wheels spinning. Poole was trying to look around Donald at the map when Donald sat back down suddenly, his chin in his palm. "Two hundred pounds," Donald whispered. "Man, that isn't much, is it?"

"It depends," Poole said.

"Well, not in this fucking war, then."

"Not in the big war, no."

"And what you want is the guy who killed the old Vietnamese. Maybe a line on Everett. Something to connect so you can take it to John Lister."

"Right," Poole said. Poole was in Donald's hands, pure and simple. So he laid it out for him, how he didn't have anyplace to go with all this information, that what he'd done was an illegal search the way he'd done it, how it could have been different if he'd thought of asking. But he was on vacation, wasn't he? That was another problem, that all this time he was supposed to be in the Guadalupe Mountains with a campfire going, watching the planets. What he really wanted was to find the gun that belonged to the fisherman; that would be the first domino and he wanted the whole chain to stop falling when he'd found out who killed Bao Do, and maybe Everett Teagarden, if they connected.

"Do you have a killer in mind?" Donald asked.

"Not the killer."

"Then a dope dealer."

"Guy named Danny Huan," Poole said. "The fisherman's son-in-law. And a guy named Jerry Donovan, also a son-in-law."

"We have two problems," Donald said. "We need a way to make a bust. Then we need a way to connect the bust to your killer. You have any ideas?"

"That's why I'm here." Poole said he didn't have any solid ideas. Maybe if he could bust the dope dealer, he could find the killer, all in one swoop. Beyond that, he said he didn't see much. D.J. was drinking his coffee, smiling, Poole wondering what he was thinking, knowing that something was about to happen. Just then, D.J. got up and asked Poole if he'd like to take a drive. It was a nice morning, only about ninety degrees in the shade and lots of humidity. Poole followed Donald up the stairs and outside in the heat. He didn't want to ask any questions now.

They got into the generic Buick. The plastic seats were so hot that Poole could barely sit. D.J. drove south through downtown Beaumont to the warehouse district, where there were brick warehouses, produce dealers, vacant lots, some trucking outfits. The car radio was playing loudly, the windows rolled down, mostly rhythm and blues from a Shreveport station. They were tunneling through the brilliant hazy sunshine, going through shadows and out again, listening to the rhythm and blues, not a single car in sight and nobody on the streets. They shot the shit for a while, Poole thinking about Adrienne Deveraux in the back of his mind, wondering where she was right now, in Houston probably, out in the backyard with her roses and honeysuckle. Poole wondered where they were headed in the generic Buick, here in this forbidding warehouse district, saying nothing, with just the music and the smell of oranges, and then they got to a parking lot surrounded by a high barbed-wire chain fence, double strands of wire on top, gate padlocked two or three times. The lot was filled with Caddys, MGs, green Jags, and some big pleasure boats, too, a cabin cruiser on blocks at one end.

It took D.J. five minutes to unlock the gate, standing in the hot sun fiddling with the padlocks. Poole followed him through the sea of cars and trucks until way in the back they came to a bass boat, a black-and-silver hog machine with black-spackled sides, deck sounding equipment, about a hundred-horse Evinrude in back. D.J. walked around the boat, running his hands along the hull as if it were a horse, looking at the motor.

"Ain't she just beautiful," he said.

"Oh, she is beautiful." Poole laughed.

"You like to fish, Tom?"

"I do, D.J.."

D.J. had put on some sunglasses. Standing next to Poole, he was a full head taller, looking at the bass boat, a finger on the hull, like he was supporting it, glints of sun off the mirrored surface of the glasses.

"I'm interested in the reefer, Tom," Donald said. "I'd like to know where it goes. It isn't a big shipment for me, but it matters, you know what I mean?" Poole said he knew. It was hot in the parking lot and Poole was sweating like a pig. "In my opinion, this shrimp boat full of reefer won't move in daylight. But maybe if we run down there tonight and hang around, keep out of sight, we might be able to follow her around and see where she goes. We'd have to be lucky. But I think whoever owns the reefer probably wants to turn on it. Why let it sit? If you're game, we could go down there for a few nights, do some fishing, see if that boat moves. If she does, we could be behind her. I don't know how that helps you with your old fisherman, much less your old bubba. But it's a place to start."

"I'm with you, D.J.," Poole said. It took him about two seconds to make up his mind.

Poole watched D.J. turn around and lean against the hull, adjusting his sunglasses. "You see," Donald said, "I don't care so much about the dope. It's a small shipment. But I don't think the owner is going to go down the coast to

Galveston or up the bay to Houston. There are too many cops between here and there. Those guys have seen it all. They'd spot this shrimper in a minute. They would smell the dope. What interests me is how these guys plan to get their reefer to Houston. Those charts you saw on board tell me maybe they have a way to catch the Intracoastal north of Clam Lake, cruise up there and off-load the shit to somebody who could take it down to Houston on the Intracoastal. If they're doing it that way, it would be a brand-new route, something I've never seen done before. That's what interests me, this new route. I thought I knew all the routes, but this might just be a new one. If it is, we might catch something larger someday. We let this one go, get something really big. So I want you to know, I don't care much about the old Vietnamese. I mean, I'm sorry he's dead. And I don't know who killed the old bubba. Maybe I'm not sorry he's dead. Shit, who knows? What I know is this. You're welcome to come along with me, stake out the shrimp boat, see where it goes. If your Danny Huan is on board, maybe you snap him up when he starts to bawl, down there in the tank. I guess I'm offering you a way to saw through the bars, all that shit. But I don't know how you're going to handle John Lister, how you're going to tell him how you spent your summer vacation."

Poole was thinking about all the red pins in that map. They were in a circle around the Intracoastal. "That would help me out, D.J.," he said.

Donald headed back to the generic Buick, Poole behind, sneaking looks at all the cars and boats, huge Blazers jacked up on oversized tires with desert suspensions, some heavy earth-moving equipment. Poole wondered where the hell the DEA had come across all of it. Captured weapons of the war, not even a dent. Donald sat in the Buick with the car door open, running the air conditioner, wiping his face with a handkerchief. It was heating up in the warehouse district, what with all the naked concrete, no trees, brick buildings baking in the sun. Donald told Poole they'd try to run behind the shrimper, and he thought he could justify a week or so, sitting at night to see if the boat moved. They'd follow into the swamp.

Poole sat in front of the AC, letting it dry his face. "They'll hear us behind them, D.J.," he said.

"Well, maybe not. I'll run in the dark with the trolling motor. It runs on two electric batteries. You'd have to be Superman to hear it, especially in a swamp full of frogs."

"You might be right," Poole agreed.

"So," Donald said, "we catch this Danny Huan unloading his dope. You scare the shit out of him, put a gun in his ear and tell him to talk."

"Something like that," Poole admitted.

"Well, something like that, then," Donald added, leaning over the hot seat.

"You know the swamp?" Poole asked. They had started to roll, bang, backing out of the driveway, cutting over to the freeway to get downtown faster. Poole could see the Wal-Mart, heavy Saturday traffic on the freeway going down the exit, people in a hurry to spend cash. The haze had settled down until you could barely breathe.

"I know the swamp some," Donald said.

"Me, too," Poole said.

Poole had cooled off finally now that they were almost back to the post office. He thought he would go home and get some real sleep, the kind you had dreams in. It looked as if he would be up all night tonight, maybe all night for a lot of nights. When he had the chance, he would go down and see Adrienne Deveraux one more time. He wanted to talk to her and tell her he had learned something from her. He wanted to tell her he trusted her and then he wanted to tell her what was going on, just to prove it. Still, he was feeling very nervy and liquid inside, like the time on the TV bust when D.J. had screamed, just before he broke down the door.

They parked in the post office parking lot and were standing beside Poole's Caprice, talking about their shitty government cars. They talked about the equipment they would need, weapons, flashlights, food. They thought they might have to stay out all night but that it was not likely. Poole didn't think it would happen slowly, watching the shrimper in the marina for days, then a lazy trip into the swamp, lying in the mangroves in the heat with the mosquitoes and gnats on you, watching the boat, waiting for someone to off-load the reefer. He thought it would happen fast. After all, these were small-time crooks sitting on twenty thousand dollars and they would want to turn it into cash. D.J. said he would gas and service the boat, ride down the coast and sit off the jetty about sundown if Poole would drive down to the marina and park someplace, walk out on the jetty. D.J. would pick him off the rocks. That way, they'd have a car at the marina if they needed it.

They shook hands, Poole wanting to tell D.J. he could back out on the deal. After all, this was personal for Poole and he didn't want D.J. into something just because Poole had a private need. He didn't, though, because D.J. had said his piece, knew what he wanted.

Poole went back to his apartment and sat in the air conditioning. While he was sitting in his chair, he tried to list his private reasons: the old woman in the hooch; his father, who had come home from work so dirty. Tran was on the list, and so was Adrienne Deveraux. He watched six innings of a ball game on TV and then was tired enough to sleep.

16

Poole was on Adrienne Deveraux's front porch, having memories. It was raining there, in the curvatures of his skull, murmuring dark rumors of rain in the faraway *villes,* netted rain in a fabric of trees that hid the mountains, and, below the canopy, barbaric orange bursts. In Vietnam, Poole would sit in his bunker and goof on the colors and listen as the weather growled away, piecing together his own ethereal peace, the only way to stay sane. Below him, other men were hiding or sleeping, playing radios tuned to the Armed Forces Network, waiting out the rain, everybody nervous and tired while Poole watched the aquamarine colors wash across the hills, trying to associate himself with something other than the current ferocity. Sometimes he associated with the damp heat, imagining himself back home, fishing in the swamps, sometimes with the mounds of base garbage, which reminded him of something he couldn't place, perhaps the oil fields, the *pop-pop* of motorbikes you saw everywhere on the roads.

Now, though, he was sitting on the front porch drinking tea, listening to Adrienne Deveraux pack her things, working the cabin down to its components, boxes of dishes, silverware, her photographs wrapped in brown paper, all the blankets and children's clothes in trunks. While he stood there in the door, a line of thunderstorms brightened over the Gulf with bulbs of lightning, like peonies on fire, but Poole kept having his memories. The rain had that faraway silky whisper to it just like in Vietnam, and his head contained the same tension, and the sea was turning purple like the rain turned purple as it came across the jungle slopes, through the invisible *villes.*

Poole was thinking about the past weeks, all his experience transformed to a network of live wires, a cracking phantasmagoria on the surface of his skin, how much all of it was like the experience of Vietnam, Poole sitting on a bunker near Duc Tho listening to the World Series on a portable radio while the rain pounded through the thick trees and the gunships whirled away like insects, terminal experiences that ended on the surface of your skin.

He had slept a little and had eaten a good lunch. He went out and got a paper and read six column inches about the old man, Everett Teagarden. A fisherman had spotted the body sitting in a lawn chair. Because it was Saturday, there wouldn't be anything more until Monday, if then, if Teagarden wasn't a thing of the past by then. The phone had rung in the apartment once or twice, but Poole ignored it. He didn't want to talk to Daddy John or Hernandez, either one. He just wanted to get on with his fishing trip, go down to say hello to Adrienne Deveraux. Down on the oil road he had considered parking right behind her place but then had parked behind the marina instead and had walked down the beach to the cabin feeling sheepish and nervous until she had kissed him and had looked at him with her marbled blue eyes, lazily almost, as if they were lovers, and had led him inside, where she gave him some iced tea.

Everything Poole thought about how to behave was being shattered by Adrienne Deveraux. It was partly the way she had taken his hand, partly how she had started talking about the packing, the matter-of-factness, which was neither threatening nor coy, how she had told him that she was taking Toby to the Finger Lakes so that they could be close to their oldest daughter while her husband convalesced. It was another phase of her life, a self-sufficient woman timing the events of her existence. Poole felt confirmed in her presence, that his night with her had been something special and inconceivably true. In the past, he had always believed you pay a price for every act you do. It was as if each human interchange was a transaction. Poole had seen himself as always on the edge of a final mistake with people. It was the result, he thought, of being a consumer.

In the background, where Adrienne Deveraux was working, Poole could hear the Brahms, the woman humming along to the melody as she worked. Behind that, way down the beach, there was the sound of a motorcycle. Pretty soon, she came out the door and sat on the porch step beside Poole, holding her iced tea, watching the waves. It seemed to Poole that his life was unfurling like a scroll and that right now everything written on it was indecipherable. As he began to talk, he was amazed that he didn't mention their night together. It was as if they had reached each other without mediation, circumspection swelling around them, getting away so that they could be themselves. Then he understood that all of his speech, his dealings with people, had been taken up with preaching or scolding. Time passed and they sat on the porch and Poole watched the sun color the water and he understood that he could address his life from another level.

The sea was roughing up. There were even whitecaps out by the swell point and vast gaps of gray water that panned toward the horizon. Below the waves, it was a green sea, with the pelicans reeling like acrobats, and there were pockets of green seaweed, too, where the waves were beginning, about two hundred yards out. Poole put his arm around Adrienne Deveraux and they shared a kiss and then Poole drank his tea and strained to see the marina, three hundred yards north, where the shrimp boats were bobbing up and down in the new weather. He could make out the dim shapes of the jetty and a twirl of terns jumping in and out of the rocks, but the wind had kicked in the sand and the spray and it was hard to see. He could taste the salt in the air and now the dim clouds had become black-bottomed toward Mexico, as if there might be a storm washing up from land.

This made Poole worry about the bass boat, wondering if D.J. could handle it in a storm or a squall. Any weather would be tough on small craft, unless they were back inland and had cover. Poole didn't want to be out in lightning, either, there were enough problems without that. Way back in the bayou, Poole knew there was cold, acid black water and running back in there without lights, the way they were going to run, would make things even harder. Poole doubted if D.J. knew Clam Lake very well, and it had been a long time since he himself had been fishing anywhere near that country. He was thinking about the weather, his arm around the woman, she touching his leg, watching the lightning out over the Gulf. They shared the first lean wing of a rain-scented breeze that was different from the hot ocean spray. The sky was muffled up in shades of purple and ocher now.

"Does my packing upset you?" she asked. She had touched Poole's arm, taking his empty glass. Poole said it didn't. He wondered if she'd read the papers, if she knew that Everett Teagarden was dead. "But you're troubled," she added.

"Bao Do," Poole said. "This whole thing. I've been thinking about it all week." He looked at her now, taking her hand. "You don't know why he wanted you to take him to Beaumont?" He had been over this once, but it was important.

"No, I'm sorry," she said. "Have you asked Tran?"

"I haven't had the chance. I'm on what you call administrative leave. The case isn't going anywhere."

The wind had drawn through the woman's hair and Poole could see the lines in her face, how the sunshine was filtering from behind with some sand mixed in, and he saw that she had been worn down as well as he, that she was tired from her packing. Poole said that Bao Do had been written off by the department but that she could trust him to keep the old man alive. He didn't tell her about Everett Teagarden or about the dope on the shrimp boat. Something kept him from it, but he couldn't put his finger on what.

"I'll tell you one thing," she said. "Tran was going to come along to Beaumont. I got the impression that he wanted her to translate." She sipped some tea. "It's odd, but I think we were kind of a delegation. I was to drive, be the witness. Tran to translate. Something of that sort. I don't know if he was having trouble with the bubbas or what. We didn't communicate well and he didn't say more."

The motorcycles created a racket down at the marina. It bothered Poole. He wondered how Hernandez was making out at home now that the news about Everett Teagarden had hit the newspapers.

Poole checked his watch. There was a gap of silence in which he didn't know what to say. Everything he thought of seemed either trite or stupid, and suddenly he didn't know how to behave again. He wanted to put his hands on Adrienne Deveraux, to take off her clothes and carry her into the bedroom and take a long time with her while the wind swept through the hurricane window. Instead, he told her he had to get going, that he knew she had more packing to do, anyway. He knew they were at the end of something and something else would take its place. So he kissed her tenderly and thanked her and they stood up together. Poole pulled on his pack of supplies and walked down the beach.

He skirted the dunes so he wouldn't run into any bikers. He didn't want to be seen going up the beach or out onto the jetty, and when he got on top of the hill above the marina, so that he could see the southern horizon, he stood in the wind and watched the ocean. There was a storm all right, well-organized, the sea growing gray as if it were freezing from the bottom. When he got to the Caprice, he took his casting rod from the trunk. Now he could see the marina clearly, kids out on the board pier, under the neon glare of the beer signs, one guy on a motorcycle doing wheelies in the sand while others were starting the bonfire. Poole could smell reefer and somebody had a boom box. He could see Janine Bonner standing in the haze beside the bait store in cutoffs and a Day-Glo tank top. He thought about the orange dinghy again, but nothing happened to the thought.

Poole sat on the hood of his car for thirty minutes and then he spotted D. J. Donald in the bass boat, the guy way out beyond the swell point, a speck tacking over the waves. Poole couldn't hear the motor over the other noises, D.J. tacking back across the swells now, the gulls rising from the jetty as he closed, Poole scrambling down the sandy hills and out onto the rocks, keeping to the side away from the marina so the kids couldn't see him from the marina dock. Poole watched the bass boat coming in, slipping his way along the rocks in the rising tide. Out over the water, the wind was whipping. D.J. made his way in slowly, running crosswise to the rocks, then back, then out, and Poole could see D.J. smiling, sitting in front with the wheel, wearing a pair of silvered sunglasses. Other than the cop grin on his face, one hand on the wheel, D.J. looked like a guy out screwing around, wearing a pair of shorts and a blue work shirt.

D.J. cut the throttle and bobbed up and down in the ocean. He had taken out the fishing seats so that there would be more room in the boat. It would make them harder to spot at night, too. D.J. tossed a nylon line to the rocks and Poole caught it and tugged the boat close to the rocks and hopped on board, D.J. helping with the casting rod and the day pack with supplies. Poole saw a leather case wrapped in plastic in the stern, what looked like an automatic weapon. There was a shotgun case up by D.J., under the wheel, and Poole knew he had a sidearm. It made Poole feel naked, all this firepower. All he had was his Smith & Wesson, one plastic jug of water. It also made Poole feel as if he was in a different league from D.J., as if this came down to firepower and D.J. had come prepared and he hadn't.

Donald backed them off the rocks. He was gabbing about the rising tide, the birds, the goddamn wind. The sun was going down and everything had a silver sheen. The sky was like tile with gull patterns in spray and haze. Under the sheen, there was a turquoise gleam. When they got going, Poole took some time to watch the mangroves and pines slide by, jade green slashes above the beach. They went straight out into the ocean, until Poole could see all the palms, hear them banging in the wind under the surf. By the time they got to the swell line, Poole could make out the shapes of all the boats in the marina. The kids had the bonfire burning now, wisps of black smoke rising, pouring north over the dunes in the wind. Poole wished he was really going fishing, that he and D.J. Donald could run over to Clam Lake with their supplies and stay out for two or three days, fish for bass and bream, maybe drink some whiskey after a full day. They might see an alligator. They could come back Sunday night like two friends on a holiday, instead of what they were, predators after a dopehead. Poole wanted the beach and the swamp to himself. He wanted an unvarnished vision of things instead of the steady sense of mission. He wanted to let go, see things from a distance, so that he knew what to love and what to fear. He sat down in the back of the boat and focused his binoculars on the marina.

D.J. was out five hundred yards, circling. While they went around, he explained the carbine in the stern, the shotgun under the wheel, saying he didn't want anyone killed just because some Vietnamese kid was turning two hundred pounds of Jamaican dope. But the thing was, they had ordnance. They could make noise if they had to make noise. Together, they worked out how they would hang back in the darkness until they saw something move on the shrimp boat. If it looked like something was happening with the dope, they would follow, but they wouldn't press anything. So they rode around the swells while they studied their charts of Clam Lake, the country along the Intracoastal down to the Houston boat canal, all the channels, trying to share their information, what they remembered about the bayous and swamps between the lake and the waterway. Poole kept an eye on the marina, telling D.J. what he could about the swamp up toward Clam Lake. Donald thought they might be headed inland toward Walker Lake, which was another ten or fifteen miles north of Clam Lake, a bigger and more open body of water, with fancy homes around the shore. It didn't matter much if they were going that far, because neither of them was familiar with the country. It would be dark mangrove, some open stretches, and hot. They passed the time that way, out in the ocean, going around on the swells, and finally they both just sat and watched the marina with binoculars.

Though he needed his concentration, something was untracking in Poole, this odd buffeting of sad nostalgia, as if he was sharing what Adrienne Deveraux was going through, way out here on the ocean with the clouds rolled up in bunches behind him and the wind spilling over the spray. He kept sweeping the binoculars down the beach to her cabin, where he could see a splatter of lights and the dark outline of the structure. He imagined her inside, packing clothes, pausing over the family photographs as she wrapped each in brown paper, how she might feel as she stored her history away. The night closed down as he watched, a surreal subtext for his vision, as though he was floating away from his consciousness and everything he saw was becoming compressed. He kept imagining himself with her, sitting in a thick sheet of light from a kerosene lamp, insects hacking at the screen, playing some canasta with her while they drank tea and listened to the Brahms piano pieces.

D.J. poked him in the arm, saying something in a high wired-on voice that Poole could hear tipping over the sound of the waves whacking the hull. The engine was making a bubbled muffle under the swells and he could see that D.J. had strained forward, binoculars over his eyes. Poole trained his on the marina and he could see someone on the shrimp boat, a swinging light, smoke boiling from the water where the engines were running. D.J. turned the bass boat around and they made out toward the swell line, over it, bouncing up and down again in a trough until they hit a space of smoother water where they turned around and sat while the waves ferried them up and down. To the south, the beach had a luminous quality that masked the flat tone of the water.

"This is it," D.J. said. "We're going fishing."

Poole got caught in the turn, falling forward as his binoculars clattered to the deck.

"Time to stop daydreaming," Donald said. Poole took it as obvious that he wasn't doing his business. He needed to be absolutely alert.

Poole got out his casting rod and dropped it over the

side as if he was fishing, thinking how it wouldn't fool anybody who knew anything about trolling. But that wasn't the point, was it? He discerned a faint boil of thunder and he could hear D.J. in the wind: "We'll stay behind this guy like we planned. I don't know shit about the weather right now, but I bet it will rough up some. If we go inland, we should be okay. Keep ready. If it rains and gets stormy, we'll talk. Just stay alive to the situation. I don't want to get killed." D.J. looked at Poole, his eyes glistening in the near dark. There was a single cabin light under the dash, making his face sparkle, bony and surreal. *Do you?"* he added.

Poole didn't say anything. He merely nodded and stayed down into the boat while D.J. looped it into two circles that were wide enough to disguise their progress south, the direction they thought the shrimper might take when it got fully underway. D.J. had gotten down on his knees and was straining over the windscreen, trying to see the marina and keep the boat moving, to stay out of the spray that was fluffing up over the bow now that the sea had become so rough. It was funny, but Poole felt suddenly exhilarated, confident about what he was doing for the first time since he'd been down to see Daddy John and had his dance with Darnell. It wasn't the danger, if there was any. Perhaps it was the people he was associating with, D. J. Donald and Adrienne Deveraux, and it was the quality of his action, the purity of it. It was action without motive, where there was no flicker of doubt about the goodness of the thing, no mediation. Perhaps it was dangerous, too, but that was a side affair. It didn't make the whole difference.

D.J. was steering with one hand, down on his knees, talking to Poole. "Look, Tom," he said, "I spent all afternoon on these map and charts. The way I see it is, if the guy heads straight down the coast toward Galveston, we take a look and do nothing. You understand?" Poole nodded, spray on his face. He trained the binoculars back on the marina and went on listening while they circled. "But if they head inland, then they're meeting somebody I don't know about. If that's the situation, then I'd like to try to make a bust. That's what I'm thinking, but it could get rough."

They were bumping through rough swells now, hard thwacks on the hull, drums and cannon. The clouds were sifting over the beach, lights twinkling inland. The shrimper had headed the rocks around the pier and was making south.

"We talk before we do anything?" D.J. said.

"At length," Poole said, smiling.

They saw the shrimper riding the swells out to sea, toward them, cutting tunnels in the water, white spray rinsing from the bow. Now the sky was spectral, a pale washed color that reminded Poole of postcard pictures he'd seen of the northern lights. It seemed something beyond his experience, repeated here in the gray-green water and the horizon. D.J. showed Poole how to work the spotlight, how you could detach it from the bow, shine it around if you had to. He told Poole they didn't want to do that unless they had to, because it would make a good target. Poole wished right then he had something other than the Smith & Wesson. He wasn't a good shot and it made him feel as if he might not pull his weight.

D.J. tapped Poole. "Fuckers are definitely headed south," he said. Well, Poole thought, they weren't going to Louisiana. That would have complicated things. Their shrimper was just a pale shape now, oblique in the water and on a line with the beach. They had a pace, slipping down toward the estuary.

"Now listen," D.J. continued, "if they do move inland, we become very careful. It will be quieter back in there and we'll use the trolling motor. If you want to know what I think, I'll tell you. If we're spotted, we could be severely outgunned." D.J. had turned on the charm. "No shit, Tom, even Mickey Mouse guys have automatic weapons in this war."

Poole knew D.J. was trying to lighten things up, make them seem more manageable than they might be. It was good psychology whether it worked or not. D.J. was saying, "This trolling motor runs on twelve-volt batteries. We can move pretty fast on them. They don't make any noise. That's the whole damn point. Why scare the fish? But let me tell you, if these guys turn and start on us, just take that pistol of yours and fire as fast as you can. We're not going to make a fight on a dark night against guys we've never seen before in a swamp, not for twenty thousand dollars' worth of Jamaican reefer. It's probably more money than they've seen in their fucking lives. They'll die for that kind of money. You know what I mean?" D.J. turned to the wheel and ran the bass boat forward. They were tipped up, with the big Evinrude running like a tractor. "You understand?" D.J. shouted over the roar. "There must be fifty different drugs of choice out there today—Smack, coke, crack, PCP, DMT, acid, reefer, hash, hash oil, mescaline, Ritalin, quaaludes, uppers, downers, cough syrup, Demerol, synthetic, organic, you name it. There's shit out there you and I never heard of, shit people put in their veins, noses, assholes. Under their eyelids, for Christ's sake. We're not going to get heavy over this thing, right?"

Poole got back to his job, studying the sea again, and there were more thunder gulps, flashes of lightning that scarred toward inland, too, and a grainy wind from the Gulf. They had gone south far enough so that Poole could see the lights of Adrienne Deveraux's cabin, and he began to drift away from himself again, just as he'd said he wouldn't. He could hear the shrimper clunking south, swells modulating the sound and then an interval, waves slapping the beach far away. He drank some water from the plastic jug and offered it to D.J., who took a hit, too. They were now dead on a line behind the shrimper, three hundred yards away. It had gotten darker and Poole could see tankers in the Gulf now, a few necklaces of light, which he knew were platforms, while inland there were more lights than he could have imagined, from houses hidden in the dunes. It was strange—all this time, Poole thought the Vietnamese were all alone on the edge of this continent, working their way inside to the good life. And now at night, way out in the ocean, Poole could see that there were other people in the dunes, hanging on, maybe wanting to get inside, too. He could see Bao Do's house as they slid down the beach, on a promontory above the water. Down below the house was a bright arm of water leading inland.

D.J. was crouched beside Poole. He was concentrating on the shrimper, a speck in white water. The sound from its engine had changed, as if it had swiveled in the axis of swells, coming from a different direction altogether. "He's going inland," D.J. said. The bass boat bumped over the waves, a flat chop that left Poole exhausted, soaking his shirt. They hit a smooth plane of water finally and Poole knew it was sluice from the estuary and they were going in.

"Goddamn it," Poole heard D.J. growl. They were about three hundred yards behind the shrimper, seeing it in flickered outline against the silver arm of water, dense black mangrove behind. "I can't believe this guy is going to the Intracoastal. He'd stand out like a sore thumb in that water. It's strictly irrigation and pleasure-boat country. Besides, it's fifteen miles or so from here to the canal and the water shallows up and there aren't any fishing boats in that far. You'd have to be a fool to take a boat like that shrimper in that far." D.J. went in toward the estuary, the waves behind them so that they tailed in the water. "My guess is we go behind this guy for about an hour and then he'll meet some pleasure vessel that will take his shit to the Intracoastal and down to Houston. Maybe he'll have a vehicle set for a land meet. I guess there are levees all up in there. I don't see the buyer running this stuff back to Louisiana, because the Intracoastal is too clogged. Besides, we've had pretty good surveillance down there. And they won't have any helicopter. That would be too high-profile." They were outside the estuary about to go in, Poole looking up at Bao Do's house, some lights in the back bedroom, probably Bhin and Jerry doing reefer, boom box blaring. The estuary was about seventy-five yards wide, full of silver ripples. "Keep your eye out," D.J. said, hard at Poole now. "I don't want some guys jumping out of the dark, hitting us with automatic weapons. We're dead motherfuckers if it happens like that."

"The fuck you say," Poole responded, his way of giving vent to the fear. His heart was pounding under the raft of noise from the hull. D.J. gave him the thumbs-up and moved behind the wheel. He shut down the Evinrude and they used the trolling motor, which made a tiny whining noise underwater. Poole pulled down his ball cap to keep the wind out of his ears so he could hear the shrimper better and then hunkered low to keep watch on the banks. They were clicking down the estuary, their noise barely audible above the wind and chop, tacking the boat back and forth from one shore to the other where there were reeds and mangrove to give them cover. Fish broke circles in the water and the frogs had begun to croak. As they went farther inland, the estuary closed to about fifty yards across and it was getting darker. More cypress and pine appeared, ragged patterns of hackberry and brush, the dunes of tule and saw grass piled behind in humps. The light was like a silk gown thrown over everything, and Poole could hear his heart still pounding inside the thickness of the evening. He had an edge on, but he was definitely not scared.

The estuary flattened into a gauzy seep of deep pools and mud flats. They were getting into swamp where the features of the landscape spread and filled, bayou where the water was lifted against the trees and levees, the water jet black and smelling of battery acid. Poole could see the shrimper just ahead in the dark, its steady *klump-klump* that told of engines on quarter speed. D.J. was standing on the bow, the binoculars around his neck.

Poole could tell that the shrimper had slowed, barely moving through the shallow water. What was happening was so logical, it gave Poole a cold feeling along his spine, despite the heat. The cypress had closed along the banks, and they were spending a lot of time in deep reeds, wallowing through them with a soughing sound, the trolling motor clicking off under the bow and wedges of moonlight sparkling on the surface, lapping noises and all the frogs and birds raising hell. There were clouds of mosquitoes, too.

D.J. came down off the bow and leaned over Poole so he could talk low. "We're in five miles or so," he said. "They can go a thousand ways now. If you're right about the charts they use, they'll go south to Clam Lake. But they've got to do something soon." D.J. looked at his watch, then up at the moon, which had risen above the eastern tier of pines, a quarter-moon, not giving off much light. Poole was sweating and he noticed that the storm threat had gone and the sky above was smooth and dark as clay, with a layer of humidity descending on them like paint. The main channel was bright as a dirty bulb, but the channels and mangrove near the banks were not. Poole wasn't worried about being seen, so long as they hugged the levees. They'd have to get hit with a spot to be seen, because the bass boat sat low in the water and was painted black, to boot. The only thing was, they might run right into something they couldn't see, like five or six Jamaicans, maybe Colombians with automatic rifles.

Poole was surprised when the shrimper turned south into an irrigation canal. The one it went down was a narrow concrete revetment with ten feet of water standing, maybe fifteen feet wide, room for the shrimper, but that was about all. Poole knew they were at the end of the estuary trip and that shit might get complicated from here out but that the shrimp boat was headed in the general direction of Clam Lake. This was a bad place, Poole knew, high-walled and full of ambient moonlight, with no place to go but ahead, no place to turn around. It would be like floating down a sewer pipe. D.J. looked once at Poole as he took the shotgun out of its case. He broke it over one knee and sat studying the canal with a worried look.

They went down through the canal for about fifteen minutes. Poole thought he had held his breath. It was as if his lungs had closed up and the pores of his skin were choking. The ticks of the trolling motor rolled off the concrete and Poole could hear the tapping of the shrimper's pistons carom off the concrete walls far ahead. He and D.J. were like a couple of ghosts until they heard the shrimper break open water, a sound like something being sucked through a pipe. They were about fifty yards behind and they couldn't see anything but a shiny nickel of light under the moon, the lake about five hundred yards across, maybe more, lily pads hugging shore and a lot of dead tree stumps on the south. It was spooky, all the mist hovering on the surface and the fish slipping in circles underwater and farther back along the banks a wrist of oaks hung with moss and dim lights from cabins far away. This is it, Poole thought to himself; the shrimper can't go anywhere from here but back through the irrigation canal. He knew the shrimper had reached the end of the line and now something else was going to happen that would include him and D.J. It had a fatality about it that Poole liked, though he wouldn't have wanted to deal with it very often.

The lake was choked by rugged country. Oaks had covered the north shore where there was a levee. Poole knew there were a few roads in the back brush that were gravel and that you could get a boat into the bayous in the daytime if you were after bass. It was snake and alligator country, too, not to mention mosquitoes. Poole watched the shrimper circle and make for the north shore, running straight down the middle of the Clam Lake in a bright pear of moonlight. Poole could make out the cabin bathed in lamplight, could hear the motor clomping in the water, its echoes returning in a double loop. Poole began to wonder to himself if the shrimper was meeting a vehicle on one of the levee roads. It would make sense. It would be good business. Maybe a truck was there already.

D.J. got them out of the canal and through the lily pads and they hugged the east shore, where there were ugly tree stumps sticking up out of the mud. The frogs were making a racket and Poole could barely see the shrimper now because of a thin swoon of fog that had seeped up from the water, but he could still hear the motor churning away, rippled waves slipping across the bow. Poole had taken out his Smith & Wesson, and D.J. was holding the shotgun across his lap while he tooled through the stumps and lily pads.

Then a gunshot slipped across the water, delicately, an echo, and then another, *pop-pop-pop,* a vast, irretrievable interlude in which Poole's skin became electric, and then another gunshot, a thin modular *pop* that had an existential terror buried in it, harmless enough to leave Poole disconnected, but scary because it didn't have a context. When the first shot sounded, D.J. had been leaning over the bow to see how deep the water was where they were cruising in the stump piles.

"What the shit?" he said, feverish with the first dish of the sound that had cupped already and was going back toward shore.

Poole had broken a fearful sweat and the mosquitoes were troubling him, roaring in his ears. And then it was silent and he was trying to discern something in the willow brakes.

It was a second later that a violent shawl erupted from the gloomy levee horizon. Poole saw a brief bouquet of color, its center fire engine red and an outer core of singed orange, something bubbling in slow motion, almost without sound. It held the shrimper in a theatrical pose until she settled back on the glaze gray water and all you could see was a ring of blue glare where the stern had disappeared. Then the sound shock hit them and Poole could discern individual oaks on the levee bank behind the boat, some cypress that seemed backlighted, and just a whiff of flame rising into a milky black sky where the moon had risen. Poole scuffled to his knees and D.J. got in the stern to kick over the Evinrude, running them through the last of the stumps and into open water that had smoothed down to glass. Poole heard some boards clap on the water and then the sound really hit him, *thud-thud.* Then the shrimper's gas tanks blew in a rushing hiss, followed by a monstrous silence. Poole was straining to see and hear, but things were going all black, oaks and mangrove receding, the moon a nearly green crescent in the smoke. Beneath the silence, like a sear, Poole was sure he could hear a *putt-putt-putt* motor noise going away through the swamp.

"We're going in," D.J. said, leaning down in the stern where he was handling the Evinrude.

They made a circle and bumped over its wake. Poole saw the shrimper clearly once when the smoke rose and he could tell the stern had disappeared into the water, blown away, and she had settled on a mud bank under the levee near the north shore. "You got any better ideas?" D.J. said across the scuttling torque of the motor. "Give with them now if you do."

Poole said he didn't and got up and put one leg over the side, trailing it through the water while they headed north in the dark, still hearing once or twice the *putt-putt* going away from him.

D.J. had stood with the shotgun in his left hand, idling back on the Evinrude so that the bass boat settled slightly in the lake, coming closer to the shrimper, so close Poole could smell a gas-and-powder aroma. It looked to Poole as if the shrimper wasn't going to burn. She was probably too soggy for that now, badly torn apart, sitting down in the mud shallows, surrounded by a sheet of unburned gasoline that you could smell on the surface, through the haze of smoke, a small line of fire working back toward the levee. The bow was on the shore, nose up to the levee, and going on her side. D.J. throttled down and hit the spot, throwing a tunnel of white through the cottony air. Poole was crouched down, D.J. behind him.

Poole had his Smith & Wesson out as they came toward shore. He could feel the lake bottom with his boaters and then he jumped over the side, feeling mud suck his shoes until he got onto some sand about twenty feet down from the bow of the shrimper. He covered D.J. while the agent nosed the bass boat onto a flat and then cut the Evinrude, jumped over, and sat hunched in a reed.

Poole didn't know what to think. His mouth was dry and his heart was pounding, but he still wasn't scared. D.J. was running his flash over the scene, which made the mangrove move in shadow, the bayou behind a curvature of mound and in the foreground the shrimper out of the water in tree stumps. D.J. knelt down. "We're fucked if somebody hits us now."

"I don't think anybody will," Poole said, breathing hard now that things had calmed down.

"I don't think so, either," D.J. said, slithering onto a mud hump, shotgun under his right arm, resting a little easier as time went by. "But I'd hate to be wrong." They were both racked up by the moment. It was that time when it would happen if it was going to. They both knew they were at the juncture where a seam could tear.

It turned out that nothing happened. There was a rotten pier jutting into the lake and the shrimper had nearly made the end of it before the explosion. Poole dragged himself through calf-deep water down by the pier while D.J. crawled onto what was left of the deck. The frogs had resumed their croaking and the noise had grown loud to Poole, nearly deafening. The moon had settled through the smoke, casting a pale green light on the water, making the lake look like a nickel again. D.J. poked around on deck, shining his flash down the hold at packages of water-slogged dope, two hundred pounds of Jamaican getting soaked. Poole could see bricks of reefer floating away in the gas-logged water, sinking, sitting up on the mud flanks.

Poole felt easier when he saw D.J. standing on deck with his shotgun down, looking around the mangrove now, where the pines rose in tiers beyond the levee.

"Very clumsy deal," D.J. said.

"Worse than that," Poole said.

D.J. had shined his flash down the mud flats. They had seen the body of a man lying on his back, half-covered by brackish water and mud. D.J. held a face in the light, a bit of white skin in repose.

"You didn't tell me Danny Huan was this clumsy," D.J. said, clicking off the flash. "Somebody really wanted this guy off their cloud. You know what I mean?"

Poole splashed through the water until he had reached the corpse. It was bruised by the blast, some fingers of the right hand missing. It gave Poole the creeps, the corpse with open eyes as the moon poured inside, a brain that had gone away, the head hollow like something out of a Halloween scene. He snapped the safety on his Smith & Wesson and put the gun in his belt, standing up and stretching while he studied the corpse. He could hear D.J. hit the water, splash toward him. Way across the lake, cabin lights were snapping through the darkness, cutting under the fog. This was a beautiful spot, Poole thought, serene in a way, a black nickel lake in moonlight, surrounded by pines and cypress stands.

D.J. was standing behind Poole. He turned on the flash and the corpse got hot and white. Poole told D.J. the dead guy was Jerry Donovan.

D.J. grunted and clicked off the flash. "This kind of puts you back to square one," he said.

"It looks that way," Poole said. He was tired, and the adrenaline was wearing away.

D.J. handed Poole the shotgun. He said he was going across the lake to use a phone.

17

Poole visited Adrienne Deveraux again just before she left for New York State. They met in the garden of a barbecue restaurant in north Houston, just across the Post Oak Road. They were sitting quietly in the shade on a hot day, shadows dappled on the sand, patterns that somehow reminded Poole of his childhood and imparted a sense of well-being. She was dressed in a smart blue skirt, and Poole told her everything about the night on Clam Lake.

It was a crazy and unprofessional thing to do, but he did it anyway. It seemed like the right thing to do somehow, whatever the cost, only Poole didn't think there would be any cost. He had driven his Caprice into the city to be serviced at a place owned by some guys he knew from his days of playing music. He dropped off his car and telephoned Adrienne Deveraux right away from a pay booth, knowing he was being silly but looking forward to seeing her again anyway, feeling sensations from insecurity to joy, knowing that he wasn't a bit out of control, though. So he used the pay phone and called her at home, taking the chance that she would be busy or surprised, that he'd find himself let down, his feelings hurt, but she answered and Poole put his emotions on the table without a second thought. He said hello and asked if she'd like to grab some barbecue. She was quiet for a long time, so much so that he could hear the TV in the background, her breathing as she thought it over. He told her it wasn't strictly business but that there was some business to discuss, that he wanted to talk to somebody, to see her. It was so quiet on the other end of the line that he could almost hear her thinking. Then all of a sudden, she said she'd love to have lunch, just like that.

Later, when he saw her drive up to the barbecue place and get out of her Cherokee, wearing her sharp blue skirt, the white blouse with pink flowers embroidered on the collar, how clean and healthy she looked, Poole knew she was there because she wanted to be.

After he called, Poole walked to a café and had some hot coffee while the guys changed his filter, put on a new distributor and some points, and changed the spark plug wires. While he sat in the café, it got to be midmorning in Houston, already damp with heat. By the time he got to the restaurant across town, it was very hot, although still pleasant in the shadows of the oak trees, the traffic sound dulled by a tier of eucalyptus, a small twinge of oil and dust in the air. Poole's back hurt him, an ache that curved all the way to his waist, soreness he had gotten from sitting against a palmetto while he and D.J. were passing the long night hours on Clam Lake before the FBI guys had come for Jerry Donovan.

First the explosion and then the vision of Jerry Donovan had pulled Poole from incomprehension. He remembered watching D.J. motor across the lake, the bass boat cutting V's in the water, D.J. standing in the bow, growing smaller and smaller, lights in the cabins cutting on and off through the fog while a fear overcame him. Thousands of swamp sounds assaulted Poole, tule rushing in the wind and the jammering of the frogs, owls hooting in the notches of the oaks. Even the water lapping on the levee bothered him, though once or twice the bats slicing down had frightened him palpably. And there were always these swords on the inside of his eyeballs that unbuttoned the unconscious regions of his mind. He started to shiver even though it was hot, even though his pants were wet and stiff with mud, and even though the fire where gasoline had smeared away from the shrimper's tanks had gone out.

How long he sat that way, he didn't know. Clam Lake was utterly still, fog rising through a gray moonlight as the shadows climbed across the water. It reminded Poole of Duc Tho on a few early Sunday mornings during the monsoon when Poole had gone topside, unable to sleep, worn out from his work at Medivac. He had watched the eastern mountains when it stopped raining and it seemed that nothing existed apart from sound, as if the entire jungle was animated. Poole could understand how jungle people could see and hear a God in everything, trees, monkeys, spiders, the mountains themselves. It would be then, taking his early-morning coffee, sitting on some sandbags, immobile for hours, watching the morning rise over the hills, that Poole learned the art of silence.

That night on Clam Lake, Poole sat there with his legs crossed, with the shotgun perched on his lap, staying just that way until he could hear D.J. coming back across the lake in the bass boat, seeing the yellow and green running lights cutting the fog, forming rings of dim halos in the wake, the man standing up behind the wheel in an attempt to see, the hull lifted slightly from the pull of the Evinrude, making speed in open water until he hit the place where the stumps were, when the boat sank back gently and the bumps returned rhythmically as he hit the wake, going in slow arcs back and forth, finding a path through the downed oaks. And then D.J. waved, holding an arc lamp, letting Poole know he was coming to shore, that it was okay and they could relax.

Poole had caught a nylon cord from about eight feet away. He tied the cord to a palmetto, pulling the bass boat through the shallows while D.J. hit the spot so he could see what he was doing, trying to keep his balance as the hull tottered. Then Poole had waded back out and held the lamp while D.J. hopped over, waded ashore, standing there in the moonlight like a surveyor, almost too relaxed for Poole, who had been tense as a coiled spring for about an hour. The running lights were their only light, except for the wedge of moon and the sizzling embers in the water that had almost gone out.

They shared a drink from Poole's plastic water jug. Poole sat back down and was uncaking the mud from his shoes. Donald rested, then jerked a thumb at the cabins across the lake. "They think all hell has broken loose," he said, swigging from the jug. "You should have seen them gathered down by their pier. They were watching this black dude come chugging through the water just after an explosion ripped all hell out of a shrimp boat. Thought I was the creature from the Black Lagoon."

"Half right," Poole said.

Poole stood again and began to feel the pain in his back. It occurred to him that he'd been suspended in his own field of concentration, a little amazed at how attentive he'd become, how it was the first time in a long time that he'd felt so situated inside an event. Now events were swarming over him and he was alive to each of them.

D.J. offered Poole a drink, putting down the jug beside him. Poole really admired D.J., probably because he had his own way of seeing, like Adrienne Deveraux had hers, both of them capable of action without meditation. They didn't question their own motives.

"We have a wait," D.J. said.

"How long and for whom? I have this need to know." Poole put down the shotgun. He was starting a worrying trend that had begun just as he heard D.J. running across the lake.

"You're still in the play, if that's what you mean."

"That's not my main problem. I had it figured that Everett Teagarden put down the old fisherman. He's dead. I had it figured that Danny Huan was Teagarden's partner. That theory isn't looking real good right now. My backup idea was that Jerry put down the old man and Teagarden. Now Jerry is fish food, faceup."

"Just so," Donald said, squatting down on the mud flat, as if it was talking that Poole wanted, they were going to do just that for a while. Poole was pondering Jerry Donovan, how his skin was glowing in the pale moonlight. He looked like a porcelain doll dropped off a windowsill, some fingers broken from a hand. "Tell me what's eating you," Poole heard D.J. say. "I know there's something on your mind."

"That's fair," Poole said, whispering, still engrossed in the enamel sheen on Donovan's face. There was a storm of mosquitoes in his ears.

"You look shot," D.J. said. "Listen up. These FBI guys are coming down from Beaumont, probably be here around an hour after first light. They can't get around down in these swamps after dark, so we're waiting until then. This is a federal thing now, good for you. That's just how it is, so you don't have to worry about Daddy John. I'm not cutting you out, and I wouldn't do that, anyway. It's just that it's a federal thing."

"I know, D.J.," Poole said. "It's okay."

"If you want, we make you disappear—like you were never here. My guys aren't going to ask you any questions.

You just fade away like a bad cold. I understand your problem with Daddy John Lister, you being here and all, and I wouldn't want you to hit deep shit with him. The FBI will do all the lab work, bomb analysis, send the body up to Beaumont and do an autopsy. Your coroner won't get his hands dirty even. They'll go over the shrimper down here and then haul it to Houston and pick it apart. You won't see much about it in the papers, this being Sunday morning and all. The focus of this will be on the drugs. The way it looks now, we'll have to talk to your Vietnamese, Tran and Bhin, probably Danny Huan. It can't be helped; I know you know that. Anyway, we'll get back to Beaumont tomorrow and clean up and have a drink and go from there. If you have any ideas, we can talk them over. But if you want to disappear, it can be arranged." D.J. looked away uncomfortably. He began to move off his haunches until he had reached a patch of dry grass about three feet away from Poole. They were so close to Jerry, they could see his hair waving in the water. "Hey," D.J. said almost conspiratorially, "I know you're concerned about your Vietnamese. I know that, man."

"I know how it is," Poole said, staring at D.J. now, trying to make him comfortable again. "I understand exactly what has to happen. I have some ideas of my own."

"I thought you might, Tom. How do you want to play this? I mean, you don't want Daddy John kicking your ass."

"Buzz me back to the marina, my Caprice. I want some sleep and some time to do my work. Number one with me is the guy who killed Bao Do. That's all I'm after."

D.J. picked up the electric lamp from the bass boat and Poole followed him out to the shrimper, splashing through knee-deep muck, Poole sitting on the hull while D.J. went on board, Poole humping up with a hand from Donald, and then the two of them onboard, Jerry Donovan down in the water, a contemplative glaze on his face. Poole had a flash and he held it for Donald while D.J. went down the steps to the hold, stairs sagging, Donald sputtering around in about six inches of water, making slits in all the packages so he could see if the dope was all there. Poole knew there would be about two hundred pounds, but D.J. wanted to see it for himself. It was just reefer, but Poole knew it was fairly fine shit—it had that bulb of seeds on the head and a yellow stalk that smelled like alfalfa, but sweeter. It was nothing special, but it had just cost Jerry Donovan his life.

Poole could tell D.J. was soaking his clothes, prowling around in the gasoline and water. The beam was on D.J. and another hole of light came through the back of the shrimper where the hold had caved out. Poole could see fog through the hold, dissipating, rising up until it was cream white on the black surface. Poole didn't feel spooky now. He felt tired and puzzled, hardly hearing all the night noises outside anymore. He just followed D.J. with his flash while the guy crawled around in the busted hold, then out through a hole and into the shallow lake, poking around in about two feet of water for more packages of reefer, kicking away the last of the embers. Donald would count the packages, call out loud to Poole, swish around and find another package, call out again. They were missing about twenty packages from what Poole had estimated at the marina, most of them probably sunken somewhere in the muck. When it got light, the FBI guys could hunt for the rest. Some they would find; some they wouldn't. The rest would make a nice present for some guy in a bass boat, sitting out in the lake in about a week.

Poole was sure he was sharing a feeling with D.J., even though they hadn't said anything. They were wondering why someone had died for this Jamaican stuff. It was good reefer, and twenty thousand was a lot of money, but there was more money than this in seeds on the federal courthouse floor. Hadn't D.J. said that himself? If it had been cocaine or heroin, sure, two hundred pounds was a life's work. But even so, it had been left behind in the water to rot. Why had someone gone to all that trouble? Poole shrugged to himself. There was only one guy to ask, and he was faceup in the swamp, looking at the moon. Maybe Poole could have asked Everett Teagarden, too. But Everett had taken a long siesta in his lawn chair. So long, Everett.

Donald had plowed back through the water and was standing under Poole. Poole leaned over and could smell his skin, gas and oil and reefer, Donald standing there in the moonlight trying to get the sticks and stems off his trousers. Poole laughed. Donald looked so much like a Rasta that he couldn't help himself. What the hell, Poole thought, they might as well enjoy the evening, despite all the shit, the shock of the explosion, which had begun to wear down. It was like Duc Tho—you had to laugh or you would go crazy inside an hour.

Poole helped D.J. onto the deck. It seemed cooler somehow and there was a light breeze blowing away the last of the mosquitoes. The fumes had made Poole queasy, but the feeling passed as the breeze picked up and they sat with their legs crossed watching the moon lilt through the oaks, grazing the tallest tree, which was hanging over them. Then D.J. got to his knees and held the electric lamp down on Jerry, Donald with no expression on his face while he peered over the side, as if the guy had suddenly shifted gears and was doing a computer analysis. Poole could tell that behind the levee there was a road on top of a wall of mud and gravel that ran along a line of oaks and willows and probably wound around the shore until it hit the cabins on the other side. Right now, the mud bank disappeared about fifty yards off, where the dark suddenly panned away. Poole was watching some possums run along the road, their eyes like marbles in the night, three and four at a time down along the tree line. Poole thought he could hear snakes flinching away in the water, but he wasn't sure. But the heaviness of the moonlight and the way the sounds seemed to crack open their contents and come falling out reminded him of the scene in Adrienne Deveraux's cabin the night he had come and put his hands on the woman's back.

While Poole was thinking, Donald jumped over the side and splashed into the water beside Jerry Donovan, landing so near to the dead man, you could imagine Jerry being annoyed. When Poole looked, Donald had leaned over so close that you could almost hear him whispering in Jerry's ear, trying to coax a moment of life from him, almost lovingly, then putting his hands on Jerry, going through his pockets, touching his head, putting his hands under the body and lifting him gently, touching the wound, too.

Donald looked up, still hunched above Jerry. "Right behind the ear," he said almost admiringly. "The second shot in all likelihood. The one we heard after the first one." Donald was shaking his head, giving Jerry back to the mud. "There's a wound under the chin, too, like this shooter hit him from below, probably standing where I am now, Donovan just where you're looking down. Surprised as shit, I'd say. Not expecting to die, get a gunshot up under his tongue." Donald stood up, backed away, staring down at Donovan as if he was framing a camera angle. "This shooter knocked him down with the first one, then put one behind his ear." D.J. was nodding, smiling. "Jesus Christ," he said, "this was cold, you know what I mean?"

Poole said something agreeable. But he was trying to think now, feeling an unease pass through him, replacing the relaxation he had been feeling just before. A mauve light had percolated up from the swamp, maybe dawn somewhere to the east. Poole saw Donald go pecking through Jerry's wallet. Now Poole looked closer at the corpse, remembering something Hemingway had written about dead bodies, how they pass through phases of color, pink to white to gray to red to an awful yellow-black. Poole could see Jerry was in the white plaster-of-paris stage, some of the porcelain sheen already gone, and while he looked at the body, he began to think about Bhin. What would she feel? He wanted to ask D.J. to go easy on the girls, especially Tran, but he didn't want to call in any favors he didn't deserve.

Poole tossed himself over the side and splashed down beside D.J. He started lecturing about Jerry, telling D.J. everything he could think of, starting with the first night he saw Jerry drunk or stoned, probably both, getting out of the yellow Charger and staggering inside the house, how Poole had input the guy's name on the state police computer in Houston and what had come up. He told Donald about Danny Huan and his problems with the old fisherman, with Jerry, too, trying to fill Donald in before it got light in the swamp and the FBI guys swarmed into the picture and Poole swarmed out. Poole told him that Bao Do wanted to go to Beaumont, but then he had been killed, and nobody seemed to know why he wanted to go. What meant something was the fact that Poole hadn't found the old .22 that everybody said the old man owned. When he finished, D.J. walked over to the palmetto and they both sat down with their backs together, tired as hell.

The light was definitely frothing up, tippets of color on the oak branches, just faint gray. "Deals like this mean one of two things," Donald mused, his voice lifting away in the cool air. "Maybe Donovan had fucked his connection and the guy killed him for it. Hey, drug deals go bad. You can read about it in the papers. It could be Donovan didn't pay somebody for a load last week, last month. If the guy he fucked over is real hard, he would kill Donovan just to send a message to the world. Hey, you fuck me and you're dead, bang-bang." Donald ducked his head around the palmetto. "That's the mentality we got here, Tom. Two-tone shoes, gold watch fobs. Real old-world values." D.J. sighed, as if he had made a mental note. "I admit, you usually get this mentality in the coke business, ice and heroin. Reefer is usually cooler." He snapped a white-teeth smile at Poole. "Still, you got these guys who will snuff you so their girl-friends will call them 'baby.' You know?"

"I know that, D.J.," Poole said.

"Then it could be something else entirely," D.J. said, leaning back on the palmetto. The breeze had slipped into the oak trees. "The usual sour deal finds the buyer taking the dope. That's why this episode is strange—the killer didn't take the dope; he just shot Jerry and went away. Hell, they blew the boat and left twenty thousand dollars' worth of dope floating on Clam Lake. Fact is, this looks very much like a message thing. I mean, they could have punched a hole in the boat, let her sink. But they blew her sky-high."

"I'm calling that too dramatic," Poole said.

There was a silence, during which Poole could hear the breeze suck through some shumard stands across the levee. Something bit him, ants maybe, crawling down on his ankles. "Yeah," D.J. said, tired now, "the dramatic kind is when some dude kills a guy because he's running dope in his territory—a turf thing. You've seen that shit come down before, guys fighting over city blocks, back alleys. This situation might be like that, Jerry Donovan, this bubba hick moves dope through somebody's exclusive territory. Whoever hit him didn't give a shit about dope; they wanted Jerry dead and his boat wrecked so it wouldn't happen again, *ever*. This guy steps out of the dark and blows Jerry away because he's into something bigger and he doesn't want this bubba fucking it up."

"I like the second option," Poole said. "I think we look for somebody familiar with the territory, somebody who knew what Donovan was doing, who didn't want him doing it anymore, forever."

They had reached a stage where tired didn't mean anything. "Got any candidates?" D.J. asked.

"Not right now," Poole responded. "Call the Drug Czar."

"He's asleep right now, dreaming about his stock port-folio. Let's let him get his sleep. Call him tomorrow morning after his croissant."

"Say hi for me," Poole said.

D.J. stretched out against the bank, looking up at the moon. Poole was trying to keep the mosquitoes off, pouring fresh water from the jug over his head, face. There was a trace of pink gracing the trees like lace, something blown in on the ethereal breeze. A premonition of light had glazed the lake and Poole could see some fish drawing circles as they rose there in the middle, under the mist, and he could see the moss in the oaks. It was hot suddenly, with a soft lilt, yet disappointing. Something else, maybe the sleeping turtles lined up on a sunken stump, made Poole think about his childhood again, the mornings when he'd ride his bike down from Port Arthur and spend the day catching carp, drinking iced tea. While he was thinking, the sun came up over the rise of trees and glinted on the cabin windows way across the lake. Poole could tell how dark and muddy the water was, almost ocher in tone, and he began to send out his own perceptions instead of staying passive, having his memories, giving something to the scene instead of taking something from it.

Then he was pitched away from it by the growl of an engine across the levee, down in the swamp. The lazy spike of gravel crunching floated through the still air, gears dropping down through second, then first, sounds going hard through the bush. D.J. got up and started putting away the gear in the bass boat, the lamp, plastic jug, the shotgun. He had covered the gear with tarp and was standing in the deep water, watching the levee road. "Now you tell me what we do," he said, tired-faced and sweaty.

"I guess I don't want front-page coverage," Poole said.

"All right," D.J. said.

"But I have a hunch. I want some time to play it."

"What kind of hunch?" Dust had tunneled in the oaks,

rising now. With the first light, grackles had laced the trees, making their ratchet sounds.

"I might be able to give you the shooter." D.J. had cranked around, a zero on his face. They were standing twelve feet apart, Poole about to wade into the shallow water, dragonflies scattered in the reeds, aquamarine streaks you could see on the brown water. It had become officially hot.

"You got a candidate?" D.J. said.

Poole had a bead on some white dust in the oak trees now where the sun was filtering through. It was beautiful, really, this hot morning way out here where every sound had a natural connection. The sky passed from rose to a bluish orange, still a moon about to go down on the far side of the lake. Poole had sloshed through the shallow water and he was right up next to D.J. "Hey, my man," D.J. said, whispering, "I thought you didn't have a candidate."

"No name, no face."

"No name, no face." Donald leaned against the hull, the sun on his face. Over his shoulder, Poole could see some boats making out from shore. "You want to tell me about it, Tom?" D.J. asked.

"Let me have a day," Poole said. Poole could hear a truck throttle down. A brown Blazer all beat to hell dropped over the tier of pines and down onto the levee, about four hundred yards away. Poole saw it flash through the shumards, then disappear in willows. When Poole saw it again, he could see two guys in front wearing shiny sunglasses.

"I'm taking you back on the bass boat," D.J. said.

"I need the day. Going to Houston."

"Take it," D.J. said, looking at the Blazer. "Do what you have to do, but come by and see me Monday when you're done. As far as I'm concerned, you're in the case if you want to be. You're out if you want to be. I can't help you a lot with the old fisherman unless he figures in this case." D.J. had headed toward the shore, where Jerry Donovan was going through the early yellow phase. "You're just a tourist now as far as I'm concerned," he said.

Poole pulled himself into the bass boat and settled onto the tarp, trying to get comfortable while D.J. walked onto the pier and hopped the levee onto the gravel road, meeting the Blazer as it stopped. He talked for a long time with the two guys, one with a bushy red beard, lumberjack shirt, about 235, the other with slick black hair. They looked like Contras to Poole, minuteman types on the government payroll. When Poole looked at their .45's, he began to wonder how he fit the picture.

Poole watched the lake, the fishing boats edging closer, so close that he could see the guys in the boats, circling now, trying to get a look at the action. The sun had come over the pines finally and the whole thicket described a rugged arc of swamp, browns and grays, vast and dirty with grackles heaped in the dead oaks at the water's edge. The sun was bothering Poole now and he knew he was bitten to a scar by mosquitoes. Then he saw D.J. hop over the pier, coming back to the bass boat. He sat still in back while D.J. settled to the wheel, and when they were ready, Poole turned over the Evinrude and D.J. backed them off the shallows and through the stumps. When they turned again, Poole moved up front, away from the fumes so he could catch some breeze as they bumped over the lake, which had burned down to a rusty red color.

Poole had to speak over the roar of the Evinrude. They were in the middle of the lake, going toward the canal.

"Before the explosion," Poole shouted, cocked into the wind, "did you hear something else?"

"You heard it, too? Engine sound, right?"

"All right." Poole laughed.

"Fuck yes, I heard it."

"Just so you heard it," Poole said, relaxed now, balanced against the windshield and the forward deck. D.J.

indulged himself in a good laugh, taking a drink from a canteen he had under the wheel. Poole took a drink, wishing it was cold beer, something that would fix his exhaustion.

It took about thirty minutes to get back to the marina. Poole got his Caprice and drove home to the apartment and took a shower, spending about twenty minutes under the hot water, listening to the radio, drapes drawn against the mall, the AC on full. He lay down on the bed and tried to sleep, but he was too wired. He dozed and took in a movie and then slept ten solid hours. He was up early and had a big breakfast and was on the road to Houston before it was hot. He had his car serviced and he made a call to Adrienne Deveraux, hoping to find her still in Houston. He made a date for lunch with her and that was when he drove over to state police headquarters, rode up the elevator, and spent an hour on the computer terminals.

It was cool and nearly airless on the seventh floor. Down behind the bank of screens, Poole tried some tricks first, playing games with the information while a steady buzz surrounded him. He concentrated on the glowing surfaces, where all the information lived.

He drank some warm tea as he waited for the data. He thought about Adrienne Deveraux, inventing for himself a future time when he would be sitting under live oaks in the garden of a barbecue restaurant in north Houston, spread out in the shade, some fresh mint on the table, finishing his potato salad. Everything centered on her eyes. The pain in his back was gone. Even as he was fixed on the pulsating green screen, he knew he would tell her everything about Jerry and Bhin and Danny Huan, that she would listen without saying anything. Maybe she would touch his hand on the table, a gesture that would fill him with great longing and tenderness. And Poole would realize that it was no longer Adrienne Deveraux he was trusting, but himself, and the unmediated moment.

Poole left the restaurant early enough that he thought he would miss rush hour. He had the sun behind him, and he had turned off the interstate onto a state road, still a four-lane, but not so frenetic. It ran down into cotton land that was black, and pretty soon he left behind the billboards and trash buildings and he was out in the bottoms. About halfway back to Beaumont, he thought about the one thing he hadn't told Adrienne Deveraux, something it was better she didn't know because it was just for Poole and D.J. right now.

Back at state headquarters, Poole had punched in the name Bonner. Because he remembered Janine, whose last name was Bonner, how she had lied to him about the orange dinghy that Poole had seen that day on the veranda of the fishing shack, Bao Do dead on the floor inside. He remembered how the woman had flustered with her coke anxiety, flushed in the face, her hands sweating on the counter while she counted out the change. So Poole punched in the name of his hunch, because he remembered the *putt-putt* sound right after the explosion and because he couldn't forget hearing that sound on the beach when he'd seen the orange dinghy rolling over the swell line, Janine with her hand trailing the water, blond hair in the breeze.

Poole sat in front of the screen while his information tracked itself down, coming back *Jack Eugene Bonner,* this quirky guy with arrests for this and that all over Texas. It surprised Poole that the guy had done some hard time in Atlanta for bank robbery, then another stretch in El Reno for lifting a crate of M16's from Fort Sill. This grew on Poole as it came back green on the black background. He could imagine Jack Bonner. An over-forty tattoo freak, wiry sociopath gleam in the eye, sandy hair and pale skin, bad temper, little popping muscles from pumping some iron. But here he had a wife named Janine who did coke in the afternoon down on the Port Arthur marina, the gal who had lied to Poole. Poole thought all this was a perfect fit. And he drove home with tunes in his head that went *putt-putt-putt,* whatever that meant.

18

Both D.J. and Poole were bone-tired, sitting in the basement of the Port Arthur Federal Building in downtown
Beaumont, in a hushed cubicle with a ventilator whisking
air in and out, Donald using a clean cloth to wipe down a
piece. They had been talking and drinking coffee while five
or six pinstripes came and went, swapping stories about
junior college basketball and jazz weekends in Denton, the
liar games that commenced when you were part of the big
coke wars, D.J. shaving off a running commentary of fuck-
ups and big deals, then going on to tell Poole about his kids,
Poole having nothing like that to share, just shooting the
shit about his dreams. Donald put away the piece, sliding it
in a desk drawer, Poole looking at him do it, not wanting to
ask about the scary black weapon.

"That was a Glock," Donald said, turning around with
a hefty smile.

"It was that plain?"

"You telegraphed it, my man." Another pinstripe went into a back room. Poole could hear the hum of a fax machine. "That piece is an Austrian-made destroyer. Top of the line, made of fucking plastic, if you can believe that. Damn thing weighs less than two pounds, can't jam, fires seventeen rounds in under five seconds. You can spray death around like paint if you want. You can sit back and squeeze, too, aim at something you'd like to hit instead of tear the shit out of everything. Take your choice." Donald sipped some coffee, grimaced. "What will they think of next?"

Poole said he didn't know. He said he thought the useful inventions were things like salad sprayers, little half-pint fishing rods that telescoped to about six inches, peanut butter with marshmallow streaks in it. Donald nodded, laughed, saying the one he liked was the electric wire you stick inside an egg, cook the thing in two seconds. It brought to mind other uses.

Poole suggested the Drug Czar requisition five thousand Glocks and hand them out like popcorn to the DEA, FBI, police forces in Los Angeles, New York, Miami, Detroit, and Houston, start studding the horizon with Glock bursts, hit the enemy with free fire zones, curfews, body counts, refugee camps. Real war, that's what it would be, civilians lining up outside Oklahoma City on the trek north away from the war zones, daylight dark with blue smoke. Yeah, Drug War I, DEA firing Austrian Glocks at Jamaicans who fired back with Israeli Uzis, Japs about forty stories up in the L.A. smog formulating new laundry detergent.

What happened that Saturday night was that the FBI had gone over the shrimper, put pieces of it in the Blazer, took Jerry back to the hospital, and interviewed Tran and Bhin. These guys were a cool, efficient bore. Donald told Poole that both women had cried for hours before they were able to talk.

The explosive had been a satchel charge, not very complicated, but good. Donovan had been shot under the chin
and behind the ear with a .22 long rifle, the charge blown
and the body burned a little, two fingers mutilated on the
right hand. Poole had gotten to D.J.'s office pretty late in
the briefing and the two of them had sat around sorting
through details of the blow, reading reports, thinking out
loud what they were going to do, lapsing into silence and
then getting silly when Donald got out the Glock. The special problem for Poole was Bao Do and how he fit into the
puzzle. About their fifth cup of coffee, after Poole had been
told about Bhin, he told D.J. about Jack Bonner, the bank
robber and M16 specialist who'd done bad time, a guy who
had a wife named Janine who snorted coke on the marina
pier.

Poole had just finished telling D.J. about Jack when he
became very tired, as if the metal hush of the room was suf-
focating him and the fluorescence was blinding him, all of it
especially grim because he'd just begun in the past week to
sense something stirring to life inside himself. Poole said
the name again, Jack Bonner, another stray piece of puzzle,
and D.J. humped forward and balanced on his elbows as
Poole thought about Adrienne Deveraux, D.J. about his
kids, both men managing their weariness as best they could.
D.J. ordered a record check on Jack Bonner and ten minutes later, the intercom buzzed and a pinstripe brought in a
manila envelope. D.J. tore it open before he sat down, and
then looked over the contents in about two minutes. Poole
was waiting, wanting to see where D.J. might go with his
Jack Bonner thing. He didn't know himself—that was the
trick of it.

"We need to make some assumptions," D.J. said, sitting
down again. Poole could hear the fax needling the air with a
nonelectric hum.

"Assume away," Poole said.

"You came down here because you thought Jerry

Donovan had killed Bao Do, some family anger thing. You found the dope on the shrimper, and that must have made you think Jerry had killed Bao Do because the old fisherman had found it, wanted to put a stop to it."

"That sums it up."

"Then you find Everett Teagarden waiting for the sunrise in his lawn chair."

"Actually, I think I said water-skiers."

"Same thing," D.J. said. "But hey, if you figure Jerry for the killer, then you have to figure that somebody told him that Bao Do was heading to Beaumont, going to blow the whistle on the pot operation."

"That's what I thought."

"Who could have told him?"

"Maybe Bhin."

"Well, if Jerry found out, it had to be from Tran or Bhin. I think that seems like a pretty good bet."

"That's how I made it."

"Well, I agree."

"Have you finished with Tran and Bhin?" Poole asked, gesturing upstairs, where he knew a bevy of pinstripes was hacking away at the two girls.

"All day long," D.J. said. D.J. gasped as though he was exhausted, as though he wanted to go home and sleep for two weeks. He leaned back and put his feet on the desk. Poole was having a hard time concentrating himself. He was that tired and having daydreams about Adrienne Deveraux, part of him returning to the cabin on the beach. They weren't sexual, these dreams, just good wish fulfillment, Poole fishing in the stringy sunshine while she was inside cooking rice and red beans, some rhubarb. And Poole was coming inside, on the porch, putting his hands on her skin again, that good brown skin, her hard belly.

"I hope they went easy on Tran," Poole said. "I don't know about Bhin, but maybe she's okay, too."

"I told them to ease up. Who knows about a suit?" The

fax stopped, but D.J. didn't move. "There is a U.S. attorney in the office with two FBI types. You know them and you know how they smell a drug bust and all the headlines and then elective office. It's worse than pussy for them. They go completely apeshit." He flicked a glance at the fax room. "Hey, I'm not in control."

Donald began to sift through the contents of the manila envelope, what looked to Poole like an eight-by-ten, some computer printouts. Poole was thinking about Tran, a nice-looking kid with a Catholic schoolgirl face, good clear skin, frail to be out on the edge of a continent, only now she was upstairs in a gray room with FBI types who knew all the tricks. Poole wanted to go upstairs and liberate the scene from its tight fascist implication, be the Lone Ranger for Tran, for Bhin, too, unshackle them and ride into the sunset on his palomino.

Donald looked up, catching Poole in his reverie, and told him he could read the records if he wanted, which Poole didn't need to read. He had seen the future on a green screen that had read out *Jack Eugene Bonner.*

"Let me run this past you," D.J. said. "If you think Jerry whacked Bao Do, you must think he popped Everett, too."

"I was thinking it. Seems like Everett might have been his partner in the reefer deal. Jerry learns how to run the shrimper and he doesn't need Everett anymore. He runs up to the old bubba's house and puts twenty cents' worth of lead behind his neck. Doubles his profit, that simple."

"Yeah, well, that doesn't explain who whacked Jerry, or why. Does it?"

"Back to square one," Poole muttered. "Look, suppose you tell me what Bhin told the suits upstairs. You trust me on that news?"

"Oh shit yes, Tom," Donald said. "It took a while. She said she knew Jerry was using the shrimper to run dope up the inlet. She knew he ran up to Clam Lake. She claims she never went with him. She says she doesn't know who the buyer was, how it was transshipped. I sat in upstairs for the first act and they treated her rough—you know the kind of scam, whipping out documents like they meant something while Bhin sits there in a bare room with guys coming and going and the most obvious two-way mirror you've ever seen staring at her. They had Tran down the hall in another room. Bhin says she couldn't control Jerry, not even about her father's shrimp boat. She was afraid of him. Maybe it's true. Who knows? The matron says she's got blue bruises on her arms, these scars on her back. She's been cuffed around pretty good. And you know these punks like Jerry—they save their good stuff for women."

"She was a victim."

"If you're asking me are they going after Bhin, the answer is, I'm not sure. If Jerry made some money and she has it squirreled away, they want it. They'd like to know how he got the reefer, where the boat came inshore to off-load it, things like that. She says she doesn't know. Right now, they're deciding if she's playing little girl from Vietnam or if she's for real. Between you and me, I think she's for real. If they find any money at the house, then she's dead meat. She's got a good chance, though." D.J. smiled, nodded. "Hey, she's not very good headlines."

"Does she think Jerry killed her father?"

The phone rang and Donald picked it up and talked for ten minutes while Poole poured himself some coffee. He was sitting in the chill of the ventilation system and the recirculated air was making him giddy. After that night in the swamp, it took a man-made atmosphere to make him sick. Donald put down the phone. "Hey, she swears Jerry didn't kill her father."

"Does she have a story?"

"Claims they were drinking together in Port Arthur."

"I heard it already." Poole tried his coffee. "Hey, I believe her."

"So do I. Man, I don't think she'd cover for that mean dead bastard right now if he killed her father. No way."

Donald had been sitting with the edge of the chair balanced against the wall, levered there, like he might topple over any second. Looking at him, Poole wondered if he looked that ragged, bags under his eyes, a yellow cast to his skin. Poole felt he was at a dead end with the old man for now and he was depressed. It was simple: Bhin had no reason to cover for Jerry, so that was out. Poole slumped forward over the desk, thinking that he probably looked a whole lot worse than D.J. The guy didn't drink schnapps and chase it with Lone Star, watch TV all night. D.J. could still go down court and jump-hook a two-pointer, pull down some rebounds.

"That guy who just called," Donald said, "told me they were cutting the girls free. FBI is out looking for Danny Huan now, just to have a chat."

"Danny Huan," Poole repeated dumbly. "What do they think?"

"Maybe he has some of the dope money. They want to tie up the loose ends. Nothing special." Donald was stretching now, tipping forward, his arms behind his neck. "You want to say anything to the girls, they're coming out pretty soon. I don't know what you want to do."

Poole didn't know what he wanted to do, either. He thought maybe he should go over to the house and offer his condolences. Would it be cool to stand around and tell them he'd served in Vietnam, that he didn't kill anybody? On a human scale, it sounded just like his scene with the woman in the hooch.

"Did they get anything from Tran?"

"You heard it the first time. Doesn't know who killed her father. Knows it wasn't suicide. Doesn't know who killed Everett Teagarden. Has no reason to think it's related, anyway. She said she didn't know Jerry was dealing. If he made his runs, he could do it in two hours. How would she know? I think the pinstripes believe her." There was a cool run on the fax again, a strip of sound that sliced the room. "They'll let them go, follow them for a week. Then they'll be onto something else."

Poole considered bringing Adrienne Deveraux into the tableau for D.J., thinking it might make it easier on Tran if she had an official witness friend. Something stopped him, not something to do with trust, because he knew Tran was going through the wringer, anyway. It had more to do with Poole's new skin, how he didn't want to use people anymore, didn't want to *investigate* them. He wanted to deal with people without stripping them down to electrons on a screen. Just then, D.J. said again that he thought Poole was back to square one with the old fisherman. Maybe the old guy did kill himself. Donald said it was something to think about.

Poole could hear Donald talking and some people outside in the hall, their voices indistinct, and then he imagined again the scene at the fishing shack that night he had turned around on the Port Arthur highway and had gone down to the beach instead of going home, brown sunshine in the shack when he got there, stripes of it on the floor from the jalousie windows. He was back with Daddy John, who was sitting in a cane chair wiping his glasses, Poole leaning on the doorjamb in the heat. There was something wrong with the picture, though, not just because it was so *uncultural,* but something else more palpable.

Poole followed Donald down the hall. They were in a pan of light that was gray and diffuse.

"Your theories are dropping like flies," D.J. said while they stood apart waiting for an elevator. "The boys upstairs have Jerry in a Port Arthur bar on Saturday, drunk as hell. Bhin confirms it."

Poole closed his eyes. He could hear the elevator sinking down through its cube. Donald asked Poole if he'd like to go out and get some oysters, treat themselves nice.

They rode up and went outside, where exhaust fumes were sitting down on the city. There was a yellow shawl on the buildings, the air so syrupy, Poole could barely inhale. Poole could see smoke from a cottonseed plant streaming in a thin line to the east, a layer above the pines, then above that a glazed sky going bronze. Out of the corner of his eye, Poole saw Bhin and Tran coming out of the post office doors down about forty yards, both of them standing on the concrete landing with their arms around each other, like sisters walking home from school, only there was a pin-stripe behind them wearing sunglasses, about six five in cowboy boots. The girls looked so small, it nearly broke Poole's heart. A beat-up yellow Charger was parked at the curb, a traffic ticket on the driver's side window and the pinstripe was lecturing the girls. Poole thought about going over and saying something, but he couldn't think of what he might say, so he decided he'd do it later, when things had calmed down. He watched as the girls went down the stairs and got into the yellow Charger. It wasn't right, how small the girls were and the big push sound of the Charger engine turning over. Poole followed D.J. to his generic Buick and they went to a clam bar near the river.

It was cooler in the bar, with overhead fans clacking around, making shadows. They were sitting on chrome stools around a Formica bar, half-moon shape, an ice cooler of seafood at one end. Poole studied a hand-written menu while the bartender smoked a cigarette. He ordered a draft beer and a dozen oysters. D.J. had mussels and fried clams and they ate some peanuts to pass time. D.J. was holding the manila envelope he'd brought with him from the post office. Poole salted his beer, dropped in a fresh lime.

"Another way it plays," D.J. said, "is that Bhin is Jerry's partner for real. She kills Teagarden. Gives her husband an alibi."

"I don't think so, D.J.," Poole said.

"Yeah, what the fuck."

The bartender served them paper plates of clams and mussels and fresh oysters, horseradish and hot sauce. D.J. sucked a mussel with hot sauce, then another. They were all alone in the bar, except for the bartender. Poole could smell the ocean about two miles away, the salt and tar smell, and the warm sand, too. The sun was being filtered through the glass all around them.

"I'll tell you what I think," Donald said, finishing a mussel and some tea. "Jerry was moving dope through someone else's territory. Simple as that. It's a helluva good idea to run the dope inland, and then all the way to Houston on the Intracoastal. But somebody thought of it before Donovan did. That's why whoever killed Jerry didn't bother with the reefer. They wanted to kill the competition, sink the old tub of a boat. They probably thought it would burn and then sink, all the dope would flush out. It just happened that we were there, found the stuff. It's an accident the hull was so old and waterlogged that it didn't burn quick enough. I'd say the guy who killed Jerry is running dope up through the estuary to the Intracoastal. When he found out Jerry was doing the same thing, he killed him."

Donald stopped for another mussel. Poole put an oyster on a cracker and then felt a breeze drift through the open door. Evening was coming off the ocean like a feather. Donald said he was sorry—he knew this idea didn't leave Bao Do anywhere but dead. Poole knew it, it was obvious. He drank some of his salty beer and ate the oyster. The clam bar was up on a truck spur near some produce warehouses. A few refrigerator trucks rolled by on the brick street, pick-ups with guys getting off work, not much else. The river was behind the bar about two blocks and Poole could see a dark crevice of water that looked oily, a few pelicans bumping on the wind. It was making him melancholy, trucks pounding along the brick street, a soft haze in the air.

D.J. wiped his mouth with a paper napkin and pushed over the manila envelope. Poole opened it and saw Jack Bonner smiling at him from an eight-by-ten, a crazier-than-shit stare that was uglier than Poole thought it would be. Old Jack Eugene, Poole thought, you crazy asshole son of a bitch. A white-noise stare seemed to break off inside Jack's head, two planks of brown in the center, as if the eyes themselves were on stalks. Jack had gray-blond hair greased back from his forehead and a pale complexion dotted by childhood acne, jaw and cheekbones like a Cajun, his whole face ferret-thin, but a tough big neck, too. Jack looked as if he'd been mauled once or twice, like he'd been shoved through a plate-glass window.

The camera had caught a glint from Jack's bald spot. Poole placed him in an orange dinghy. What else was there to do?

D.J. stabbed a clam. "He's a bub, ain't he?" he asked. The light had changed. Poole was getting a flutter of mauve in the haze, something flattening out through the streets.

"He sure is a bub," Poole said. Poole riffled through the computer records.

"Like they say, Tom," D.J. said, motioning the barkeep for more tea. "If you can't do the time, don't do the crime."

"He can do the time," Poole said. "He also owns an orange dinghy that goes *putt-putt* in the night."

"*Putt-putt-putt,*" D.J. said, a grin on his face, wiping some hot sauce with his napkin.

Poole dropped the manila folder. He drank some beer and lime. "I think this bub Jack Eugene killed Jerry Donovan."

"It's worth looking into." D.J. pushed back his paper plate. "If Jack Eugene is running drugs up the estuary to the Intracoastal, then Jerry was screwing up his scene. Jamaican reefer is shit compared with the stuff they have in white powder. Cocaine does weird things, you know?" D.J. leaned over the stool and refilled his tea glass from a pitcher behind the bar. "This Jack Eugene looks strange to begin with, and if you add coke, there's no telling how strange he might become. He ain't that pretty."

The bartender had gone outside and was standing beside the curb watching evening drop. "You should see Jack's wife," Poole said.

"You mean Janine?" D.J. said he'd like to see a picture of the lucky woman who had it so much on the ball that she'd walk down the aisle with Jack. "Can we use her?" D.J. said.

"Can we use her?" Poole repeated. Poole was thinking that maybe they could handle her some, scare her, give her a reason to snitch on Jack. Sometimes that worked, but only if you had a wedge you could drive between the happy couple, like seven or eight years in jail. Poole bit his lip and drank some beer. Here he was talking about using people again. Maybe this would be the last time, ever. That would be something, wouldn't it?

"Shit, man," D.J. said. "I think Janine would be more crazy scared of bubba Jack than she'd be scared of the DEA. What do you say?"

Poole looked out the open door at the barkeep, who was having a smoke. Poole said he thought D.J. was right, that she wouldn't scare so easily, not with Jack Eugene in her rearview mirror. Besides, Jack would have someone behind him, someone behind that someone. Old Jack didn't have the brains to run coke all by himself, and he didn't have the connections and wasn't that good. Poole slid down a last oyster and turned around on his chrome stool. He could hear some gulls fussing over the river canal. D.J. was leaning against the bar, elbows on the counter, looking out the door at the empty street.

"You didn't read that file folder too close," D.J. said. He glanced at Poole, who was staring at the case of fish. His knees felt weak, like he might fall off his stool and go to sleep.

"What do you mean?" Poole asked. The colors had gotten behind Poole's eyes, baked gray, white, some sallow orange where the sun had streaked dirty glass.

"Jack didn't kill your fisherman. He didn't kill Jerry, either." Poole felt his head pound, turned and looked at D.J., who was far away now, down a tunnel of untuned distance. "Jack got a DUI in Houston six months ago. He's doing his weekends in lockup down in the county jail. Goes in at six and comes out at six Sunday night. That puts him in jail when the old fisherman was killed. It puts him in jail when our boy Jerry lost his life. Whoever pushed those two over, it wasn't Jack Eugene." D.J. put a toothpick in his mouth, ducked down, frowned at Poole.

Poole felt the breath go out of him. Something sank away and it was a few minutes before he could think again. The bartender had come inside and was washing dishes. All the pieces of Poole's puzzle were fading out.

"Hey, I'm sorry, man," D.J. said. "I know Jack Eugene looked good for it."

Poole managed a weak smile. "What are you going to do, D.J.?" he asked. He didn't want to be cut out. That was all he knew.

"I follow Jack, whoever, up the estuary. See where he goes. See whom he meets, who meets him. Same scenario, only I bust the son of a bitch if I can."

Donald opened a napkin and moistened his fingers, rubbed the paper across his mouth. He grabbed the check and smiled at Poole. Poole's back was hurting again. Maybe he had sat too long over the counter. Poole started to say something, but before he could, D.J. said, "Hey, I know this stops you cold with your fisherman. Hey, I know that." He tapped the check on the counter. "I don't know what else to do but land on whoever is running that putt-putt up the estuary and to the Intracoastal. If it happens to be Jack Eugene, then I land hard on his head. But, hey, I give you my word, if he knows anything about the old man, I'll give you the pitch. You hear it first, okay?"

"No problem," said Poole. Poole was facing Donald, their knees almost touching. "Do something for me, huh? I mean it, D.J. I want to go along with you. I want to go along up the estuary."

"Oh man, why you want to do that?"

"I mean it, D.J.," Poole said. "I want to go along. I made a promise to myself. After Bao Do, there are no more corpses for me. No more cowboys and Indians. This is my last act."

"Oh man," D.J. said. "You leaving the force?"

"Two weeks, maybe three. Whatever it takes to find out who killed the Vietnamese. Then I'm out."

"Shit, I know how you feel." Donald was really seeing Poole now, you could tell, the way his eyes had come to rest on Poole's chest, stayed there. "But how does it do you any good? We don't know where Jack Eugene is. We don't have a decent line on his thing. Just that putt-putt shit, so I have to stay out by the marina, catch him when he comes by in his orange dinghy. I don't know how long it will take. Also, my man, he'll go up the estuary at night, if it is him, or whoever, and the dude will be absolutely dangerous. Hey, Jerry got popped in a rude way, you know? I'm planning on taking the bass boat, travel light and smooth, see what I can see. So how are you going to help Boa Do on a complex deal like this?" Donald looked at the empty street, sky heat-locked, starched out and blank. "Besides, what do I tell Daddy John, the Drug Czar, too, when you get your ass shot. What do I tell your momma?" D.J. tried to smile.

"Send my momma white lilies. Fuck Daddy John."

"Yeah, well I wouldn't mind that last part."

"No, I mean it," Poole pleaded. He tried to sit straight, despite his back. Poole was aware of the necessities, how D.J. had a DEA job to do. It was Donald's game now and

Poole wasn't really a player and no agent wanted a non-player getting hurt. Poole was trying to conjure some crazy way to explain it to D.J. without taking him all the way back to the hooch, describe for the guy his new skin and how it had grown overnight, the years he'd spent drinking schnapps and watching TV while thinking about Lisa Marie, how it had all dovetailed to an emotional silence that had snarled Poole's whole character.

"I don't know, Tom," D.J. said.

Poole was aware he had said something, but the words were out of his mouth, free. "I know a cabin," he'd said. The words had winged away unsupported by thought, Poole just saying it. "About two hundred yards south of the Port Arthur marina. You can sit on the porch all day and all night and watch the pier, the jetty. You can see everything, man. We just sit on the screened porch and watch for the orange dinghy. When it goes by, we just get on our pony and ride."

Donald was drinking his tea, sucking ice cubes. The bartender finished washing dishes.

"All right, Tom," D.J. said. "Hey, it's not the cabin. That's nice. It's more personal with us."

Donald drove them around south Beaumont until they found a Dairy Queen. Poole sat under some dusty oleanders, eating a cone, white blossoms dropping in the heat. He and D.J. decided that it would be the two of them in the cabin, D.J. would get a federal search warrant, the FBI would follow Janine around, see what she was up to. If they could get a line on Jack Eugene, it would give them some advance warning, but it would be up to D.J. and Poole to get the job done. If they got in trouble, there wouldn't be much help way out there in the swamp. Poole reflected on what it would be like out there, worse than following Jerry in the shrimper, a darker night, and Jack Eugene, if it was him, a lot rougher case, a sociopath sitting on a load of coke.

Poole felt his heart running like a ticker tape, as if someone was hammering nails. He knew he had taken a chance offering the cabin like this without calling Adrienne Deveraux. Then he listed the things he needed to do. He needed to see Tran and Bhin, tell them he was sorry, that he was still on the case and wouldn't let their father slide away. He needed to get some supplies for the cabin. He needed to call Adrienne Deveraux, and he needed to get some rest. When he thought some more, sitting under the oleanders in the canted sunlight, he knew he wasn't frightened of Jack Eugene or anything like that. He was frightened only because he was quitting his job and leaving Beaumont and Port Arthur behind. It was giving him fits, an anxiety he couldn't position on the screen.

D.J. circled around and dropped Poole off at his Caprice. Poole drove over to the river to be alone and collect himself. He sat in his car and tried to think who might have killed the fisherman, how he could get a fix on the position of the case. It took about an hour for his anxiety to come away from itself, and then he went home and took a shower and sat listening to classical music on Public Radio. The phone rang later; it was D.J. calling to tell him that the FBI had searched the yellow Charger and found a rusted .22 Colt. They had found it in the trunk, under a bulk of scrap and old tires. There were no prints and the gun was so fucked up, it wouldn't fire. D.J. said he knew Poole would be interested.

It didn't get Poole far, but at least he knew he was right about the gun. The fisherman hadn't used it to kill himself. Somebody had come in and blown him away and left a different gun. Poole decided if he could get through the next few nights, he might be able to prove who'd done that.

19

Poole was thinking about his father when he saw the dinghy. He had been absentmindedly shuffling a deck of cards while D.J. crushed some ice for the cooler in the other room. He was hoping to get himself some rest later on the box springs in back. Poole had put a glass of tea on his forehead, letting a trickle of water run down his skin while he pictured his father in his mind. Then he saw the dinghy.

The memory was an inexplicable change of mood for Poole, who had been wired for three days. They had been inside the cabin all that time, both of them as taut as piano wire, taking turns watching the marina and the swell line with binoculars, sitting up late some nights playing gin rummy and drinking tea, taking walks down the beach when they needed some exercise, beachcombing and talking about life and Jack Eugene. They were trying to stay alert and catch a glimpse of the orange dinghy, although their nerves were shot and they hadn't slept well in the heat and the steady wind that made the air electric.

At that point, shuffling cards, D.J. in the side room crushing ice, Poole's mood clicked to something else, and in his mind's eye he saw his father coming home after work, tired and dirty, sitting down on the sawhorse in the side yard of their Port Arthur house, his face contaminated with a frown of despair, leather brown from the sun.

Putting down the cards, touching them to the table, Poole remembered his father's face exactly while he massaged his forehead with cold water, getting a lock on an ancient scene, how his father had wistfully pulled a bottle of whiskey to his mouth, a glove-sized half-pint of off-brand bourbon, how the fading light had struck the glass and made a few stars in it, his father drinking without pleasure and the bottle falling back into the shade. Poole had been terribly frightened by the event, its simplicity, its stark reality, the smell of the whiskey. Later, at his father's funeral, he had suddenly remembered the scene and it had gained power over him in a sudden mysterious rush and he found himself associating his father's face with other scenes in his own life, as if his father's pain had overflowed into his own. These twin remembrances embraced Poole and he forgot to feel the cards and the icy glass on his forehead. He placed a hand on the screen for balance and saw the dinghy out on the swell line. Bare green water, silky pullulating glare, an orange wrinkle.

He sat there with the tea draining down his forehead, along the bridge of his nose, banging his head on the screen in absolute surprise. He yelled for D.J. to get his ass out on the porch right now.

The afternoon had taken on a bruised look that was very threatening, and now the sun had gone behind the mangroves in the west and was washing up over the ocean until everything had a crushed look, the color of the waves deeply filtered by brown, the sky utterly suffused except for some gray clouds over Mexico.

Poole heard D.J. moving through the cabin. He focused his binoculars on the water, trying to discern another flash of orange out beyond the swell line where the waves were curling beneath the surface, flattened into a gray-blue expanse with only a few gulls winging up in the breeze, suspended there, and some pelicans farther out, flying north to the jetty, one thin dark line. There was a silence, and then Poole squinted and he could see the orange shape of a hull submerged slightly by the swells, popping back again in deep relief, but there. He got up and went outside on the steps with the binoculars and now he was able to see over the waves, two figures in the dinghy. Below the breeze, he could hear a thin *putt-putt,* maybe a fifty-horse Mariner.

D.J. edged out and stood behind him. Poole could sense him there, breathing, while Poole studied the progress of the dinghy, just to make absolutely certain and get a clear fix, locking in his radar while his mood changed to wired aggression again. Some lights blinked on the platform rigs in the Gulf and a few stars sprinkled the horizon. The marina and the jetty were lapsing to fuzzy gray and just then Poole felt his hands quake. He concentrated and then he finally calmed until the shape and size of the man in the dinghy appeared. The guy was wearing a black T-shirt and a ball cap. There was a woman with long blond hair and skinny arms in the front of the boat. She was trailing one hand in the water as they skimmed along. The orange hull caught some sunlight and flashed.

The images were mixing for Poole, gathering on the binocular lenses in swarms. Poole could see Bao Do on the floor of the fishing shack. He could see the hooch through an awful brown seethe, and Janine Bonner chewing her fingernails while boom-box music played in the marina store. He could see Jerry Donovan getting out of the yellow Charger, staggering drunk. Poole felt D.J. press past him, saying something to charge Poole up, then D.J. saying, "No shit, there he is" as he stood just beside Poole with his binoculars.

Back at the post office in the cool basement office of the DEA, when he had shot the shit all afternoon with D.J., Poole had started to get himself to the psychological point where he thought he could go see Tran and Danny Huan. He had driven down to the river and had gone home and showered and stood for a long time before the sliding glass door looking down at the parking lot and the Wal-Mart. Just then, Poole knew he needed to see Tran, that what he had to tell her was important. Then he would call Adrienne Deveraux and ask for the key to the cabin, lay it on the line. He'd tell her the absolute truth.

So that night, he drove back to the marina. Coming over the oil roads, he had a clear view of the stucco house with its lights flooded through to the ocean backdrop, like every bulb in the place was glowing, keeping away all the ghosts. Tran answered Poole's first knock. She was just as pretty as Poole remembered her, but overwhelmed, her eyes large and hollow and red-rimmed, a Catholic schoolgirl freshness shredded by grief. Poole thought he saw an expression on her face that said, Hey, you can't come in here, especially now, and Poole saw Bhin across the room in the kitchen nook, all the mascara drained down her cheeks, fan blowing across the floor, grains of sand in the air. He was tuned now to the smell of citronella and tobacco smoke and the faint sweet marijuana odor, too, which he rediscovered while Tran held him up at the door, standing there and saying nothing until she whispered she had nothing against Poole, that she knew he was trying to help. Adrienne Deveraux had told her as much.

Poole had edged himself inside the house. Danny Huan was looking at him the way a cat might watch a robin, locked in but not too hopeful. Danny didn't move a muscle, sitting on a kitchen chair, maybe expecting Poole to arrest him. The house had a feel to it, as if every second something was in the balance, tick-tick-tick, an existential clock was running and you could hear it inside the walls. Poole nodded at Danny, tried to make contact, but the guy just sat there without shifting gears, not a flicker. Some guys got over that stage real quick, became hangdogs you could whack all you wanted, hit them with a newspaper and they shit outside, curl up so you can whack them again. But Danny was giving Poole the cat look, features frozen shut.

Tran offered Poole some hot tea. He could smell pork and rice from the kitchen, and when he walked to the nook and put a hand on Bhin's shoulder, Tran poured him some. He was soaked through with sweat and the hot tea made it worse, but he drank it anyway as a gesture to the family, laying out how he felt about the death of the fisherman, Jerry, too, saying he wasn't there to hassle anybody, not Danny, that he just wanted to make contact. He thought Danny relaxed some, and he let them have it, how he thought he could prove who had killed Bao Do, but it would take some time.

He had been in the house for fifteen minutes when he told Tran he was quitting the Sheriff's Department, but not until he busted the guy who killed her father, Jerry, too. He told her he would come back and say good-bye on his way out of town, because he was going somewhere away from here. He didn't know where, but he was finished being a cop. Poole felt faint after the speech, all those black eyes watching him with a flickering sense of belief. He took in all the attitudes: Danny Huan taut inside his awareness; Bhin starting to cry, having a hard time relating right now; Tran relieving her shyness by staring out the picture windows that looked over the ocean. Poole could see her biting her lip in the window's reflection and he thought about putting his hand on her shoulder, but he had to admit he didn't know the rules, what was allowed in this society, so he backed away across the room.

Poole left things that way. He drove back to Port Arthur and called Adrienne Deveraux from a sheriff's substation where he could get ammunition without questions. He told her the absolute truth, just as he had promised himself he would, and she told him to get the key from a real estate broker in Beaumont, that she understood the problem exactly. She told him to be careful. He mattered. Call her when it was done.

That was then. Now, Poole saw D.J. come through the screen and put his binoculars around his neck on a leather strap. He was following the dinghy as it bounced over the ocean. They both could see a lean-muscled male sitting in back, Poole fascinated by how sharply he was coming through in the gray light, blue background. Poole could see Janine, too, smoking a cigarette, trailing her hand in the water. Poole left D.J. on the porch and went around the cabin and locked the side door from outside and shut all the hurricane windows. Something made him remember the shudder that had passed through Adrienne Deveraux when he told her he thought he knew who had killed Bao Do, a quick intake of breath.

Poole went about collecting his gear, some water jugs, a canvas bag with the shotgun, his Smith & Wesson, a Glock. He met D.J. on the beach and they hustled down the oil road toward the marina, on the run, going up the hills, Poole lagging behind D.J., who was in shape, until they had gone up over the dunes above the marina, where D.J. had left the bass boat on a trailer, with an FBI guy keeping watch from a campsite, pretending to be a fisherman on vacation. They backed the Blazer down the hard-packed beach until they had the trailer in the water. The FBI guy was helping them stow their gear. Right then, they were about fifteen minutes behind the dinghy and they wanted to get going, head south for the inlet while circling out of sight beyond the line the dinghy was taking. It was risky, because they didn't want to get spotted, and they didn't want to lose Jack Eugene in the mangrove. If they did that, they'd have a hard time picking him up later when it got dark.

They walked about two feet out into the surf and launched the boat with the help of the agent. All their gear, including food and water, was in plastic bags, two walkie-talkies, candy bars, ammunition, two infrared lenses for night-vision tracking, a first-aid kit, and some flares. There wouldn't be any helicopters helping them out, no TAC squads busting in to save their asses, so if they got down to the flares, it would be a way to mark the spot where they died. Simple as that. In the mangrove, they would be alone with Jack Eugene.

D.J. kicked over the Evinrude while Poole clambered over the side. He was wearing jeans and a black cut-off sweatshirt, tennis shoes, making him invisible in the dark. D.J. sure as hell would be. D.J. pulled the boat through the low surf, backing out to keep the surf down, going out about two hundred yards until they headed south at full throttle, cutting through the chop while Poole organized gear in the back. It was getting dark and Port Arthur was sifting an orange bulb up into the sky, a fuzz on the horizon in the northeast, the lights on the platforms glowing on, like ionized webs. As he watched the lights on the water and in the dunes where the shacks were, spray was cooling him down. He could see the breeze clicking in the palms and palmettos, and he had a clear view of a cloud bank over Mexico, boils of purple at twenty thousand feet. D.J. had throttled up and they were bumping hard over the water now, the spray boiling over the bow in a solid mist, thwacks on the hull, as if somebody was pounding it with a trash can lid. Poole watched Adrienne Deveraux's cabin go by as they went south, then Tran's house on the promontory.

Poole crawled up front and sat beside D.J. They had their guns in canvas and plastic on a narrow shelf under the wheel, their maps and flashlights and some flares, walkie-talkies and batteries in tarp back by the engine, infrared viewers on thongs around their necks, where they could get to them fast. Jesus, it was beautiful out here, Poole thought, going under a cliff where the estuary cut inland. The water was gleaming silver where fresh met salt, a ribbon all the way up to Walker Lake, about fifteen miles. In his days at the cabin, Poole had dreamed every possible scenario, how things might be up the inlet in the swamp, fiddling with the maps while the mosquitoes buzzed against the screen. Together, he and D.J. tried to decide how they would react if someone got shot, laughing nervously. It was bad luck to dwell on it, but you had to be prepared.

D.J. headed them inland, hitting rough water as Poole banged his sore knee on the instrument panel. Considering the circumstances, D.J. looked calm, almost serene, leaning against the wheel with the palms of his hands, dressed in navy blue trousers and a blue work shirt.

D.J. throttled back when they hit the estuary and the boat sank down, and Poole was amazed at the silence. You could hear water hitting sand and way in the mangrove you could hear a fifty-horse Mariner modulating through tunnels of thicket, maybe a mile ahead. They had made up their fifteen minutes now, and Poole knew they would catch Jack Eugene pretty soon at this rate. D.J. raised some speed and ran up-throttle for a while until they reached a bank of stunted pines on the far shore, running cleanly though it to the ragged edges of mangrove and mud flat, moving out into open water, then back again where the shore showed gum and pine trees, some willows. Poole looked back and caught a last glimpse of Bao Do's house, two hundred yards away in a blue-glazed sundown, then it was gone for good.

Poole wiped down his lens and tried it on the swamp ahead. D.J. looked down at him and smiled, and Poole could see a narrow black edge of mangrove raised slightly from the surface of itself, like an artifact appearing in a dig, and then he thought he could see a dim outline of the dinghy hugging the mangrove about three hundred yards ahead. Poole stood so he could see more clearly and then he tapped D.J. on the shoulder. It was Jack Eugene all right, and he told D.J. to change to the trolling motor. They were coming to twists and turns as the estuary corkscrewed. Now they had to keep the Mariner within earshot. It would be nice if Jack Eugene was going straight north to the Intracoastal through Walker Lake, an L-shaped oxbow that was part bayou and part swamp, full of vacation houses on the far side, a narrow canal leading to the Intracoastal. Between here and there, there were lots of offshoots where Jack could disappear into mangrove, but that wouldn't make much sense, because there really wasn't anywhere to go. Maybe portage the coke two or three miles to a road, but that seemed a lot of trouble. The whole point was to take it all the way up the inlet. That way, you didn't have to use roads, carry anything heavy overland. D.J. and Poole just assumed Jack was going up to Walker Lake to meet somebody, the buyer. In this dark, they'd try to be right behind him when he made contact.

All they did was run straight on for thirty minutes, about two hundred yards behind the dinghy, most of the time Poole able to see it in his scope, losing it for a minute, then finding it again, keeping the Mariner locked in because he could hear it running slow. Poole guessed they'd come four or five miles through mangrove, wide channel, but getting narrower, tunnels shooting off to the side through oak stands, some banked levees. The air was humid and Poole could barely breathe. The mosquitoes were thick, so much so that every few minutes Poole had to stand up just to catch a rest from the bugs. The smell was ferric and very dense, almost surreal, with frogs screaming under the thin drone of the electric trolling motor.

D.J. punched Poole on the arm. They were gliding past the cement irrigation canal where they had followed Jerry

Donovan, which meant they were six miles from the ocean. Poole remembered the spot on the charts they'd studied in the cabin. Jack Eugene would have to go all the way to Walker Lake now, because there weren't any landings until then, just flat swamp backed by levees, miles of oak and palmetto waste. They were on mud flats, stretches of shallow water masked by mangrove and tiered by pines and oaks, backwaters that led away to dead ends thick with bugs.

Poole swigged from the plastic jug and offered some to D.J., who took a long, sloppy drink. Poole sat back, using his infrared for a long time, lulled by the swish of the water slapping under the hull, trying to catch some breeze, but there wasn't any. D.J. was hunched over the wheel. They were passing so close to mangrove, he would have to bend low when they hit rough stretches. There was so much bug noise, Poole was surprised. He couldn't even hear the Mariner. Pretty soon they hit a current and drifted sideways into the middle of the channel. D.J. looked back at Poole, cocked his head, and Poole understood they had shut down the trolling motor. They were drifting now, just drifting.

They were dead in the water, drawing through the current under a shawl of stars. Poole sensed D.J. pull taut under the wheel, crouching now, trying to hear something other than the frogs. Poole knew then he'd lost the sound of the dinghy. When he looked, he couldn't locate anything in the infrared, either. The fragile clouds had parted and they were alone under a sheet of moonlight that fell down like dust, and Poole had the funny feeling that he was in the air, flying over thick jungle, that he could put out his hands and touch rice paddies flooded under green monsoon. He couldn't hear the *putt-putt-putt* anymore. Something had closed down the line between them and Jack Eugene. "This doesn't make sense," he heard D.J. mutter. They were tilted into the current now, D.J. starting to look worried.

"Maybe Jack is at his meet," Poole said.

"No way, man," D.J. whispered, looking down at Poole, who was crouched over the hull, trying to hear. Everything was screwed down tight. Poole could feel his muscles, bones in his chest. "We're only ten miles in. Walker Lake is still on ahead. He can't off-load cocaine in a place like this." D.J. had taken a paddle and was trying to get the boat straightened up in midchannel. They were becalmed in a puddle of moonlight about fifteen feet from the mangrove. They could have hung a target on themselves—it was that dangerous.

"No roads, no lakes. What the hell is going on?" Poole was staring at D.J.'s own empty stare, going to say something about the frogs, but they got sideways in mangrove and both had to shove hard with paddles. The heat was terrific under the canopy of brush.

Poole tried counting the things that were wrong. He was confused by the noise of the mangrove, the frogs, and dizzy from the hard, close air. They were in a channel about forty yards wide, overhung by mangrove on both sides, banked by levees that held stands of tupelo and sweet gum, willows clutched down in the shallows. Clouds were drifting in the static water like white peonies. D.J. shrugged and started the trolling motor again, just to give them some control. If they were going to lose Jack Eugene somewhere in this channel, there was nothing they could do about it now.

They got up some speed with water washing back from the bow, messing up the cloud reflections, wave on wave rolling back from where Poole was crouched over the edge as he tried to catch a sound from ahead. They were making about two or three knots, just barely moving. Poole couldn't see anything but mangrove and black water.

It was a strange experience, seeing the black-vectored shapes of things outlined in red. Poole couldn't hear the Mariner and he couldn't see the shape of the dinghy, either. He began to believe Jack Eugene had cut into one of the side channels, although he couldn't imagine why. The channels ended in tule and dune and palmetto waste, but in his mind he thought maybe the bubba had cleared some brush away and covered it with camouflage, made himself a lean-to and had a way to get the coke transshipped from there. Poole had studied the maps and he knew it was miles over the scrub before you hit a hunter's path that bisected the Intracoastal Waterway about five miles above Walker Lake. Poole moved back in the boat to get away from the hum of the trolling motor and tried to stay with the infrared lens. Then, hunched down in the hull, he let his eyes rest where there wasn't any breeze at all.

Poole put down his scope and drank some water. The plastic jug was at his lips when he heard a thin whine like scree breaking down a slope, like bees, and then he heard D.J. mutter something under the sound of the trolling motor, and suddenly a larger sound broke through the mangrove just ahead. Water thumped away from a stand of willow and someone beat a drum. The worst scenarios flashed through Poole's head. He was hearing a sound that was absolutely wrong, and he knew they were heading into a worst-case scenario for real, something they'd talked about in the cabin, something on paper. Poole saw that D.J. had ducked behind the wheel and was peeking over the windscreen.

A concentrated whine burred out of the mangrove. Oh man, Poole thought for an instant, before his mind closed down. It was like a sound he had heard in Vietnam, when Special Forces would come out on Saturdays and practice shooting arrows at targets. Poole would sit up on his sandbags and watch them under the hot sun. He could remember the sound the arrows made, barely audible, then a *whip-crack* that nearly made you sick if you tried to remember it. It was like that now, only Poole was connected to the sound only by a black corridor and a fibrous vector of water. His mind was disconnected all of the sudden and he felt very peaceful. D.J. was studying the moonlight, smiling, perhaps a question in his eyes, but nothing panicky, nothing like that. It was almost as if they were back on the porch playing gin rummy, watching the sunset. Exhale, bright blue smoke on the horizon, both of them drifting through an evening.

Just then the windscreen exploded. Poole's phase of peace ended with one breath. He was going to tell D.J. he thought he was seeing blue smoke, maybe exhaust. They had come out on the lee of some shiny mud flats, the moon low against the opposite mangrove, and Poole had seen the blue smoke, shadows on the foliage, a tier of pines. He could still hear the breeze high up in the trees. He had put down his paddle because he had his arms full with the plastic jug, the scope. D.J. held his shotgun, looking back at the Evinrude. Poole thought he might kick it over and get them moving because of the dark and the silence. Poole saw D.J. motion for the starter, just a jerk, when the whole windscreen burst open and shards of glass funneled into a cone shape, D.J. uttering a cry inside a sweep of blood-covered particles.

Seconds later, Poole heard the blast and saw the dinghy running out of the mangrove just ahead, explosion, glass, motor sound, dinghy thumping over a huge wake, bouncing down on a crest of water, just like arrow motion. He felt pain before he heard sound, a smoky coldness on his cheek as if it had been sliced. He knew D.J. had gone down in the hail of glass, screaming something Poole couldn't hear. D.J. appeared again, fumbling for the shotgun just as Poole felt another frosty spot, this time his ear, then something buzzing and totally ambiguous as the exhaust smoke misted up over the dinghy and a huge wave crested against the bass boat, Poole down sideways now and the dinghy roaring in.

Poole knew D.J. was hurt, down on the deck with one leg stuck through the spokes of the wheel, a rag doll with both hands over his face, trying to kick loose his leg. Poole thought he could help D.J. if he could get to his knees, but forces had knocked him down, first the blast, then the wake tipping the boat up and dropping it hard on the water. Poole was hugged by gravity in a blizzard of plastic jugs, rope, tarps, maps, as if things had been compressed, the pressure released, confusion at the wellspring. A second clear blast brought Poole out of his drowsiness, like an alarm clock for his nervous system, only this time he was sure he had been raked by metal fibers, only it was shotgun pellets creasing through the hull. Another wake threw Poole down again and he lay there helpless in a Tilt-A-Whirl environment, only it was Jack Eugene firing a shotgun.

When he finally saw Jack Eugene, it was through a red flash of fire, Jack Eugene riding back in the dinghy above the wake, holding the fifty-horse Mariner in one hand and a shotgun in the other. He was riding the Mariner at full throttle, going round and round, using the wake to swamp the bass boat, to get Poole and D.J. in the water, then cut them to ribbons with his motor blades, either that or he would just rip them to hell with buckshot. It occurred to Poole that Jack must have been waiting for them under the cover of a mangrove, buried deep, using the dinghy's shallow draft to ride just above a mud flat with the Mariner on idle, making hardly a sound.

Poole felt cold slices on his cheek. He wondered how badly he was hurt, how badly D.J. was hurt, if D.J. would ever get his foot out of the wheel.

Poole wondered how he was going to get off a shot. Jack fired again from the port side, somewhere in the dark, and Poole ducked, stupidly, as if he could avoid something. He knew more pellets had torn into the bass boat and he heard D.J. shout again, his pants ripped up the side and the white moonlight on his leg. D.J. was cursing, trying to reach for the wheel. Poole kept thinking how cold his face felt. It was like a dream now, a slow-motion reverie.

He struggled forward against the weight of another

wake. This time, he found space for his motion, just behind an amplitude of water, a rhythm he could get used to if he studied it, Poole hitting his head on the dash, groping for the Glock that was under there someplace. He had no idea of time; he just groped for the Glock, keeping his head down, hearing the dinghy turn and come back starboard with another wake and another shotgun blast that tore the wheel all to hell. Poole rose and fired the Glock just as the bass boat struck the high side of the amplitude, way up on a ridge of black water, with the dinghy below in a trough, so that Poole could fire down, just for an instant held steady in a berth before the shotgun hit again. He didn't hear the Glock and he wondered if it had misfired. D.J. had said it couldn't happen; it was Austrian. It was only after he heard the frogs again that he knew things had changed and that the sequences were different.

Poole pulled himself over the hull and watched the dinghy circle off into mangrove, then straighten and disappear into the mud flats underneath. The Mariner had throttled back, just a dull pull of sound in the brush. D.J. was on one elbow, looking up at Poole, sweaty-faced, surprised, starting to poke a finger in the crease of his pants where the shotgun blast had ripped them open. Poole's forehead hurt. His neck was sticky and stiff and he had a cold feeling on his cheek. He helped D.J. get his foot away from the wreckage of the wheel and they both lay on the deck, breathing hard.

D.J. was on his back, stargazing. "Son of a bitch hid in the mangrove and waited for us." He picked at his pants, which were shredded.

They drifted with the current until they went past some mangrove, where they could see the stern of the dinghy. The Mariner was churning up mud, and Poole could see a dark balloon of it skimming away in the moon glow. He didn't know how long they drifted, but soon he could see the edge of Walker Lake, a flat channel with cabin lights far away, reeds and tule clogging the shoreline while the current pulled them toward open water. Poole wished they could float that way all night, drift around and around in the flat brown water, go in circles forever until the sun came over the rim of lake, shining through the oaks.

"D.J., how are you?" Poole asked.

D.J. had gotten up on one elbow now. His face seemed slick with blood, but Poole couldn't tell. It was as if D.J. was trying to place himself in context, legs, arms, various moving parts.

"I'm okay, man," D.J. said.

They were about thirty yards into the lake. The mangrove was behind them. Poole was sitting on some broken glass, what felt like bedsprings. One of the seat cushions had been blown apart.

"He's a cautious guy," Poole said.

"Old Jack Eugene," D.J. said, trying to sit up now. "He hit me, but I'm okay."

"We've got to go back," Poole said. It was as if they'd wounded a tiger and it had run off into the bush.

"Fine with me," D.J. said. "But I think you fucked the bubba up good"—big smile—"you ask me."

20

Poole had taken the motor from D.J. and they'd turned her around with what was left of the wheel, a stump you could steer with. His mind was numb, so dead inside that his hands didn't shake. He was more frightened there in the dark pool of the lake than when he'd first heard the shotgun blasts. Then, at least things were happening too fast to think about. Now, though, D.J. was leaned back against the hull, his leg on a seat cushion, trying to wrap it with tarp, tie it down so it would stop bleeding. Poole was using the wheel pulley gears to run the trolling motor around, and when he got the Evinrude going, they turned back toward the channel.

Poole poked at D.J.'s leg with his fingers, got the trouser leg up, but it was plastered into the wound, so he settled for a quick look and tied it up with gauze from the first-aid kit. He told D.J. it wasn't too bad, but Poole didn't like it much. It wasn't bleeding too much, but he didn't want it to start if D.J. began to thrash around. In the dark, D.J. might bleed to death, just go cold with a big smile on his face. D.J. helped get some strips of tarp tied around the leg and he told Poole he could hack it. In Vietnam, if a guy said he could hack it, you sent him back, so Poole relaxed and went to work on the pulley gears, getting them turned around, headed back into the channel.

The Evinrude sputtered out. Poole got in the back and discovered a beehive of buckshot in the gas tank, a few spackles in the back of the carburetor well. Up front, he got on the trolling motor and backed them thirty yards into the water hyacinths that lined the shore, then trained his infrared on the levee and used the night sight to find the starboard side of the dinghy buried in mangrove about sixty yards away. D.J. was sitting in the bottom of the boat, looking out over the windscreen, holding the shotgun through a wedge of broken glass, Poole on the other side with the Glock. They meandered through some thicket until Poole got the hang of the pulley gears, when he made for open water again. There were dunes rising behind the mangrove, swales of sand and pines that smelled like resin. Poole was frightened, and he wouldn't have been surprised if he let loose on nothing in particular, some indistinct sound. He had seen the same reaction in Vietnam, guys so scared, they poured thousands of rounds into the gaping dark, tracers arcing away into palm fronds, hillsides, empty villages, rearranging the jungle to suit their fears.

This scene was changed by Janine Bonner. They hadn't gone too far when they heard a woman crying, breaking into gagged screams they heard above the frogs. As soon as he heard her, Poole relaxed. He didn't think he could be in too much shit, because if Jack had been up and around, he would have whacked Janine, made her shut up. They were fifteen yards into the channel when Poole dropped over the side and gave the pulley wires to D.J., walking in the shallow water, trying to guide the bass boat with a shoulder and keep an eye out for Jack. He held the Glock in his left hand, out of the water.

Poole plunged through some reeds and found Jack Eugene on his back in the dinghy, shot all to hell. He couldn't find the shotgun. It must have gone overboard when Poole let loose with the Glock. Poole had seen a lot of chest damage—it was the worst—but he hadn't seen too much to match this particular hole. It surprised Poole how much damage he'd done in under five seconds. Poole heard the bass boat coming up behind him and he flashed D.J. a thumbs-up just as the guy dumped himself over the side, one leg wrapped in tarp. He splashed through the water and helped Poole look at Jack while Janine howled.

D.J. said he thought that Jack had gone into the mangrove and backed off the Mariner so he could wait and listen while the bass boat moved through the channel. Maybe Jack had heard them somewhere in the channel. Maybe it was an accident, or maybe he planned it this way. Maybe he always stopped and listened just before he hit the open water of Walker Lake. Both of them saw that Jack had an infrared, so he had probably seen them. It took balls for Jack to pop into the mangrove and wait that way, then hump out like a cave bat and start firing the shotgun while he circled his dinghy. You had to hand it to Jack, the wiry, muscled guy with stringy blond hair and bad skin. He had some tools, too. He had a fifty-horse Mariner that could lift the dinghy out of the water like a motorcycle on flat earth, a death roar and a big wake, a dragon breathing fire. He had four or five pounds of coke, too, in plastic bags down under the board seats of the dinghy.

Janine was covered with Jack's blood, splotches of it on her halter top, sprayed into her hair. She was cold, too, rolled up into a glassy-eyed ball, shivering in the back of the dinghy like a naked turkey. D.J. slogged through the slick mud until he could get her out of the dinghy, then made her lie down on the sand in shallow water, trying to get her to shut up. Poole heard D.J. talking to her like you might talk to a puppy.

Poole counted four plastic bags of coke, maybe eight pounds in all when he was through, the bags punched into two orange crates, It looked to Poole as if Janine had been sitting on the crates, riding on all this coke and getting a big kick out of the symbolism no doubt, but now she was hysterical, and the drug wasn't doing her any good. Poole thought this was a fortune in coke, but he knew it was just a good day's haul for D.J., nothing special. He hopped into the dinghy and sat down on the crates, resting for a while as D.J. calmed the woman down. He used his infrared to scout the shore of Walker Lake, an outline in dark gray and red with oaks and pines, terraced houses on the far side, away from the shore, piers and docks and a little marina farther to the northwest. The levees stopped about halfway around the east side, and the vegetation stopped, too. It looked like a five-mile ride across.

Poole almost laughed when he heard Janine beg D.J. not to kill her. "Oh please, I'll do anything." Wet and shivering, she was trying to hold D.J.'s hand. It was pathetic how frightened she was, but Poole couldn't blame her. He felt the same way, only he had a Glock.

D.J. told her to calm down, that they weren't going to kill her. They were cops, for Christ's sake. He told her she was in a world of shit but that they weren't going to snuff out her life. He patted her on her shoulder when she had crawled close enough. She kept begging D.J., as though she hadn't heard a word. D.J. got her out of the shallow water and put his arm around her waist. She stopped crying, but she was still shaking. The shock had soaked into her bloodstream. Poole knew that pretty soon she would turn pasty white and begin to chill, and then she would go numb. He thought he saw some signs already. She had backed off and was sitting up in the sand, staring at her toes.

Once Janine went into shock, it took about ten minutes for Poole and D.J. to start their routine. D.J. explained to Janine that she would do about fifteen years if she was lucky, but then, she might go down for a felony murder. That would mean she might go up to state prison, where some burly guy would stick a needle in her arm, and then *boink*, she'd be history. "Don't worry," he told her, "it doesn't hurt. You just go to sleep and you don't wake up. It's like what happens in the dog pound. You've heard about that, right? Then your body goes up to the university, where students hack it to pieces for science."

Janine was moaning, trying to dig her way through the shallow mud and water on her butt. For a second, Poole thought the whole thing was harsh. He admired D.J. for doing it, though, and then before he thought much more about it, he started in on Janine from the other side of the mirrored door, telling her he wouldn't let them do that to her. Trust old Poole, Tom, he'd see she wasn't *boinked* in state prison. All she had to do was be nice, tell them about Jack. Poole told D.J. to take it easy on the young woman, Poole smiling at Janine, who was babbling like a kid. Then he sat down on the mud right next to her so he could talk into her ear, both of them coming at her now from different sides.

In about fifteen more minutes, they had Janine to where she would shit nickels if they told her to make change. Dimes, quarters, half-dollars, pesos, too, if that's what they said to shit. Poole found a towel in the dinghy and dried her face, playing the friend while D.J. sat off on the levee and pretended to brood, to reason with Poole, telling him they ought to duck her in the mud and get the truth. D.J. would tell Poole to take her out into the brush and tear off a fingernail, then Poole would tell her not to worry, that he wouldn't let the guy do that. Poole watched Janine take some coke out of her jeans, a vial with some powder wrapped in aluminum foil. She shook some onto the back of her hand and snorted it right there, her eyes going bright in about ten seconds, getting her head tight while she told them everything she knew in a rush of words, hiccuping, running her finger around her gums to get really tight.

Janine pulled up close to Poole and measured her distance from D.J. She had a coy little-girl grin on her face, pure coke theater, which Poole knew all about. Poole had a good view of her bloodstained halter top, tufts of blood and tissue on her neck, and he could see how bright her eyes were in the dusky moonlight. She was racing toward a dream and she might shit herself getting there. Holding her skinny arms around her knees, she told Poole she didn't know where Jack got his stuff. It was told in a whisper, to Poole's face, as if they were lovers having foreplay. Janine said she'd gone with Jack once or twice, for kicks was all, and he'd always have a good stash, like four or five sacks, and she would get maybe two or three ounces for her time, give Jack some head on the way. But Jack usually went up the swamp alone. Tonight, he'd been wanting her company because he was lonesome.

Poole was listening good old boy–style, with one hand on a knee and his butt in the water while Janine rubbed a leg on his thigh. Both times she'd gone with Jack, they'd crossed Walker Lake to a big house with a wood pier and pleasure boats docked on either side. A guy would come down from the house, walk out to the pier, and pick up the coke. By the time he hit the wood pier, she and Jack would be trucking back out into the lake. She got good looks at the guy, but she didn't know who he was, and Jack never talked about him at all. That surprised Poole, because guys like Jack tell women like Janine everything. They get drunk and they brag; they can't help it, because the shit they're into is too damn exciting. All Janine knew was the size of the house, about two acres of grounds and some pecan trees for shade, a porch and some stone steps going down to the pier. She told Poole they would go across the lake and glide into the wood pier and Jack would yell something and the guy would come down the steps and Jack would dump the crates onto the pier and then they'd back into the lake and make it back to the marina for the late show, which meant they'd go up to Port Arthur and do coke all night and shoot some pool.

D.J. hobbled off the levee and dragged the bass boat into some shallows, under a willow-banked levee and shumards in deep shadow. Poole left Janine in her coke puddle and went out to the boat, the two men standing beside the hull in about six inches of mud and water.

"I know what you're thinking," D.J. said before Poole could open his mouth. "But I wish you wouldn't think it."

For the first time since he began with Janine, Poole felt his face. He resisted the temptation to scratch at the series of cuts. "Janine doesn't like you," he said, turning to D.J., who was stowing a flashlight under the wheel.

"No shit," D.J. said under his breath.

"I want to go across the lake," Poole said.

"Too dangerous, Tom."

"If I go across, we can make a bust. Janine says you go to a big house on two acres of pecans." Poole grabbed D.J. on the arm, stopped him. "Bubba paradise. Let's fuck it up."

D.J. raised his leg out of the shallow water and picked at it, getting some trouser and tarp out of the wound. Poole could see how black it was, bulging out of the torn material, but it didn't look as if it was bleeding. Behind them, Janine skittered onto the flank of the levee.

"Suppose," said D.J., "we take Janine back to Port Arthur. Tomorrow, we come out to the house with a search warrant."

"Too late," Poole said.

"Nobody gets hurt," D.J. replied.

Poole was getting ruffled. They were having a debate in the fringe of a mangrove, about thirty yards south of Walker Lake, stink lifting through pines, gray water lapping at the levee.

"Suppose I put on Jack's ball cap. I take the dinghy and you follow me across the lake in the bass boat. I make the drop, bust the guy when he comes down the stairs."

"Foolproof," D.J. said.

"Close as."

"This guy has an infrared, just like Jack. He comes down the stairs and kills you. How foolproof is that?"

"Hey," Poole said. "We sit Janine up front in the dinghy. He looks in the scope and sees the blonde. It relaxes him quite a lot." D.J. cracked a smile. "Right?" asked Poole. "You think I'm right?" he repeated.

"You're very free with this girl," D.J. said.

Poole could hear it ticking: She's not a player.

It didn't matter to Poole. He had to have Janine in the dinghy if he was going across the lake. She had to guide him to the right house. He couldn't afford to meander around in the lake, hoping some guy was going to come down and relieve him of eight pounds of coke. So, to Poole, the girl was necessary. Poole had only surprise, the Glock, and Janine Bonner, in that order, and with all three he could run across the lake and make the drop, maybe bust the guy on the other side. Poole was telling D.J. all this when he began to see him in a moment of drifting moonlight, scissor cuts in his face where the glass had raked him under the right eye, some braised skin and a big cut on his chin, one over the forehead that showed white bone.

"I'd go myself," D.J. said. Poole laughed quietly, more nerves than anything else. "I can't pass."

They sloshed through the water over to the dinghy and got Jack under his arms and dragged him out of the dinghy, and *spat-splash* over the side he went, facedown, Janine looking at them in terror. Poole could tell D.J.'s leg was hurting him now, and he told him to take it easy. Still, Poole thought it would be a shame to get this far and not go on across the lake to the big house. D.J. told Poole the girl might not make it. She might freak, do some coke, pull her own plug. It was too much to hope she'd keep quiet. She could get Poole killed and wouldn't that be a trip? They debated this, dragging Jack across the mud to where they could sit him up on a levee bank under shumards and a stand of gums. His T-shirt shredded apart and they could see his guts now, a red bubble stomach, white stuff that looked like worms.

They sat down beside Jack and talked. Janine was down the way doing more coke. D.J. leaned back against a mud bank, trying to get the weight off his leg, keep it out of the water. Poole knew it would be throbbing right now, needles and pins. D.J. mentioned that he'd like to go back to the bass boat and get a walkie-talkie, call up the Drug Czar and ask him what the hell he thought about all of this, an untrained sheriff's detective driving a cokehead across a dark lake. D.J. shrugged when Poole didn't speak. Poole walked over to the bass boat and towed it back to the levee. D.J. got his leg over the side of the boat and together they dragged Jack toward the hull, Poole in the water, D.J. down in the stern while they hefted Jack up and over.

Poole tried to think and catch his breath. He was thinking about the house on the other side. What if there were two or three guys up in the house? What if they killed Janine, who was maybe not a player? Poole was standing in the muddy water with his face burning, watching D.J. try to sweep up some broken glass with his hands, make himself a spot to sit down on the tarps. D.J. found his shotgun and sat with it cradled over his lap, looking at Jack, telling Poole he'd be about five hundred yards behind. If something happened, it would take about ten or fifteen minutes for him to catch up. So if something did happen, get the fuck out and fast. End of story.

Poole took three clips for the Glock. He stood in the shallow water, going over scenarios with D.J. What it amounted to was that Poole would get on the Mariner hard if he smelled trouble. He'd find D.J. and together they'd head back across the lake and hide someplace dark. With only the trolling motor, D.J. wouldn't move very fast, so Poole would pick him up. They'd let Jack float around, hope some fisherman didn't find the guy stewing in the heat, this big hole in his chest. It would scare the shit out of anyone.

D.J. was sitting in the bass boat while Poole went over to Janine. She was in a fetal zombie phase, sitting in a dark ring of mud with her legs against her chest and neck, her pasty white skin covered with grime, fluffs of blood on her halter. She looked terrible, and Poole tried to sweet-talk her down from her heights, telling her they were going across the lake, presenting it to her like she had no choice. She was gurgling and choking, but softly, looking at Jack in the back of the boat with D.J. Poole felt sorry for her. He wanted to tell her to go on home and do some more coke, watch TV and eat Moon Pies. But he didn't. He knew things for her wouldn't end so simply.

Getting Janine in the dinghy was like dragging a ball and chain through honey. Her legs were shock-rubber and she had a runny nose that dripped on Poole. She kept rubbing her gray-green eyes, making them water, hair soaked, strands like straw on her shoulders. What a Gumby, Poole thought, almost calling her that out loud. He finally got her in the front of the dinghy on one of the plank seats, put a blanket around her, and told her to keep quiet. Poole found a fifteen-gallon gas can under the backseat and pull-started the Mariner. They were humping under fumes, churning water, Janine started to shiver, looking back at Poole and seeing Jack, too. D.J. propped his leg over the hull and tapped Jack on the shoulder with the shotgun, smiled.

"Hey, don't be a hero," he called.

"It's a war," Poole said. Janine hunched forward, ran a finger over her lips.

"If it's a war, where's the Drug Czar now? And Daddy John? Where the hell is he?"

Poole had made off slowly. They were running under a cloud of mist and fumes and Poole could see now how huge the lake was, completely black center, clouds bouncing overhead. It was hard to tell the lake from the forest behind it.

"You take care," Poole called, going away.

"Ain't no TV cameras," Poole heard D.J. call back. Then Poole heard him say, "Hey, man, good luck."

Janine rolled herself into a ball and ducked under the rim of the dinghy, huddled there like a kid. Poole could see her tiny shoulders, the straps of the halter top coming down over them now, her legs crossed because there wasn't any room. Poole could reach out and grab her if he had to. She was a good stretch away, but now she wasn't making any sound at all. Haze had covered the water and Poole saw more stumps under the levee. They looked like human forms under a canopy of oaks and willows. He fingered the Glock in his belt, touched the Mariner throttle, got them going a little faster so they nosed up. They were progressing north across Walker Lake, cutting the mist until Poole could see it roil across Janine, strike him, fall back. He couldn't hear D.J. at all, couldn't see him, either.

Poole had nothing to do. They were way out in the middle of the lake when his thoughts overcame his muscles and he began to think about his father again, seeing his face, like the face had been *unearthed,* rising up through the haze. Poole felt as if he could reach out and touch it. Leathery and smelling of whiskey, the face tormented him for a second. None of it made sense when the scene called for immediacy, when Poole was gripping a Glock in his right hand, when he should be concentrating on the cabins and vacation houses two miles across the water. But he felt himself drifting with his father, situated somewhere other than here and now.

Janine turned, a weak expression on her face, drip-dried down to her last ounce of coke courage. She was trying to steer Poole starboard, pointing at a clutch of lights on the verge of the levee. Poole could see that her eyes were still bright from the coke. Getting the vial out of her jeans, she snorted another line or two, white powder on the back of her hand, sniffing, rubbing her nose, trying out a little coke smile on Poole. He didn't care if she snorted five or six ounces if it got her through her reality holes. He put one of the electric lamps on the seat with him so he could have light if he needed it. He wanted D.J. to see the dinghy if there was trouble. He tried to see the shore with the infrared, but all he could see was a mass of haze that looked like a blank wall.

They reached a pan of shallow water and Poole moved forward and grabbed the girl around the neck without warning, surprising her. He could feel her flinch, her body grow taut, and then he creased her neck with his elbow. He didn't want to hurt her, but he didn't want her to cry out, either, so he split the difference. Poole was full of a distinct circumspection because they were only three hundred yards from shore and he could see the expensive dark summer places. Against Poole's face, the girl's hair had a pasty consistency and he could smell her sweat and perfume. He could feel the tiny veins in her neck pounding. He was whispering to her now, sweet words, saying he needed to know the exact house, where the pier was, the lights. He was trying to scare her—as if she needed more scaring—but he wanted to be the source of whatever was going to happen, ease her away from her fear of whoever was in the house, make her fear what would happen if she lost control of herself. Then he softened his grip, winning her fear with a little kindness, then he scared her again, and so on and so on.

Poole had his right arm around her throat, the Glock grazing her temple, left hand back on the throttle, easing down into a pane of smooth water where the haze had settled about three feet high. The girl was nodding, trying to tell Poole it was a big house on the right, with a patio made of concrete and cypress, all these boats bobbing down at the pier below it. They were in a glaze of water hyacinths, some with big teardrop blooms. The girl was crying softly. Poole thought that any moment she might throw herself overboard. Inside himself, Poole wanted to let her go, let her slide away into the brown water, but then he thought about Bao Do, Jerry, too, and he knew this was something the girl ought to be doing. Poole told her he would shoot her if she fucked up.

The girl pointed at a house, one with a mansard roof and long patio, blazing with light. It was a pine and cypress–board house with a sloped and manicured lawn that tipped toward the lake, huge pecan trees cut around the grounds in a semicircle. Beams of light were shooting into the lake haze and Poole could see a figure on the patio, just at the edge of the glass door, a big hulk in a loose print shirt, trousers. He was sliding the door back with one hand, pausing, maybe scoping them with an infrared. Poole let go of the girl and told her to keep quiet, that this was just about over and it was going to be okay. She slid away from him.

Poole down-throttled and went another hundred yards while he watched the man on the patio. Poole had him spotted with his own infrared. He could see a pistol held down by his side! He was just standing on the porch while Poole went dead ahead. Poole felt overloaded with anxiety. What if there was a signal? What if the guy opened up and let them have it? He knew D.J. was out in the middle of the lake somewhere, cruising on a twelve-volt motor with Jack Eugene in back, no help at all. It could be that Janine was holding out on him, but he figured that was a long shot, since she was so freaked. But then, maybe Janine didn't know if there was a signal or not. In that case, they would both find out pretty soon.

Poole was about fifteen feet from the end of the pier when the big guy started down the stairs. The lake was like a mirror now, and they were only about forty yards from shore, with the guy standing behind pylons and two speed-boats. Poole could smell sweet gum and the lush aroma of cut grass. Poole wanted to get all the way to the pier, where there was cover. He didn't want to take any career-ending chances now. He had decided he'd let go with the Glock if anything seemed out of place, if there were loose seams in the fabric of the bust. A gray moon rode in on low clouds, but the only real light was coming down in waves from the house, a soft filter between the guy and Poole.

"Hey, Jack," the big guy yelled. An echo bounced at Poole across the breeze-sweet water, a halo that surrounded him. "Have we got a problem?"

Poole didn't know what he meant. The guy was balancing his pistol on top of a pylon, looking out at the lake with an infrared scope, relaxed, but in a posture that Poole didn't like right now. Poole hit the pier, bounced, cut the throttle back to idle, throwing up some fumes. "Hey," the big guy shouted. "I think there's some asshole behind you—out on the fucking lake."

Poole looked back, but he couldn't see D.J. at all. It was a pitch-black mirror. The guy had taken a few steps onto the pier, walking slowly, stopping to take a good look at the dinghy. Poole was making some calculations, click, click, his mind coming up blank.

Then the worst thing happened. Janine screamed suddenly, one piercing loud note that struck Poole as nonsensical, a completely discordant thing. Before Poole could think, the guy had fired, *bam-bam,* setting up a chain of echoes, all of it happening so fast that Poole had no time. He couldn't tell if the other guy was firing out into the lake or at the dinghy, but then he heard another quick shot and saw the guy scramble back across the pier and take cover behind a pylon again. Janine was screaming now, steady and insane, and Poole knew that the fabric had torn to hell. When he saw the big guy on the lawn, upslope and scrambling through the wet grass, Poole let loose with the Glock.

Poole was balanced against the pier, the dinghy sliding away slowly. He thought for a second he might fall into the water, but then the clip exploded away from the plastic gun and there was a hot ball of blue flame, some smoke, and then he could hear the girl screaming again. What had D.J. told him? Seventeen rounds in under five seconds? It seemed to Poole that he could hear breaking glass, but then he found himself in a ridiculous posture, spread-eagle against the pier, the dinghy half gone, and then he could hear D.J. yelling his name out on the lake.

Poole pulled himself onto the pier and let the dinghy go. He fumbled another clip into the Glock and lay flat on the pier while Janine drifted away, did two small circles in water hyacinths, and then it was so quiet Poole thought he could hear clouds grazing the moonlight. The gums were racing in the breeze, too, and there was a curious web of smoky fumes on the water where the Mariner was idling. When he looked up, he thought he saw the big guy drag himself onto the porch.

Poole spent about ten minutes lying flat on the pier, until D.J. glided in behind him. The girl was out of the dinghy, trying to hide behind it in shallow water. D.J. grabbed the pier. Poole could see that Jack Eugene had toppled over onto the Evinrude, rag doll–style.

"You Glock somebody?" asked D.J., crawling up front in the bass boat so both men could see each other.

"Fuck if I know," Poole replied. "It's war, isn't it?"

Poole grabbed a nylon rope and tied the bass boat to the pier. He helped D.J. over the side and both men lay on the pier, breathing hard, close together. Poole told D.J. he was glad to see him. He said he thought he'd shot somebody but didn't know who it was. The guy had crawled onto the porch, and he might be hurt. They could see the whole house in light, broken glass patio door, empty white spaces inside.

Poole crawled to the front of the pier, near the steps, and listened. A breeze leaked through wind chimes. Hummingbird feeders were swinging between baskets of fuchsias. Nice, Poole thought, very comfortable, upscale, just a few miles from the Intracoastal, the perfect place to off-load some coke. Poole could see a guy on the porch now, two feet over the edge, one hand on the patio door, lying there on his stomach. When D.J. got to the front of the pier, they separated and went up the lawn toward the porch on opposite sides. They hid in shadows and waited for a while, then went toward the middle, where the big guy was down.

It was Daddy John Lister on his stomach, flowered shirt, khaki pants. Poole thought, I just Glocked Daddy John Lister. The man was lying face down, the right heel of his foot blown away entirely, up to the ankle. His Tony Lama boots were ripped to shit, heel gone, a portion of bone showing through the pants leg, blood all over the shingle porch. That must've hurt like hell, Poole thought.

Poole looked at Lister, whose face was ashen white and vacant, beaded in a cold sweat, the fat pig face as smooth as ivory, pupils dilated. He was moaning and unconscious, making bubbles on the corners of his lips. Poole felt his cold forehead. There was a pulse in the temple. Poole was sure Daddy John would live through all this, but there would be no more morning walks through the courthouse, no more glad-handing and backslapping.

D.J. sat down, his back against the cypress wall. The patio door was shattered, broken glass everywhere.

"You just shot the sheriff of this county," D.J. said. "I'm surprised at you, Detective Poole."

Poole was squatting in the lotus position in a blood-soaked circle. They were smiling now, D.J.'s face caked with dried blood, the wound on his leg black where blood had soaked the gauze and trouser leg. Poole found a piece of door glass and looked at himself in the reflection. The left side of his face would take some patching.

"This must be Daddy John's place," Poole said.

"Nice spot," D.J. said.

"You think if we check the Intracoastal, we'll find he has a boat?"

D.J. straightened his leg. "Sure," he said. "He takes the coke from here to the Intracoastal. From there, he takes it down to Houston or has someone do it for him. It was a sweet setup." D.J. patted his leg and grimaced. "I guess this was too much money to ignore, even for Daddy John. I've seen it all, Tom. This war is about money."

Poole was looking at two big houses, downshore about three hundred yards. He was starting to get the stupid shakes. They decided to sit and rest for a while, then see if there was anybody in the house. Poole said he'd go down to the neighbors and tell them what was going on while Poole telephoned for help. They wanted to get an ambulance and a search warrant. There was no sense fucking up a good bust now that they had the time.

"Sorry about your fisherman," D.J. said, closing his eyes. Fatigue had worn them both down. "I don't suppose all this gets you very far with him."

Poole was trying to think himself out of the shakes. He could see Janine, hunched against the dinghy in about four feet of water, white shoulders and an orange hull, steam rising through the water hyacinths. She looked so pitiful, Poole thought somebody ought to take pity on her. He didn't have anything to tie off Daddy John's leg and stop the bleeding. Maybe he would bleed to death, and wouldn't that be too bad! Poole was looking at Janine, who seemed to be staring at Jack now.

"How do you see this D.J.?" Poole asked, turning his attention back from the weird scene out in the lake.

"Jack Eugene and Daddy John ran coke up the estuary. When they found out Jerry Donovan was using the estuary to drop off his reefer, they killed him."

"Everett was Jerry's partner, the guy with the expertise on a shrimp boat."

"That's how I see it."

"That's how I see it, too," Poole added. The wind chimes were very soothing. Poole could have gone to sleep in a bed of broken glass, blood, shreds of Daddy John's boot.

"Jack was in lockup Friday night when Everett Teagarden was shot. So we have to assume Daddy did the deed."

"You see him for that?"

"Well, who else?"

"Yeah," Poole mused. "On Friday night when Teagarden was killed, a buddy of mine was watching his house. I went up to relieve him about eleven that night. He hadn't seen anybody drive up the road that skirts the lagoon."

"The killer came by boat from the river side."

"That's how I see it, too."

"What's wrong with that? Daddy John knows the river."

"That gives Daddy John credit for more balls than I thought he had."

"Hey," D.J. said, pointing out at the dinghy, still drifting, pulling through circles of light at the edge of some water hyacinths. "You got maybe several hundred thousand reasons out in that dinghy for Daddy John to grow balls."

"I guess so," Poole said. "But about the fisherman. . . . I know Daddy John killed him. I know it for sure."

"What?" D.J. said, surprised. "You're sure?"

He took D.J. through the whole thing, telling him how he'd had a call on the Port Arthur highway on his way home after a long Saturday, how he'd turned around and had gone back to the fishing shack, how he'd found the old man, Bao Do, dead on the floor. He had been going home to drink beer and schnapps, watch TV until dawn, but he turned around and that's when the whole thing started. What started Poole thinking was the flash he'd seen out on the water, Poole standing on the veranda of the shack, nursing a headache. When he had looked, he had seen a guy in an orange dinghy staring at the shack through binoculars. He asked himself why a guy would be looking at the shack through binoculars. Then Poole had gone inside the shack and looked around at the seines and nets and gas cans, and he'd studied the old man on his side, a pool of blood under him.

The fisherman had been dressed all in black. He was a tiny guy and it had unnerved Poole, the way the afternoon light filtered through the shuttered jalousies. It had brought back all his Vietnam angst, the hooch. Poole didn't expect D.J. to understand completely, but he knew D.J. was getting the drift of his experience. Poole had become vaguely nauseated and he couldn't breathe, so he had to go outside and stand on the veranda. While he was outside, waiting for Daddy John, he started his train of thought that led to the orange dinghy. The guy had turned out to be Jack Eugene Bonner, skipping one of his DUI weekends.

Only then, Poole didn't know it was Jack. Then he stopped thinking about the orange dinghy for a long time. When he finally thought about it again, he was on his way to see Adrienne Deveraux and stopped at the marina store, catching Janine in a lie. What cinched him was when he'd been down at the cabin and he'd seen the dinghy again, out on the swell line under a bruised clouded sky, Janine in the dinghy, her blond hair in the wind, teasing her hand through the water. At that point, Poole still thought Jerry had offed the fisherman, but he didn't know why. He thought it had to do with Bao Do going to Beaumont. Now, it turned out that someone was Daddy John. It wouldn't do if Bao Do reported the reefer operation to the sheriff. He would have to investigate, shut it down; the news would get out. Maybe the old man had found out about the coke operation, too. That would be a real motive.

A single thought had stayed with Poole. It had emerged the afternoon he and D.J. went out for clams and oysters, then down to the Dairy Queen for a cone. Poole had taken a ride by himself down by the river. Sitting in the car all alone, he featured himself standing in the fishing shack in a terrible heat, dusty rays slanting through the jalousies. Poole remembered Daddy John wiping his glasses, walking out the back door of the shack and down the jerry-built steps, right up a dune to where he'd parked his car. At that time, Poole hadn't given it a thought.

But then at the Dairy Queen, under the pink oleander blooms, Poole pictured Daddy John looking through the fishing gear, the crates, gas cans, going out a door that Poole hadn't noticed, one that looked like a closet. It wasn't natural. Or maybe it was too natural, as if Daddy John had been in the room before. Neither Poole nor Mirabelli had noticed the door. Yeah, Poole thought then, Daddy John has been here before.

Poole made some connections then, like maybe the old fisherman had phoned the sheriff's office for an appointment and was going to blow the whistle on a dope-smuggling operation. The sheriff couldn't let that happen. And so he shot him and let the investigation die.

"Can we take him down for it?" asked D.J. "You got any ideas?"

"Why not?" Poole said. They would start with the .22 Colt, trace it back, straight police work. They had Janine now and Poole knew she would sing her heart out once they got her in one of those smelly, dank rooms in the basement of the federal courthouse. Maybe if they asked around, someone at the sheriff's office would remember the dead fisherman who called in for an appointment. Poole said he'd stay around for the trial and then he'd be leaving.

Poole heard Daddy John gurgle. He was rolling his eyes. Poole told D.J. he'd go down to the next house and make a telephone call. D.J. grinned, shook his head. He said he'd go see about Janine, try to be nice. It went against his better judgment, but he would do it, anyway.

Poole was in pitch-darkness under some pecan trees. He could hear the wind in the leaves and he could hear a sprinkler going *schick-schick* somewhere. The Bermuda grass was warm and rich as hay. He was walking away from the house, down a driveway lined by honeysuckle bushes, behind that a stand of pecans, the lake whispering out in the night. It would have happened differently if he had seen both cars first, the powder blue Cadillac and the tan LTD with a custom kit on the back, but he didn't. He was just about to cut through the pecan trees when Darnell Lister stepped out of a shadow and leveled a police .38 at Poole. He scared the shit out of Poole with the way he looked, deranged, such a wild gleam in his eyes that Poole thought something had popped loose inside his head. His face was cut to hell and it looked as if he might lose an ear.

"Keep quiet, fucker," Darnell whispered.

They were about twenty yards from the house, around in back, which was really the front. The cars were on a circular drive, near a flagstone walk leading to oak doors.

"Stay cool, Darnell," Poole said. "It's all over. No more killing. Okay?"

"Fuck you," Darnell said.

He had moved over and Poole could see him now. His cute pink Izod shirt was covered with blood. He must have been standing at the glass doors when Poole fired the

Glock. "This isn't over until I say." He waved the gun in a semicircle. Poole was supposed to move up the drive, work his way around Darnell. "Move, goddamn it," Darnell said.

Poole had no choice. He walked up the drive about ten yards until he was directly in front of the path. Darnell was behind him, just to one side.

"Call the nigger," Darnell said.

"There's no place to hide," Poole said.

"Tomorrow morning, I wake up in Tegucigalpa with two million in the bank. Think about it." Darnell was up to Poole now, just behind him in some honeysuckle. Poole could smell him, his cheap aftershave. Going through Poole's mind was everything he'd been trained to do in a situation just like this. He wasn't going to call D.J., give up their only gun in a hostage situation, even if he was the hostage. Darnell would have to shoot him. That would be what Darnell would have to do. Then he'd have to deal with D.J.

"Was it worth it?" Poole asked.

"Come on," Darnell said, "call the goddamn nigger."

"You were the one who did Jerry. You did Everett, too."

"Well," Darnell said, "Jack was busy."

"Three men dead," Poole said quietly. "Four, if you count Jack. Call it off, Darnell."

"Those fucking idiots," Darnell growled. Poole could tell from his voice he was out in space, disconnected from his lifeline now. "Can you imagine Jerry Donovan and Everett running shitass reefer up the estuary? They were going to fuck us up."

"Well, they did."

"Come on, call the goddamn nigger."

A line of pure reflection rinsed through Poole, winglike, an airfoil of thought. Poole sensed that he was at the center of sound, wind rippling through the pecan trees. It was almost as if he could hear each leaf tremble, all the katydids and frogs at the edge of the lake making a terrific racket. Poole decided he would say something to Darnell, something sassy, wide of the mark, maybe give his last few moments some pizzazz.

"Why the hell did you baboons have to do the old fisherman?" Poole wondered if he would hear the firing pin, or if things would simply blister suddenly and go black.

"That was Daddy John," Darnell said after a while. Poole thought the guy might be crying. He wasn't sure, but it wouldn't surprise him. "That damn fishhead called the sheriff. Squawking about his son-in-law smuggling dope. He couldn't talk English, but you could sure as hell tell what he needed done. And if he had come up to Beaumont, the DEA would have gotten involved, the whole thing would have gone up in smoke. One day, Daddy just went down to have a talk, calm him down some. The old slant went into a rage. Daddy did what he had to do."

"Just for the money."

"One hell of a lot of money," Darnell said quickly. "Hurry up now and call the damn nigger. I know he's up there. What's he doing, anyway?"

"Just tell me about Everett. That was really stupid."

"Shit," Darnell hissed. "Nothing is easy. To old Everett, twenty thousand dollars is a lot of money. We're talking millions here. When you came up to Daddy's house last week, I knew we'd have to do Everett. We couldn't have you talking to Everett, him scared, big headlines about the new pipeline to Houston."

"You do him from the swamp side?"

"Hell yes. I took Jack's dinghy around toward the far side of the bay and came up behind him. It didn't matter. That old bubba was drunk on Dixie, just laid there." Darnell was making circles with the gun, moving Poole farther up the flagstones, keeping honeysuckle between himself and Poole. Darnell's face was sweat-glazed.

"Not that it matters," Poole said, seeing Darnell again

in moonlight, his ear like a pad of hamburger. "How'd you get Jerry?"

Darnell smiled, a bleak characterless blast. "Jack wired the shrimper before he went down to Houston to do his damn DUI weekend. We didn't think old Jerry would take her out again, not after Everett, but he did, damn fool. I drove up here to the house, where we kept the dinghy, went on down to Clam Lake." Darnell put a hand on Poole's right shoulder, the .38 back under his waist.

Poole had one more thing. "Jack's down in the dinghy," he said. "He's going to tattle on you."

"I seen him," Darnell said. "It don't make no difference."

"They'll find you in Honduras, wherever you go."

"That's fine," Darnell said.

"Look at Noriega. You don't have that kind of suck even."

There was a convulsive silence as Poole fought through the collapse of his thought.

"Then, that's what they'll have to do," Darnell said. He was making a wide circle with the gun barrel, its curvature leaving a trail on Poole's retina. "Now call that goddamn fucking nigger."

"Fuck you, Darnell. Tee it up." Poole was looking at the guy out of the corner of his eye. This last bit had really frosted Darnell. He looked like he was busting a gut. Poole wasn't going to let Darnell kill D.J., drive the LTD down to Matamoros, hop a jet to Honduras. No fucking way. "Fuck you, man," Poole said. "Let's do it." Poole gave himself no chance. He could see Darnell, just behind him, across the honeysuckle.

Then Darnell's head disappeared. It came apart like a tomato, fleshy pulp, stem, seeds, a trail of white mucus. Poole fell into the honeysuckle, hearing the roar of a shotgun, or maybe its echo out on the lake. He could see Darnell down, his feet twitching, half his head plastered to the side panel of the LTD, giving off little risers of steam. D.J. appeared around the hood, looking down at Poole.

"Now I killed me a public official, too," D.J. said.

"Jesus Christ," Poole said.

D.J. stabbed Darnell with the shotgun. It was going to take a spatula to get him in a body bag.

D.J. offered Poole a smile. "Daddy John came to, looked at me, and said, 'Darnell.' Then he passed out again. I looked inside the house and saw blood all over the dining room floor where you'd busted in the patio door with the Glock. I figured Darnell was around somewhere, so I came around the house to warn you."

"I appreciate it," Poole said. "Darnell was the one who did Everett and Jerry. Jack was busy, in jail." Poole knew they wouldn't talk about it anymore. It was done.

D.J. helped Poole out of the honeysuckle. He told him that Janine had gotten in the bass boat with Jack and they ought to go out and see about her now. It seemed to D.J. that a night like this might take some of the party out of Janine, calm her lifestyle. Poole allowed as how that might just be right.

21

Poole was at four thousand feet, going up in high desert, with the Davis Mountains ahead, like brown ziggurats in the middistance, under a Giotto blue sky. He had been going uphill at thirty miles an hour all day, downhill at sixty, but it wasn't bothering him. The VW bus had cost him only two hundred dollars and it had the heart of a mule, the soul of a belly dancer. It made him feel about twenty-four years old again. Besides, Poole wasn't going anywhere. He had no particular destination. He didn't even have a map beside him on the seat. All he knew was that he wanted to see some dry country for a change, get up high where there was no humidity, where he could really see the country and drive. Way up here, there seemed a crackle to each sensation. The browns in the granite boulder foothills, then dark red clay, then the pearl gray expanse when he had hit sage country, mesquite. Even the black-and-white feathers on the roadrunners had a vibrancy.

He drove all night, not intending to do it. He had come out of the Hill Country past Austin and had witnessed an awesome sunset that had spread over the horizon in a blaze of pink and scarlet, red-tailed hawks perched on each telephone pole, light snagged in the last of the scrub oaks. Then he was in the mesquite country just as the sun set, and he decided to keep going. He passed where a grain elevator posed against the suffusion of sky. Black clouds banked to the south, moving toward him as he drove. There was something good about being so far out in country nobody wanted anymore.

After the sun had fully set, he nearly stopped driving. But he bought some powdered doughnuts and milk at a service station and decided to go some more. Somewhere from his youth came the memory of a song by Tex Ritter, "Deep in the Heart of Texas," with a yodel break in the middle. How beautiful the chorus was, how sad, too, when you listened to it carefully. Poole had asked his father to play it once on a jukebox in Port Arthur, and he had remembered it ever since. Then when the stars came out after dark, Poole knew he would drive all night. The highway was absolutely empty, a straight black road, the stars were burning down, and he was humming the Tex Ritter song. How could he stop driving?

It got cold later and Poole drove with the heater on, though it wasn't delivering much heat. It was a forced-air contraption that fed heat right off the engine, producing some mildly warm air through a vent under the window. He drank milk and ate doughnuts, feeling so happy that his heart warmed him. Poole knew that his experience was one of the last pure pleasures in imperial America. He had the real road, not the high-pressure delivery system of freeways and their franchise food, bypasses, but an old two-laner through small towns that were dying. He felt free, looking at the mountains and the ranches.

During the night, Poole thought a lot about Adrienne Deveraux. He gave her up for a final time somewhere near Alpine. The afternoon he left, Poole ate lunch with her at a Mexican restaurant in Houston. He held her hand under the table. He kissed her good-bye under a live oak on the patio. Everything smelled dusty and good. He knew then he wouldn't see her again, that there was no way. She would be living in the Finger Lake country, far away from where Poole wanted to be, which was in the high desert, the Rocky Mountains—somewhere dry where he could have an orchard and some bees, a big summer garden for tomatoes and squash and cantaloupe. Poole had decided to teach piano again, perhaps give private lessons or get a job teaching high school band. He could always scratch out a living. That wasn't the problem with modern life, modern America. The problem was something else.

Adrienne Deveraux had given Poole all she had to give. She had given him love and a deep appreciation for the moment. She had been honest and now she was going away. What more could Poole desire? The woman had shown him another way to behave.

There had been no trial. It disappointed Poole a little, but in the end it had turned out for the best. Daddy John had copped a plea in order to avoid getting *boinked* by the death needle up at state prison. Poole had been through every stage. Daddy had looked like shit at the bail hearing, right foot casted up and bandaged, face gray, wearing an orange jumpsuit, trying to hide from the cameras. D.J. had gotten a kick out of that, this bozo who made a living from being a media star all of a sudden camera-shy. The main thing was that Poole knew Tran and Danny Huan had a chance now to hang on to the edge of their new continent. He knew he had made up something to himself, a debt he owed to the woman in the hooch at Duc Tho.

Before dawn, the sky turned pink and it rained. A huge thunderstorm rode up from Mexico and dumped about ten minutes' worth of wet blue drops on the desert. Poole was beyond Alpine in big rock country and the rain turned the highway cobalt-colored, an extravagant gray mist in the hills above. The sage smell was overpowering. The rain had released it, and Poole thought he could smell right into the heart of the country, which was why he'd come in the first place. He laughed out loud, he was so happy.

But the big thing happened just after the thunderstorm. Poole had been thinking, making judgments, like he wasn't going to live out the American nightmare anymore, no more credit cards, straitjacket of consume and destroy, buy and sell. No more mailboxes stuffed with circulars from the discount electronics warehouse. He had been making resolutions, all probably necessary and true, but then he came over a hill and he could see the Davis Mountains, boulder cones and a whisper of morning-white clouds, the feathery relief of window ice. And Poole finalized his plan. He would try to love the land first, get rid of his self-focus, then he would see if he could find some people to like, as well.

And then he saw a rainbow drawn south of the highway. It disappeared into a horse pasture, all the colors brushed by cloud. When he saw it, he nearly ran off the road, hitting shoulder, kicking up some sand, running the old VW back onto the pavement, moving on. Poole was going thirty miles an hour, but he didn't mind. It gave him more time with the rainbow.